The Wilkerson Farm Murders

by
Greg Wilson

Chapter One

The moped appeared from nowhere, speeding around the corner in the middle of the road. Vicki Wilkerson saw a splash of colour and a rapid blur. She reacted instinctively, yanking the steering wheel to the right and slamming on the brakes. The driver of the moped reacted with equal speed, screeching around to the left and somehow managing to avoid the front edge of the car. Vicki felt the wheels judder as the vehicle crossed onto the grass verge to her right and, as the car pulled to an awkward halt, she heard the roar of the moped's engine behind her. The rider had lost control of the vehicle and the motorbike was skidding on its side onto the opposite verge. Vicki looked round in alarm, too late to see the cyclist come off the bike.

It was Akash Antonelli, her boyfriend, who let out a cry of surprise. 'Jesus!' he exclaimed, glancing out of the passenger window. 'That was bloody close.' Akash was a handsome, gangly young man in his early twenties, with an unruly mop of curly dark brown hair and, most of the time, a relaxed expression. It took a lot to unnerve Akash, but this had done the trick. He looked back at Vicki. 'Are you all right, doll?'

Vicki Wilkerson nodded numbly, her hands clamped to the steering wheel.

'Your reflexes are a lot better than mine,' Akash said. 'I think I'd have hit him.' He craned his neck to look back at the road.

Vicki lifted herself up in her seat and finally let go of the wheel. 'Is he all right?' she asked, breathlessly. Her view was not as clear as Akash's. What if she had killed him? What if he was seriously injured? She peered back through the rear window and saw with relief that the man was moving, extricating himself from under the heavy bike.

Akash undid his seatbelt and pulled open the passenger door. A blast of cold air swept into the car from the outside.

'Careful of the road,' Vicki warned him. They had come to rest on the right-hand side of the lane, but Akash was seated to her left. It was a little confusing, driving a British car on a French road. Akash had been at the wheel most of the way from Calais, but Vicki had taken over for the last couple of hours, as they drew closer to her parents' farm. She was less likely to get lost, although she had only been here once before and she was still getting used to driving on the other side of the road. They had left the motorway well behind them, and the narrow country lanes of Southern France required a degree of caution that Vicki had been happy to exercise. But nobody could have avoided that moped. It had been in the middle of the road, roaring around a blind curve. The driver had not had any thought for oncoming traffic.

Akash checked the way was clear and then stepped out of the car.

Vicki reached for her phone. *I should call for an ambulance,* she thought. *Just to be on the safe side.* A quick look at the display, however, showed that there was no signal available. Vicki was not surprised. There had been no coverage the last time she had been out here. They were not far from the farm, though. If she needed to, she could probably walk to the house from here and use the land line to raise the alarm.

She unbuckled her safety belt and pulled open the car door. It was cold outside – bitterly cold, for early April – but she had a coat on. The edge of the door jammed up against a mound of grass on the side of the road, but she managed to squeeze through the gap. She made her way around the back of the car, a green Nissan Micra, and stood for a moment, observing the scene a little way down the road.

The moped was lying on its side, on the opposite verge. It did not look to be damaged, at least not from this distance. Her eyes flicked to Akash, her beanpole of a boyfriend, as he helped the helmeted cyclist to his feet and back onto the verge, out of the way of any traffic. Boyfriend. *Well, fiancé now,* she corrected herself, with a smile. That was the good news they were going to pass on to her mum and dad, when they arrived at the farm. Not that daddy would think it was good news. She frowned. Giles Wilkerson – her father – could be a little crusty, but he had promised to behave himself this weekend. Vicki was

2

determined to keep him to his word.

The owner of the moped was limping slightly. He was moving off the road, with Akash's help, but he did not look to be seriously injured. *He could have concussion though*, Vicki thought.

A car was coming up the road towards them. The driver slowed down to take in the scene but Akash waved to her that everything was okay, and the woman continued on her way.

Vicki hesitated for a moment, then crossed the road to join them. The cyclist, still in his helmet, had his hand pressed against a tree to support himself. He was lucky he had not hit it.

Akash was all smiles. 'I think he's alright,' he said, his eyes twinkling and his breath forming a cloud in the air.

Vicki shifted her gaze to the helmeted figure. '*Comment allez-vous*?' she asked. How are you? A bit of half-remembered French.

'He's English,' Akash said. 'From London, apparently.' Evidently, the two men had already exchanged a few words.

The other man dropped his arm from the tree and spread out his hands. He mumbled something to Vicki, but she struggled to catch it through the helmet. The man was tall and lean, though not skinny like Akash. Actually, there was something familiar about him. Something in his bearing. 'Robbie!' she exclaimed in surprise, as he pulled up the visor. It was her brother, Robert Wilkerson. Even with just the eyes and nose visible, she could not fail to recognise him. She gazed at the helmeted figure in wonder. 'What are you doing here?'

Robbie Wilkerson unfastened the strap at his chin and quickly pulled off the helmet. 'What do you think? Same as you.' He handed the helmet to Akash, who stashed it on the ground.

Vicki frowned. 'Come to visit mum and dad?'

Robbie nodded. 'Special occasion. How could I miss it?' His voice, though, was dripping with sarcasm.

Akash was standing between the two of them, looking confused. 'This is your brother?'

Vicki nodded. The two had never actually met, although she had told Akash all about him. All the dubious details. Robbie was the black sheep of the family. He was *persona non grata* as far as her parents were concerned. 'Dad will have a fit,' she breathed. 'He won't want to see you.' Robbie had fallen out with his father a few years ago and the two of them hadn't spoken in an age.

'I don't care,' Robbie said. 'It's mum I've come to see.'

Akash scratched his head. 'She invited you down, did she?'

'Not exactly invited. You're…Akash, is it?'

The curly haired youngster nodded. 'Pleased to meet you.' He extended a hand. Robbie looked down at it dubiously, but took it anyway and gave a half-hearted shake.

Another car flashed by on the road, and Vicki glanced at the over-turned moped. *Oh my God.* She had almost hit her own brother. 'How are you feeling?' she asked. 'Oh, Robbie, I could have killed you.'

'You very nearly did,' he growled.

Vicki didn't understand what he was doing on this particular road. 'Why did you come this way?'

'I told you, I was heading for the farm.'

'But the farm's back there. The turning.'

Robbie shrugged. 'I thought it was the next one along. I've never been here before.' He winced slightly.

'Are you hurt?'

'No. No bones broken. Just a few scratches. My leg's a bit sore.'

Vicki exchanged a quick look with Akash. 'We should get him back to the house. It's not far from here. They've got a phone. We can get a doctor out to look at you.'

'I'm fine,' Robbie insisted. 'I don't need a doctor.'

'Somebody should…'

'Stop fussing, Vick. I'm fine. Just need a lift, that's all.' He shot her a grin.

Vicki smiled back. 'You won't be told, will you? It is good to see you.' And it was. It had been so long since she had last seen her brother. And now here he was, in the flesh. She couldn't stop herself then. She grabbed hold of him and gave him a big hug. 'Oh God, I could have killed you.'

'Yeah, you want to watch where you're going sometimes,'

4

he joked. 'Get off, you big lump!'

She banged the back of his shoulders with mock indignation. 'It was all your fault. You were in the middle of the road!'

'Ow!' he exclaimed, not entirely in jest.

Vicki pulled back sheepishly. 'Sorry. Let's get you into the car.' She glanced at Akash, looking for help.

'What do you want to do about that?' Akash asked, gesturing to the moped.

Robbie didn't care. 'Leave it, mate. I think it's probably a write off.'

'Since when have you ridden a motorbike anyway?' Vicki wondered. As far as she was aware, he didn't even have a driving licence. He had certainly never taken any lessons.

'A while now,' Robbie said.

Akash was feeling a bit of a spare part. 'I could walk it to the farm if you like,' he suggested, looking down at the moped. 'If it's not that far. Shouldn't really leave it on the roadside.'

Vicki smiled. That was Akash all over. He was always happy to muck in and help out, whenever it was needed. Her dad thought he was a waster and a layabout, but the truth was somewhat different.

'How far is it, did you say?' he asked.

'The turning's about a hundred metres, up on the right,' Vicki said, gesturing towards the curve in the road. 'Then it's about half a mile. It's the second farmhouse along. You can't miss it. Are you sure you're all right doing that?'

'Just so long as I can get it up,' Akash said, with a sly wink. He moved across and gave the vehicle a speculative pull. It looked heavy but, once he had got the measure of it, he was able to lift it up.

'Be careful, darling!' Vicki called, blowing him a kiss. He grinned and gave her the thumbs up; then Vicki returned her attention to her brother. 'Come on, you idiot,' she said, giving Robbie her arm and helping him across the road to the car. Robbie was hobbling rather, but at least there were no broken bones. She hoped she hadn't done him any permanent damage. She would get somebody to have a proper look at him at the farm, no matter what he said.

5

She propped her brother against the side of the car, pulled opened the passenger door and helped him inside. Then she headed round the back and squeezed into the driver's seat. Once she was settled there, she took a moment to compose herself and then stared across at her brother. 'I can't believe it was you,' she said.

'Yeah, what a way to meet up.' Robbie chuckled.

'Seatbelt,' she said.

'You said it was only a hundred yards.'

'Seatbelt,' Vicki insisted, struggling not to smile. 'This might be a bit bumpy.' She waited for him to do as he was told, then switched on the engine. The road looked to be clear both ways. Slowly, she bumped the car off the verge.

The farmhouse was a dilapidated building nestling halfway along a small dip in the hills. It was one of four small holdings off the main drag and had been unoccupied for some years before Vicki's mum and dad had moved in. Quite a lot of English people bought up old properties in this part of the world, for use as holiday homes or as somewhere nice to retire. The French tended to prefer modern buildings, so her dad said. There were signs of life at the "château", as she drove down the mud track towards it. Daddy always called it a "château", though it wasn't that big. Smoke was belching out of the chimney stack and, as the car made its way down, Vicki caught sight of her mum standing in front of the barn, chopping wood. Vicki smiled.

Marion Wilkerson, her mum, had always been a very practical woman, more so than her father. She was stocky without being fat. She had a wide, friendly face – pleasant if a little weather-beaten – and a mop of short reddish brown hair. At the sound of the car, Marion put down her axe and gave Vicki a short wave. She was dressed in dungarees with a heavy woollen jumper over the top. It was barely midday and it was surprisingly chilly out. Vicki had the heater on in the car at full blast. It was much chillier than normal for this time of year. But unlike Vicki, Marion was not one to pay any heed to the

6

weather, good or bad.

Robbie Wilkerson was regarding the farmhouse with some scepticism. 'Jesus, what a dump!' He shook his head in mild dismay. 'They paid good money for that load of old rubbish? It's practically derelict.'

The building had certainly seen better days. The stonework was crumbling and there were shuttered windows along the front, not all of them glazed. It was a big building, though, the front stretching some ten to fifteen metres, with a barn at one end and a huge expanse of lawn out front.

'You should have seen it when they first arrived,' Vicki said, turning the car onto the driveway leading up to the house. 'They've done a lot to it already.'

There were flowers in the window boxes and the garden – which was more like a field – had recently been mowed.

'You mean mum has,' Robbie guessed. Marion was the practical one of the family. Giles, their father, would always help out, but he had problems with his leg and couldn't do much physical work these days.

'Daddy's done his bit,' Vicki insisted, pulling up the car and switching off the engine. The prospect of Robbie and her dad in the same house was a little worrying. 'Be nice, Robbie. This is their special weekend. I don't want any rows. Oh, here comes mummy.'

Marion Wilkerson had abandoned her wood pile and was making her way towards them.

'Don't worry,' said Robbie. 'I'll be as good as gold.' His tone suggested otherwise, however.

Their mother, at least, was all smiles. Vicki undid her seatbelt, pushed open the door and rushed around to greet her. 'Hello mummy!' she said, enveloping Marion in the biggest of hugs.

'Welcome home,' her mum said, with a soft smile. 'I was hoping you'd get here before the others. How was the journey, dear?'

'All right most of the way. We had a bit of an accident at the top of the lane.'

'An accident?'

'You'll never guess who we ran into?'

Robbie took this moment as his cue to open the car door. He pulled himself out of the passenger seat with a big grin on his face. 'All right, mum?' He smiled.

The look on Marion's face was priceless. 'Robbie!' she exclaimed. It took a lot to surprise their mother. Without a second thought, she stepped forward and embraced him.

'Ah, get off!' he yelped.

'Mum, don't!' Vicki said, thinking of all the bruises. 'He… he's been in a bit of an accident.'

Marion pulled back sharply. 'An accident?'

'Nearly got run over.' Robbie grinned sourly. 'By my own sister, can you believe it?'

Marion frowned, gazing between the two of them, unsure if they were joking. 'I'm not sure I follow, dear,' she said.

'Robbie was speeding around the corner on a motorbike. Well, a moped. He nearly went over the bonnet. But he's fine.'

'A motorbike?' Marion's voice was sharp. 'Robbie, those things are lethal.'

'Yeah, so you always said. Don't worry. I think it's a write off. Won't be riding that again.'

Marion eyed her son up and down carefully. He was tall and solid looking with a wide mouth, light blue eyes and short, honey-coloured hair. His default expression was one of practised scorn, but Vicki knew there was a tender heart beneath the surface, and their mother knew it too. 'Are you all right though, dear?' Marion asked, with some concern.

'Yeah.' Robbie shrugged off his discomfort as casually as he could. 'Just a bit of a bruised leg.'

'And what about your young man?' Marion asked Vicki, looking past them into the car.

'Akash?' Vicki smiled. 'He's bringing the moped back. Walking it back. It's just down the road. He'll be here in a few minutes.'

Marion Wilkerson was quiet for a moment, taking this all in. 'Well, you have had a busy morning. You'd better come inside. You're the first to arrive. We've got a full house this evening, dear.' This she aimed at her son.

8

'Oh yeah.' Robbie grinned. 'Happy anniversary, by the way.'

His mum dismissed that with a hand. 'That's not until Sunday.' She glanced back at the house and grimaced. 'I'm happy to see you, Robbie. I always am. But your father....I'm not sure it was a good idea, you coming here today.'

'It's a good opportunity,' Vicki put in, earnestly. 'This has been going on for far too long. We should try and put it all behind us.'

'That's all very well, dear,' Marion said. 'But your father, you know what he's like. He can be very stubborn. He won't be happy, Robbie. I'm not sure he'll let you stay.'

'He can't refuse now,' Vicki insisted. 'Robbie's hurt. He needs somewhere to rest.'

'Of course.' Marion nodded. 'You let me handle your father, Robbie.' She managed a smile. 'It is good to see you, dear. I get so worried. You should have...you should have texted me at least.'

Robbie scratched an earhole. 'I thought you couldn't get a mobile signal out here.' He winced slightly, as he shifted his weight from one leg to the other.

'Not at the farm. But in town we can. You'd better come inside. I'll leave the wood for now. Vicki, you can put the kettle on.'

Vicki nodded. 'I'll just get my things from the car,' she said. She watched as her mother led Robbie up towards the front door. Marion Wilkerson, at least, was pleased to see her son.

Giles Wilkerson was on his knees, tucking in a bed sheet. Vicki pulled up at the top of the staircase and smiled at the sight of her father, crawling about on the wooden floorboards. 'Hey, daddy!' she called out. Mum had said he would be up here, getting the place ready.

The room was at the far end of the house, on the opposite side of the building from the living room. The last time Vicki had been here, it had been completely inaccessible. It looked like her parents had done a lot of work in the meantime. The staircase was new, unvarnished and without a handrail as yet.

Giles looked up from the floorboards and his eyes widened. 'Victoria!' he exclaimed, his puffy bespectacled face lighting up with joy. 'What a nice surprise! We weren't expecting you until later.'

Vicki grinned and moved carefully into the room. 'We thought we'd get here early and give you a hand before the others arrived,' she said. The room was awkwardly proportioned, with wooden beams cutting across the diagonal roof. A small window at the far end gave out onto the front of the house. There was no furniture, except for the mattress, a small table and a metal clothes rack to one side, which looked as if it had been stolen from a department store. Daddy had probably picked that up somewhere for a song. He loved a good bargain.

'I thought I heard a car,' Giles said. 'I thought it might be the neighbours. I wasn't sure if they'd be coming down this weekend.' He lifted himself laboriously to his feet. Giles was a portly man of middling height, grey haired and balding, with functional glasses and a rather loud jumper. In summer he always wore Hawaiian shirts and short trousers but it was too cold for that just now, so he was sporting a pair of red corduroys instead. He beamed at Vicki and, keeping his head low in deference to the beams, he came forward to give her a hug. He had a slight limp that was noticeable whenever he moved. He had been in an accident a few years before – a parachute jump, for charity. He had landed badly and broken his leg. It had been fixed up but he had been a little unsteady on his feet ever since.

Vicki pressed him to her as tightly as she could. She had always been a bit of a daddy's girl – Robbie had teased her mercilessly about it when they were kids – and she had been rather sad when her parents had upped and moved to France, as it meant she would see them less. She missed her mum too, of course, but she had always been closest to her dad. 'Mummy said you'd be up here. Are you all right on those stairs?' The thought of him, with his dodgy leg, clomping up and down such a steep staircase was a little troubling.

Giles pulled back. 'I'm getting better with the stairs now,' he said. 'I'm not even using a stick these days.' He spoke softly, his voice mild and light. 'But your mother does all the hard work. All the heavy lifting.'

Vicki glanced around the room. 'So who are you putting in here?'

'Your mother and I. I just brought a few clothes up.' He gestured to the rack and a small pile of clothes lying on the floor beside it. 'Marion thought it would be nice to let someone else have the master bedroom. We're putting your Aunt Betsy in there, and we'll put David and Emma in the far room.'

Vicki smiled at the mention of her aunt. Betsy Klineman was the live wire of the family, loud and often quite rude, but very funny. Strictly speaking, she wasn't really an aunt. Betsy and her mum had been at school together. Vicki had known her her entire life. 'Is she really bringing her young man with her?' she asked.

Giles nodded darkly. 'I'm afraid so. You know what Betsy's like. But your mother will be glad to see her. And as she's come all this way, it's only fair we put her up properly.' Her dad was nothing if not a good host.

All the same, the farmhouse was pretty basic, and Aunt Betsy was not known for living quietly. 'Does she know what she's letting herself in for?'

Giles rested an arm on the ceiling to one side. 'We told her it was rustic, but probably not,' he confessed. 'Although it's a lot better than it was.'

'I know. It's all wired up now.' Vicki was impressed. The last time she had been here, in October, the only electricity had been from a junction box in the living room. They'd had to run wires across the floor for lightbulbs and for the oven. Now there were lights in every room.

'We had an electrician in,' Giles said.

Vicki found a switch beside the door and flicked it on. The bulb fluttered into life. 'Very impressive,' she said. Even if there was no lampshade.

'Oh, that's not the end of it. We have a shower now, too, as well as an indoor toilet. Your mother did some of the plumbing for that. We've put in a couple of makeshift walls.'

'I saw.' Vicki had passed the bathroom on her way through to the workshop. The walls looked to be made of plywood. 'So where am I going to be sleeping?'

Giles gestured to the stairs. 'Well, now.' Vicki moved out onto the narrow landing. There was a stone wall to her left and a sheer drop to her right. Giles popped his head out of the door behind her. 'Did you see the ladder opposite the bathroom?'

Vicki moved onto the stairs. 'What, you mean the one leading up to that hole?'

Giles nodded, taking a moment to steady himself on the landing behind her. 'That's the one,' he said. Vicki reached the bottom step and looked back. Giles was following her down, using the wall to balance himself. He was wheezing badly. They really did need to put a handrail in here. 'Your mother hasn't had time to do much in there yet, but I thought you wouldn't mind.' He reached the bottom step and took a moment to catch his breath. 'You and your young man.'

Vicki rolled her eyes. 'He does have a name, daddy. Akash. Akash Antonelli.'

Giles pursed his lips. 'Akash.' He nodded, with a hint of disapproval.

Vicki stifled a laugh. Daddy had never approved of any of her boyfriends, but he seemed to have taken a particular dislike to Akash. In his opinion, the boy was not good enough for her. She dreaded to think what he would say when he found out they were planning to get married. That was not the only news, of course. 'Daddy, you have to promise to be nice to him. We've both come all this way and it's meant to be a happy occasion.'

Giles inclined his head. 'I shall be very polite.' He adjusted his glasses.

'No, not *polite*, daddy. Friendly.' Vicki laughed. 'I know what you're like when you're being *polite*.'

'All right, all right,' Giles agreed, with good humour. 'I'll be friendly. Even if he does start playing that awful guitar of his.'

'He's a very good guitarist,' Vicki said, loyally. And she meant it. Akash had insisted on bringing the guitar with him.

He had aspirations to be a musician and he certainly had the talent for it. She loved watching him strumming away, lost in a world of his own.

'Oh, I don't disagree,' Giles said. 'It's his taste in music I question.' He smiled. 'Don't worry, Victoria. I'll be as good as gold. I promise.'

'Thank you, daddy.' She gave him another hug and kissed him on the cheek.

'We haven't decided what to do with this room yet.' He indicated the workroom, a hangar-like space which ballooned out from the bottom of the staircase. It was enormous but dimly lit, with a set of exterior doors off to their right, through which a modicum of light flickered, and lots of small holes in the roof, way above. 'Your mother wants to use it as a workshop.' There was already a lot of bric-a-brac in here. A work bench, various tools. Lots of junk too, things daddy had bought. Magazines and boxes piled up underneath the stairwell, in front of a locked interior door. Giles did like to horde somewhat and it looked like this was the place where a lot of it was being stored. But there was room for work too. Mum had probably cut a lot of the wood for the stairs in here, with a little help from a local handyman or two. 'You know what she's like,' Giles added. 'She loves her DIY. And then over here...' He moved across the workshop towards the far door. 'We'll use this as a pantry and wash room, since we've already got the plumbing.' He stood at the doorway, looking down into the utility room. It was in here, in a corner, that the new bathroom had been erected.

Vicki came to a halt beside her dad. 'And your wine rack as well?' she teased. Dad was very fond of wine. He had ambitions to grow his own grapes, at some point.

'Eventually. That's certainly the plan. We're hoping to begin planting in the spring. But it will be a few years before we see any results. In the meantime....' He smiled. 'I shall potter about and look after your mother.'

'She'll look after you, you mean.' Vicki chuckled. Mum and dad had always made quite an odd couple, but they complimented each other. Marion was the hard working, outdoor type. She liked to make things and was never happier than when planing a plank of wood or banging in a nail. She never kept still. Dad was a much gentler soul, happy with his books and a good bottle of wine. He liked to potter around the markets, finding all sorts of bric-a-brac. He did a bit of cooking, though, and fancied himself as something of a gourmet. Not that he didn't do his bit too, as far as the household was concerned. In fact, he did most of the domestic chores – the washing, the cleaning and the cooking; anything that didn't involve heavy lifting. Mum took care of the heavy duty work and any of the technical challenges.

'Where's your luggage?' Giles asked. 'I'll show you to your room.'

'I left it in the kitchen. Daddy.' She hesitated.

Giles looked back from the doorway. 'What is it?'

Vicki took a deep breath. It was better to tell him now, about Robbie, rather than letting him stumble into the living room and finding him sitting there. 'We've got a visitor,' she said. 'We ran into someone on the way here. Just up the lane.'

'Oh?'

'Now, you're not to be cross.' She sighed. There was no easy way of breaking the news. 'It was Robbie.'

There was a very long pause, as Giles digested the news. He put a hand up to steady himself on the door. 'Robbie? He's here?'

'He's had an accident,' Vicki said, anxious to avoid any awkwardness. 'He fell off his motorbike. He's okay, but it's been a bit of a shock.'

Giles considered this for a moment, his eyes hardening behind his oval spectacles. The two had fallen out quite spectacularly some years before and he was unlikely to welcome the boy with open arms. 'But what is he doing here? What's he doing in France?'

'I don't know. He said he was coming to see you. Well, to see mummy.'

Giles pursed his lips. 'He can't stay here.'

'Daddy....'

'We have guests. I'm not having Robert upsetting anyone...' Giles was not a man to lose his temper, but he could be very stubborn.

'It's only Uncle Dave and Aunt Betsy. They know what he's like,' Vicki protested. Robbie had always been prickly with people, even before he had fallen out with his father.

'I'm not having it.' Giles was firm. 'It's not acceptable, Victoria. He should not have come. It'll upset your mother.'

'But he's here now,' Vicki insisted. 'And he's got nowhere else to go.'

'That's his fault.'

'Oh, daddy! Don't you think this has gone on long enough? You should talk to him at least.'

Giles looked away, and adjusted his spectacles awkwardly. 'I can't just…'

'For mum's sake. You know how hard it's been for her. And this is her weekend. We don't want to ruin it for her…'

'I didn't ask him to come here, Victoria. It wasn't me who started this.'

'You can't still be angry about the money.'

'It wasn't the money. It wasn't even the embarrassment. It was what he did afterwards. How can I forgive him for that?' His eyes burned angrily, though his voice was as softly spoken as ever. 'I was in hospital, for goodness sake. He didn't even come to visit me. He didn't try to apologise. And what he put your mother through.'

'I know, daddy. But she's out in the kitchen with him. She's making him a cup of tea. She's forgiven him. Why can't you? I know he did some horrible things. But he's your son. It's not as if he killed anybody.'

Giles considered that for a moment.

'Do it for me, daddy, if not for him.'

He let out a heavy sigh. 'All right. I'll hear what he has to say for himself.'

'Thank you, daddy.'

Giles closed his eyes. 'You're a good girl, Victoria. I promise I won't make a scene.'

Vicki smiled as Akash wheeled the motor scooter through the

doors. The barn was on the east side of the house. The doors were enormous and it had taken quite a bit of effort to pull them open. The building shared a wall with the main house, but was on a lower level. A set of steps led up from it to the living room. Akash had donned Robbie's helmet, to walk the scooter down the road, and his face was obscured as he manoeuvred the vehicle into position. It was a sensible precaution. In England, you could be arrested for not wearing a helmet, even just walking, and it was probably the same in France. Vicki stepped back and watched as he found the mounting and moved the bike onto its stand.

Akash rested the moped in front of a sofa, which was covered over with a sheet. The barn was every bit as cluttered as the workshop, though a lot of the stuff here had probably come with the building. The place was gloomy but Vicki had already flicked on the lights. There was a lathe off to one side and, up against the wall, what looked like a ping pong table, its two ends collapsed and standing vertical together. At the far end of the barn, accessible by a crude wooden ladder, was some kind of hayloft.

Akash removed his helmet, shaking out his curly brown hair, and placed it on the front handles of the bike. He grinned at Vicki as she came across to him and gave him a kiss. 'Thanks for doing that,' she said.

'Hey, no worries.' He glanced down at the moped with an appreciative eye. 'I don't think it's in too bad a nick. It might not be a total write-off.' He scratched his nose. Akash was a good looking young man, with a boyish face and dark brown eyes. 'Your Uncle Dave knows about bikes, doesn't he?'

Uncle Dave was another one of the guests this weekend. He was a school teacher, and had taught for a term at the local comprehensive where Akash had spent his formative years.

'He used to turn up on one.' Akash grabbed the handlebars and chuckled at the memory. 'Huge great thing it was. Much bigger than this.'

Vicki smiled at the thought. 'He does love to ride.' Her Uncle Dave had always been a huge motorcycle enthusiast. She remembered him sitting her up on the seat of his bike, when she

16

was a little girl, much to her dad's disapproval. Dave had been as much a part of her childhood as Aunt Betsy, though he was not technically a relative either, just a family friend. He had moved away from Hounslow now, but for a time they had all lived quite close to each other. 'I don't think he would know how to fix them,' Vicki said. She pulled out her phone from a pocket to check the time. 'He should be landing about now.' Dave and his girlfriend were flying out to Bergerac this morning, along with Aunt Betsy and her young man. Vicki looked back at the moped, imagining Dave, with his enormous legs, trying to fit onto it. 'I don't think it's his kind of bike.'

Akash plonked himself down on the seat. 'So where do your reckon Robbie picked this up? It's got French plates on. You don't think he nicked it, do you?'

Vicki was appalled at the suggestion. 'No, of course not. He wouldn't have stolen it.'

Akash wasn't being mean. She had told him all about her brother. 'He does have form for that sort of thing, doesn't he?'

'I know. But that's in the past now.'

Akash nodded amiably. He patted his lap. 'Come here.'

Vicki smiled, pulled up the hem of her dress and sat herself squarely on his lap. His arms gripped her firmly around the waist. It was nice to feel the warmth of him. It was quite chilly out here in the barn. Vicki was wearing a cardigan over her dress and thick winter tights, but it felt like the middle of January rather than early April. She didn't care though. She had Akash with her. She turned her head to face him, and kissed him again on the lips.

'I love you,' she said, staring into his dark brown eyes.

Akash grinned back at her, lifting a finger to touch her nose. 'Quite right too.' he chuckled, squeezing her tightly and kissing her back. 'Love you too, doll.'

'Are you glad you came?'

'Yeah. It's gonna be great. Breaking bread with Mr Flint.' He chuckled. His old school teacher. 'And it's nice for you to see your mum and dad. I know how close you are to them.'

'It feels like I've come home,' Vicki said. It sounded daft, when she put it like that. This was only her second visit to the farm. But wherever mum and dad were, that was home for her. Vicki kissed Akash again and they remained locked together. She could feel him waking up slowly beneath her, despite the cold. She pulled back for a moment and looked him in the eye. She could see the mischief there.

'There's a hayloft at the back,' he pointed out, nodding towards the rear of the barn.

Vicki shook her head. If it hadn't been so cold, she might have been tempted. 'It's too chilly.'

He rubbed her belly and a hand fell on her breast. 'I'll soon warm you up.'

She pushed his shoulder back gently. 'Not here. Mum's just outside. She'll hear us.' Marion was out the front, chopping wood. It was cold enough outside now, but it would be absolutely freezing when the sun went down. The house had no central heating and they would need a proper fire to huddle around. Marion had replaced the hearth in the living room with a large wood burner. That would keep the living room warm at least. The funnel stretched up the old chimney flute, through a hole in the ceiling, past the bedroom where Vicki and Akash would be sleeping tonight, and up to the chimney pot above. Hopefully, the bedroom would feel the benefit too.

Akash was miming disappointment.

'Maybe later,' she said, kissing him again. 'After supper.'

'All right, doll.' His hand rubbed against her belly and Vicki placed her hand on top of his. There was a baby growing inside her. A little person. It seemed strange to think of it. Akash knew, but nobody else did yet. There wasn't really much of a bump, even though she was four and a half months gone. Her mum must have felt it though, when they had hugged. Vicki wondered if she had put two and two together. 'Hard to believe there's a little Antonelli in there,' Akash said, with a broad grin.

'A little Wilkerson, you mean.'

He nodded. 'So are you hoping for a boy or a girl?'

'I don't mind,' Vicki said, 'just so long as it's healthy.'

'It will be,' he assured her, squeezing her hand. 'When are we going to do it? When are we going to tell everyone the good news?'

Vicki had already made up her mind about that. 'At supper.' That seemed like the best time. It would give the whole family an extra little thing to celebrate, on top of the house warming and her parents' anniversary. 'Mummy will be so pleased,' she said.

'What about your dad?'

'I think so. When he's had the chance to think about it.' She slipped off his lap. 'He'll enjoy being a grandad.' She looked down at her clothes, and brushed away the crumples near the hem of her dress.

'How did he react, when you told him about Robbie?'

'He was very calm,' Vicki said. Her dad had entered the living room ahead of her. Robbie had been sitting on the sofa in front of the wood burner, with his trousers off, a loose shirt hanging down, covering his underpants. Vicki was a little disconcerted, when she saw the bruising on his left leg. It wasn't just black and blue; there was dried blood as well. Robbie had refused to let them call a doctor, but Marion put some antiseptic on it, just to be on the safe side. For a moment, when the two of them entered the room, nobody spoke. 'Daddy could see Robbie had been in the wars. He asked him how he was. Once they'd started talking, mum and I left them to it. She went out to chop some more wood, and then you got here.' Vicki frowned, gazing at the steps leading up to the living room. The door was shut. *I hope everything is going all right.* 'I haven't heard any raised voices. I'm hoping…I'm hoping they'll find some common ground. They need to put it all behind them now. This has been going on for too long. It needs sorting.'

'It'll be fine, doll,' Akash said, pushing her gently up and then standing himself. He moved around the motorbike and pulled back the dust cover on the sofa behind it. 'This looks all right.'

'Dad must have picked it up somewhere. He's always finding bargains.'

Akash plopped himself down onto the cushion and gave it a bit of a thump. Vicki moved across to sit next to him. 'They can't chuck him out on his ear now, can they?'

'No. No, they can't. He'll have to let him stay the night at least. He's got nowhere else to go.'

After the falling out, Vicki had been the only one to stay in touch with Robbie. They had exchanged messages even when he had been abroad, and Vicki had passed on his whereabouts to mum.

Akash scratched his chin. 'I never really understood what it was all about,' he admitted. Vicki had made a point of shielding him from the ins and outs of it all. It wasn't fair to put all her burdens on him. But she had never concealed anything either. 'I mean, I know he stole some money and then buggered off,' Akash said, 'but we all do stupid things when we're young, don't we?' He slid a hand into his coat pocket and pulled out a packet of Rizlas. The action was quite deliberate. At twenty-four years old, Akash was not long past adolescence himself, though he was a few years older than Vicki.

'Not here!' she said, her hand sliding down to her stomach. 'The baby.'

'Oh, yeah.' He nodded, pulling out a pouch. 'I'll save it for later.' He started to roll a joint.

'Don't let daddy see you doing that!'

Akash laughed. 'He's not *my* dad. Not yet, anyway.' His fingers worked expertly to lay it out in his hand. 'But he's family, isn't he? Your brother, I mean. You forgive and forget.'

'It wasn't only the money. If it had just been the one time...'

'He stole your dad's credit card, didn't he?'

'Not just *his* card. And he dropped out of university at the same time. He was studying economics.'

Akash linked the ends of the paper and sealed up the join. 'Yeah, I remember you saying.'

'Dad paid out a fortune in fees. But Robbie hated it. It was three years of torture, he said. So he dropped out, and decided to go off travelling. Daddy was livid. If Robbie wanted to take a gap year before starting uni, or even afterwards, dad would probably have come around to the idea. But to throw off his studies at the last minute like that.'

Akash grinned, stashing the joint behind his ear. 'Yeah, that would never do, would it?'

'Dad was absolutely livid. He refused to give Robbie any more money, so Robbie stole half a dozen credit cards from his friends. On my birthday, too. If it had just been the family, it might have been all right. But we had a lot of guests that weekend. A bit of a party. And Robbie stole the lot.'

Akash whistled in mock appreciation. 'That took a lot of nerve. Not exactly clever, mind you.'

'No. He didn't really think it through. He never does. But he managed to spend quite a bit of money before the police caught up with him. He booked a flight to South America, and got as far as Madrid before the police found him.'

Akash raised an eyebrow. 'So he ended up in prison.' That much Vicki had already told him. 'Seems a bit much, for a first offence.'

Vicki looked away. 'It wasn't exactly a first offence. He was caught shop-lifting before that. Quite a few years ago. This time, he was given a suspended sentence. Two years. He was supposed to report in every week, but he never bothered to turn up. And so he went to jail.' Vicki shuddered at the memory of it. Seeing him behind bars like that. Seeing how much it had hurt her mum and dad. It was an awful time. 'Even then, daddy might have forgiven him. But then he had his accident, just after Robbie got out.' Giles had been doing a parachute jump for charity, and had broken his leg. 'He ended up in hospital, and Robbie didn't even come to visit him. He didn't speak to mum either. He knew she was at the hospital, so he went home, got on the computer and stole from him all over again. Dad's never been very internet savvy. He had all his passwords on a sticky note by the screen. Robbie...he broke into dad's bank account and transferred ten thousand pounds to his own account.'

'Jesus. That's a lot of money. And the bank just let him?'

'He had to phone them to confirm it, but he had all the passwords and the birthdays and all that.'

'And then he buggered off to Africa?'

'That's right. Dad was so upset, when he came out of hospital.'

21

'I'm not surprised. Not much of a homecoming.'

'He'd been all set to welcome Robbie back into the fold. That was the stupid thing.'

'And now he turns up here, out of the blue. And we nearly kill him.' Akash chuckled.

'Don't laugh about it,' Vicki said. 'An inch or two either way...I dread to think what would have happened.'

'It wasn't your fault, doll. And he's all right, isn't he? Just a few scrapes and bruises.'

'Yes. Yes, thank goodness.'

'You kept in touch with him, though? All through this?'

'Yes, we've texted. Emailed. Well, you've seen.' Vicki had been determined not to lose touch, even though she had sent two or three messages for every one she'd got back. 'And I've always kept mum up to date. She tries not to show it, but she does worry about him.'

'Only natural.' Akash gazed down thoughtfully at her belly. 'Let's hope *our* little monster doesn't turn out that way.'

'Robbie's not that bad,' Vicki said. 'He just gets a bit angry sometimes.'

'Just needs to meet a good woman,' Akash reckoned.

She nodded. 'It would do him the power of good.' She glanced across once again at the living room door. 'Do you think I should go and see how they're getting on? It's been twenty minutes now.'

'You might as well. It looks like nobody's stormed out, anyway.' He pulled Vicki close to him and kissed her. A lascivious look played across his face. He gestured to the hayloft. 'You sure you don't fancy a quickie first? I've never done it in a hayloft.'

Vicki laughed and rolled her eyes. 'Later,' she said, standing up. She moved across to the front of the barn, listening for any sounds from the house, but she couldn't hear anything. Her mum must have finished chopping up the wood out the front. She hesitated, at the bottom of the stairs. Perhaps it would be better to wait. She didn't want to interrupt, if Robbie and dad were having a serious heart to heart. Better to let them get it all out of their system. Robbie could be pig-headed sometimes, but

22

so could Giles. In many ways, the two of them were rather alike, though neither of them would ever admit it.

In the distance, she could hear the sound of a vehicle; a car coming down the lane. She looked to Akash, a mass of curly hair still sprawled out on the sofa. 'Someone's coming,' she said. 'It must be Uncle Dave and Aunty Betsy. It must be their taxi.'

Akash rose up from the sofa, dropping the dust cover back on top of it. He pulled his coat around his shoulders and grinned at Vicki. 'Let's go and say hi, then.'

They stepped out of the barn together and Akash gave a friendly smile to Marion Wilkerson. Vicki's mum was standing with her axe by a pile of wood, gazing across the field at the approaching vehicle. She wasn't smiling, though. Her heavily lined face was creased in concern. For a moment, Vicki could not understand why. Then she realised that the vehicle was not a taxi.

Two smartly dressed gendarmes were driving towards them.

Chapter Two

Emma McNamara was struggling not to laugh. Dave had told her that Betsy Klineman was a force of nature, and he had not been kidding. It was all Emma could do to keep a straight face. 'You should have seen the dress,' the woman blabbered, her hand tapping the edge of the seat rest between them. 'I was saying to Nicholas, that dress was gorgeous. All the lace and fripperies. I was the maid of honour, you know. The train was half a mile long. Honestly, I was still at the church door when Marion was saying her vows.' She chuckled.

Betsy Klineman was a large woman in her early forties, not fat but big boned, and colourfully dressed, her face plastered with make-up. For all that, she was an attractive woman, with an angular head and a matt of dark brown hair, but it was the mouth that really drew Emma's eye, the perfect white teeth flashing constantly

Her attention was beginning to flag, however. Emma was happy enough to sit next to her on the flight out to France, but Dave had been right: Betsy Klineman could talk the hind legs off a donkey. They had been in the air for almost an hour now and the woman had barely drawn breath.

It would be nice to get away for a few days, though. Emma loved her job – at a veterinary clinic in Hythe – but she enjoyed a bit of a change from time to time. She didn't know any of the people she would be spending the weekend with. Betsy was a complete stranger, as was her bloke, Nicholas, a shy young man in his early twenties, who was sitting with Dave two rows in front of them. She didn't know Giles and Marion Wilkerson either. They were old friends of Dave's, apparently. They had bought a farmhouse in the south of France and decided to move out there permanently. This weekend was intended to be a late house warming as well as a wedding anniversary. If they were anything like Betsy then the whole thing was going to be a hoot.

'And you'll never guess what,' Betsy continued. She was

still talking about the wedding. 'When they got to the bit about "any just cause" not to go ahead, one of the little kids farted.' Emma laughed and Betsy shrieked at her own comment. 'Really loudly. It was totally deliberate. The little monster. He'd been holding it back, just for that moment. I was telling Nicholas, it brought the house down.'

'I can imagine.'

There was a gentle ping as the seatbelt light came on, and the captain's voice came over the speakers, momentarily interrupting the flow. It was a budget airline, so they had all been jammed in together, but Emma didn't mind. It was a relatively short flight and it looked as if they would be coming into land soon. The captain confirmed that over the tannoy. Outside the window, there was nothing but clouds. The temperature at Bergerac was a chilly two degrees Celsius, the captain said.

That got a coo from Betsy. 'I said it was going to be cold, didn't I? I was saying to Nicholas, bring your thermals, love, it's going to be freezing.' She shrieked again. 'And in April, who'd have thought it?'

Heavy snow was in the offing, the captain added, as she wished everybody a safe onward journey.

'I saw the forecast before we went,' Betsy said, as Emma refastened her safety belt. 'They said there might be snow. I was saying to Nicholas…'

Emma nodded again, beginning to zone out a little. It was quite amusing – entertaining even – the endless monologue, though she felt a bit sorry for Betsy's boyfriend, if he had to put up with it twenty-four-seven. 'She's a diamond,' Dave had said, before the flight, 'but only in small doses.'

Dave Flint was Emma's boyfriend. He was some years older than her, but he had a youthful outlook. A school teacher by trade, it had been his idea to fly out with Betsy and Nicholas. He and Betsy were old friends of the family. He had been best man at the wedding, while Betsy had been chief bridesmaid. Apparently, the two of them hadn't seen each other in years. Emma was pleased that Dave had invited her along for the ride. They had been dating for a couple of years now. Betsy had already asked her how they had met.

'I was coming out of the gym,' she said. 'I saw him parking up his motorbike. I had to check it out.' The bike was a top of the range Harley Davidson. An old man's bike, sure, but still impressive. They had got talking. 'I've always been a bit of a biker chick,' Emma confessed. 'There's nothing quite like the open road.'

'Dave's always loved his bikes,' Betsy agreed. 'He turned up at the wedding on a motorbike.'

'Anyhow, I bumped into him at the gym a couple of times, then we went for a coffee and things took off from there. There's a bit of an age gap.' Dave had just turned fifty, while Emma was a little shy of thirty. The girls in the office teased her about that relentlessly. They called him her Sugar Daddy, though he didn't earn any more than she did. 'But we get on so well. We have a lot in common. If you like someone, you like someone. And Dave's great to be around.'

'He is,' Betsy agreed. 'I know what you mean, lovey. I was saying to Nicholas, people can be so small minded. He's gorgeous, don't you think, my Nicholas?' She gestured a couple of rows forward to her own young man, whose blond hair was just visible over the top of the seat. Emma nodded politely. 'He's so shy, though. We met at work, did I tell you? He was doing some temping in the office. Wouldn't say boo to a goose. But I brought him out of his shell.' She laughed. 'I'm such a cradle snatcher, aren't I? Oh look, there's the airstrip.' She pointed a finger out of the window.

The plane had circled round and was now heading for the runway. A bald head peered back from a couple of rows in front. Dave Flint grinned across at them. Even strapped in with his seatbelt on, he towered over the lip of the seat. He was all arms and legs and had to be seated opposite the doors, so he could stretch himself out. He gave her a wink and Emma replied with a thumbs up. A few more minutes and they would be on the ground.

'Blimey, you weren't kidding!' Emma chuckled, as they moved

out of the arrivals lounge and onto the concourse. 'She didn't stop talking, the whole flight. I was creasing up!'

'I did warn you,' Dave laughed, as the doors slid open in front of them.

'You did. You did!' she agreed.

The big man shivered as a wall of ice hit them. 'Bloody hell, it's cold.' The arrivals lounge had been nice and snug but, out in the open air, the temperature wasn't much above freezing. Dave put down his rucksack.

'You're not exactly dressed for the Arctic,' Emma observed drily. She already had the hood of her coat up and was about to put on some gloves. Instead, she bent down and unflipped the lid of Dave's rucksack. 'Here, put this on.' She pulled out a scarf. 'We don't want you freezing to death.' Dave grinned and quickly wound it around his neck as she pulled out a woolly hat to go with it.

Emma gazed up at the great lump as he pulled the hat over his head. He was a giant of a man, six feet six in his stockinged feet. Emma wasn't exactly a short arse, but Dave towered over her, a mass of skinny arms and legs. He wasn't the best looking bloke in the world. The small blue eyes and long, thin nose were nothing to write home about. A straggling grey beard added a bit of character, and the woolly hat covered a fair amount of hair, below the naked crown. If anything, he looked like a retired basketball player. But there was more to a bloke than just his looks. Emma had dated her fair share of handsome idiots. A pretty face and a nice bum were all very well, but if you wanted a relationship to last, you needed someone who was on the same wave-length as you, someone with a twinkle in their eye who could make you laugh. If they had that, even if they were years older than you, then you were on to a winner. Dave put his coat back on, over the extra jumper, and zipped up the front.

The sky was a blanket of cloud, darkening even in the early afternoon. 'We'd better find a taxi,' Emma suggested. A road snaked past them towards the exit. 'Shame we couldn't have brought the bikes with us.' It would have been fun, rocking up to the airport in London and trying to persuade the airline to let the vehicles on board. She smiled at the daft thought.

'Give us a minute,' Dave said, pointing to a taxi sign. 'I'll just go and grab one.'

She watched him go. There was a bench nearby but she didn't really want to sit down again. She had been sitting for an hour and a half already, and the bench would probably be freezing anyway. *Welcome to Santa's Grotto,* she thought, her breath a chilly cloud in front of her. If the snow really did start to fall, perhaps they could organise a snowball fight, when they got to the farm. That would be a laugh. Dave would certainly love it. He was a big child, in many ways. A very big child.

Betsy Klineman had disappeared into a small shop, with her bloke in tow, to buy a few last minute items. "*La Boutique Des Délices*" the sign read. What exactly the '*délices*' were, Emma had no idea. All she could see were postcards, magazines and tubes of crisps.

She smiled at the pair on the other side of the glass. Nicholas Samoday, the boyfriend, was buried under a pile of snacks Betsy had grabbed from the shelves. She was chattering away to him, while the two of them quietly ransacked the small shop. Betsy was quite well off, by all accounts. Absolutely loaded, according to Dave. And several decades older than Nicholas. Not that Emma was going to cast any stones. She couldn't help but feel a bit sorry for the bloke, though, buried under all that rubbish, listening to Betsy blabbering on. He was quite cute looking, with a rounded face and a mop of blond hair which cut across his eyes. He wasn't really dressed for the cold either. He had a coat on, but it was a light one. Not thick enough for these temperatures. According to Dave, he was the son of a mutual friend; someone else who had been at Giles and Marion's wedding, all those years ago. Presumably, he wouldn't even have been a twinkle in somebody's eye back then. Betsy was notorious for her affairs. 'She's a right slapper,' Dave laughed, albeit with affection. 'Loves her toy boys, does Betsy.' The woman had been quite upfront about it on the plane. She had worked her way through a whole string of young men, by all accounts. And why not? There was no harm in having a bit of fun, so long as everyone was grown up about it.

Emma's eyes drifted from the two of them to the newspaper rack just outside the boutique. Her French was non-existent, but she didn't need it to understand these headlines. They confirmed what the pilot had said on the plane: heavy storms were expected. Like as not, they were going to be snowed in at the farm for a day or two. She rubbed her hands together. *I hope it's warm there.*

They were guaranteed a warm welcome, at least. Marion and Giles were a smashing couple, according to the big man. When Dave had booked the flights, a few weeks ago, they had had some hopes of warm weather. Early April was always tricky – you never knew what you were going to get – but it was only when they were packing their bags that it became apparent just how bad it was likely to be.

'Do you want to give it a miss?' Dave had asked her, on the phone last night. They didn't live together. They had separate flats. 'We don't have to go.'

Emma was not going to be put off by a little snow. So long as they got to the farm before it hit, that was all right with her. And if the return flights were delayed or cancelled and she couldn't get back to work next week, well, that was just too bad, wasn't it? Besides, she knew how much Dave wanted to see all his old mates. He hadn't seen much of them of late, since he had moved away from Hounslow; and now with the Wilkersons moving to the south of France. So, they might be forced to stay a few days longer than they anticipated. Work could hardly complain if the airport was closed down for the week. The girls at the clinic would be jealous, though.

Dave was lumbering towards her, grinning and waving. 'The taxi's just coming,' he said.

Betsy was leaving the shop, with Nicholas in tow.

A vehicle pulled around the bend towards them.

'Just in time,' Emma said, grabbing hold of the luggage. The first flakes of snow were beginning to fall.

Dave Flint sucked in his cheeks and shook his head with mock gravity. 'A double bed? That's no good.' He pretended to grimace. 'What will people say? She's young enough to be my daughter.'

'Granddaughter,' Emma put in cheekily, standing by the bed.

Marion Wilkerson had shown them into the room where they would be spending the next three nights.

Dave jerked a thumb at Emma, continuing the pretence. 'She'll have to sleep on the floor and she won't be happy. Not in this weather.'

A small window gave out to the front of the house and the snow was falling persistently now. Dots of white had already spotted the grass as they'd clambered out of the taxi a few minutes earlier. The cab driver had not been able to pull up too close, as there were already three vehicles in the drive, so Emma and the others had to unload the boot and carry their luggage the last few metres.

One of the vehicles was a police car. Two gendarmes had been standing at the front door, bidding their farewells. That was something Emma had not been expecting to see when she arrived at the house. 'You didn't tell me they were criminals,' she teased, quietly, as they made their way over. The officers waved a respectful hand as they passed her by and returned to their car. The visit was more of a courtesy call than a criminal investigation, as it turned out.

In the bedroom, Dave was now crouching down theatrically and peering underneath the bed. His joints clicked a couple of times as he did so. 'Thought I'd better check if there was anyone under there,' he joked. 'Just to be on the safe side.'

Apparently, a nearby farmhouse had been broken into in the last few days. A couple of vagrants had set up home there for a night or two, helping themselves to food and beds, while the owners were away. That was why the gendarmes had called, to ask if Giles and Marion had seen anything amiss over the last week or so, and to warn them of possible break-ins. A few things had gone missing from the house before the intruders had left.

Marion had met the new arrivals at the door. She was a solid, no nonsense woman in her mid-forties, with a wide face

30

and a practical manner.

Her daughter Vicki, who was with her, was a little more diffident, though her smile was equally sincere. She was short and slim, with a bland but not unattractive face. She had straight honey blonde hair which reached down to her shoulders. Betsy Klineman had made a particular fuss of her.

Introductions were handled swiftly and there was much exchanging of news and gifts. Betsy was jabbering so much, it was several minutes before Marion had managed to disengage and show them all to their rooms. Betsy and Nicholas were given the middle bedroom, while Emma and Dave were put at the far end.

Dave lifted himself up from the bed. 'Well, I suppose we'll have to make do,' he said, with a twinkle. He looked from Emma to the woman of the house.

Marion showed no signs of taking offence at all the daft banter. She was obviously used to Dave's sense of humour, though she had no intention of being drawn into it. Just as well really, Emma thought. Marion was clutching a bottle of wine in her hand, which Dave had presented to her on the doorstep. A good vintage, too. He was never stingy with things like that.

'Well, I'll leave you to determine the sleeping arrangements,' Marion said. 'I'm glad you could come, dear,' she added to Emma. 'And thank you for this.' She lifted up the bottle of wine. 'Giles will appreciate it. I'm sorry he wasn't here to greet you. A bit of a last minute crisis. There's been so much to do.'

'That's all right,' Emma assured her. 'All adds to the fun, doesn't it?'

'I'm not so sure about that,' Marion said. 'We certainly weren't expecting the police to turn up this afternoon.'

'Your French is very good,' Emma said. She had overheard her saying goodbye to the gendarmes. She hadn't understood the words, but she recognised a good accent when she heard it.

Marion beamed with pride. 'I have lessons twice a week, in Duras. Well, I'll let you settle in, dear. Dave. Giles is so looking forward to seeing you. Come through to the kitchen when you're done, and Vicki will get you something to drink.'

She moved to the door, intent on heading back to the living room, but before she got two metres, Betsy Klineman started shrieking at her.

'This place is gorgeous!' Betsy exclaimed. 'I was just telling Nicholas…'

Thankfully, the door swung back behind Marion at this point, cutting off most of the babble. Emma rolled her eyes and grinned at Dave.

'We're going to have to walk through there, every time we need to go to the lav,' he pointed out.

Emma nodded. That was going to be fun, in the middle of the night. 'I don't suppose they've got a po in here anywhere, have they?' She glanced around the room. It was a pretty functional affair, with bare stone walls, a chest of drawers and a double bed. The only decoration was a landscape painting above the bed. It would do the job, though. There was a rug on the floor and a portable electric fire next to the bedside table. The fire was plugged into the wall and three bars were glowing red, doing their best to heat up the room. There were several doors in here, including one out to the front, and an internal door at the back. 'Perhaps we can nip through there,' Emma suggested, moving across. She grabbed the handle but the door was locked. 'Or perhaps not.'

Dave was already trying the exterior door. It was on a latch but it was not locked. Dave pulled it open and a blast of cold air filled the room. 'There you go. We can go outside, if we need to.' The front lawn was barely six feet away. 'Plenty of bushes out there.'

Emma laughed. 'Oh, you'd love that, wouldn't you? Forcing me outside in the middle of the night, just to have a pee.'

Dave shrugged good-naturedly. 'Getting back to nature. Nothing wrong with that.'

'My arse would freeze off before I'd even got my knickers down. I'd be a block of ice.'

'Don't worry.' Dave closed up the door. 'I'd come and dig you out in the morning. Well, after breakfast, anyway.' He returned to the bed and sat down on top of it. The ceiling was a little bit low in here, for someone of his height, and he had to

32

stoop whenever he was standing up. He looked like a giant in a doll's house.

'You're going to have to watch your head,' Emma said. There were wooden beams across the ceiling and the frames of the doors were particularly low.

'That'll make a change,' he grumbled, lying back on the blanket but keeping his feet on the floor.

'Are you going to fit on that bed?' Emma wondered. The mattress was wide enough for two, but barely long enough for the likes of Dave.

'No problem,' he assured her. He put his head on a pillow on the left hand side, lifted his legs up onto the blanket and then wriggled his feet across to the opposite corner, so that he was lying diagonally across the whole of the bed. 'See. Perfect fit.' He looked up at Emma in apparent innocence.

'And where am I supposed to sleep?'

He shrugged nonchalantly. 'The floorboards are quite comfortable. And you'll be right next to the radiator. Or you could lie crossways. Head here, legs down there.' He gestured to the diagonal. 'Just have to go underneath halfway.'

Emma laughed. 'It wouldn't be the first time.' Whenever they shared a bed, he would somehow contrive to end up on top of her; or to pull the duvet away, though only ever in jest. She looked down on him affectionately for a moment, his ridiculous, gangly frame as out of place as ever, spread out over top of the blanket. 'You stupid sod.'

That was what she liked about Dave. He never took anything seriously. When they had started dating, two years ago, it had been just a casual thing. She had liked him from the get-go but she never expected it to be anything more than a fling. She certainly never wanted to move in with him or make any particular commitment, and she still didn't. But she was happy to drift along, enjoying his company, never getting too serious. And somehow, they had become a couple. Dave had been through the wars, before they met. He had been diagnosed with cancer and had lost most of his hair in chemo. It had come back on the lower part of his head, but not anywhere else. 'I'm as bald as a baby's bum down there,' he often joked, gesturing to his crotch. 'No sign of life at all.' He hadn't been kidding either. It had been quite a novelty at first, when they started going out. He was given the all clear after a couple of years but he still had regular check ups. And here they were, two years later, a couple. They got on so well together that there had never come a point where Emma wanted to end it. She still wasn't sure if she was in it for the long haul, but she was happy to coast along. Living apart probably helped, stopping things getting stale. When Dave had told her about the reunion in France and asked her if she wanted to tag along, she'd jumped at the chance. Anything for a change of scene. It had certainly been entertaining up to now.

Emma left Dave to unpack his stuff and went to freshen up. Betsy Klineman was rabbiting away to Marion in the middle bedroom, so she was able to slip past them with just a smile and a wave. She moved into the living room.

Vicki Wilkerson, the daughter, was on kettle duty. The girl shot her a friendly smile. The living room served as a kitchen too. A row of units stretched along the back and west wall; a sink, an oven, even a dishwasher. A large dining table dominated the centre of the room. A sofa and a couple of armchairs sat opposite a metal fireplace, which was blazing away nicely. There was a cabinet with a television inside in one corner, but it wasn't connected up to anything.

Emma moved across the room. The roof was a little higher than in the bedroom, so she didn't need to watch her head as she passed under the thick oak beams.

'How is your room?' Vicki asked her. She was a slim, diffident creature, her blue eyes lost beneath pencil thin eyebrows. She didn't look like her mother at all, though they were a similar height.

'Warming up,' Emma said, her hands stretching out in the direction of the wood burner. The kettle was just coming to the boil. Emma placed her wash bag down on the dining room table and moved over to it. The floor was cobbled underfoot, though a carpet was spread out beneath the table itself. 'It's very nice.

Dave's marking out his territory. I thought I'd better leave him to it.'

Vicki's face lit up at the mention of his name. 'It was so good he was able to come.'

'You couldn't keep him away. He's been looking forward to this.'

'He's part of the family,' Vicki said. 'I've known him since I was a girl.'

'Yes, he told me. Said he used to bounce you on his knee.' Emma laughed. 'Lucky you didn't get vertigo.'

'I gather you've been together for a couple of years?'

'Yes, on and off. He's great fun, Dave. Well, you know that, perfect "uncle". Where's the bathroom? Out back, your mum said?'

'Yes, just through there.' Vicki gestured to a door at the rear of the living room, on the left-hand side. 'I think…Nicholas, is it?' Betsy's young man. 'I think he's in there at the moment.'

'Oh, right. Never mind, I can wait.'

'Would you like a drink? The kettle's just boiled. '

'I wouldn't mind a glass of water, actually.'

Vicki nodded and poured her out a glass from the sink.

'When did *you* get here?' Emma asked her. 'This morning?'

'Yes, about midday,' Vicki said. 'Me and Akash. He's my boyfriend.'

'The curly haired bloke?' Emma had seen him when they arrived.

'Yes, that's him. I'm not sure if Uncle Dave recognised him, but they do know each other. He taught for a term at Akash's school.'

'Small world.' Emma took a sip of water.

'It was a few years ago now. But he still calls him Mr Flint.'

Emma leaned back against the table. 'It's a nice place your parents have got. Very rustic. I wasn't sure what to expect.'

'I hope you won't be too chilly. We put the heater on in your room.'

'Yeah, it's just starting to take the edge off.'

'I slept in there the last time I was here,' Vicki said. 'The bed's very comfortable. Did you see the painting on the wall?'

'What, the landscape? Yes, I saw it. Who is it? Some local artist?'

'No. My dad did it,' Vicki said proudly. That would be Giles Wilkerson. Emma hadn't met him yet. 'He's very talented.'

'He must be. I shall have to have a proper look at it.' Emma suppressed a smile. The daughter of the house seemed rather earnest. Still, nothing wrong with bigging up your parents. 'How old is this place, anyway?'

'Oh, hundreds of years,' Vicki said. 'Seventeenth century I think.'

That sounded about right. Emma glanced up at the ceiling. Three large wooden beams supported the roof. Two of them were dark and old – clearly part of the original house – but the third was light and more recent.

'Nobody wanted to buy it,' Vicki said. 'Dad got it for a song. He says the French aren't really interested in places like this. They like new buildings. The house was pretty run down when they bought it.'

That was an understatement. Emma could see the appeal, though. Something to get your teeth into. 'It needed a lot of work, did it?'

'It still does,' Vicki admitted. 'But mum's done so much in six months. We barely even had electricity when I was out here last year.'

A distant flush interrupted them – someone finishing off in the bathroom – and a minute later the intervening door opened. Emma suppressed a smile as Nicholas Samoday – Betsy's young man – appeared at the door and did a double take at the sight of the two women staring across at him.

'Oh, hello,' he mumbled, attempting a smile.

'Hello again,' Vicki said, warmly.

Emma grabbed her wash bag from the dining room table. 'What are the facilities like?' she asked, moving towards him.

'They're okay,' Nicholas said, not quite meeting her eye. He stepped to one side and looked across at Vicki. 'Erm…which is my room?'

'I'll show you,' she said.

Emma left them to it, moving through the far door.

'Oh, mind the step!' Vicki called out to her, just in time.
'Thanks!'

The utility room at the back of the house was gloomy, what little Emma could make out of it. It was cold too, with no heating. Wind was starting to whistle against the stone walls outside. The wall to her left, however, seemed to be made of plywood. It was only a little taller than head height, with no ceiling above it. She peered up and saw the roof of the house way above, with little bits of light flickering through. Vicki hadn't been kidding. This part of the house looked almost derelict. What had it been originally? she wondered. A stable? There was some light, from a bulb hanging above the makeshift wall to her left. *I'm guessing that's the bathroom.* There was a door a few feet along and another makeshift wall, around the corner. It looked like the whole place had been put up in a hurry, doubtless for the benefit of the guests.

Emma reached for the handle. The door wobbled under her grip, but before she could pull it open she heard a noise coming from behind her. She glanced back and saw a figure in silhouette, standing in the frame of a door on the opposite side of the room. 'Who's that?' she called out. She raised a hand to her forehead.

'Hello,' the figure replied. A man. 'Who are *you*?' He tripped down the steps from the doorway, moving into the light. He was lean and tallish, in his early to mid twenties perhaps. Quite fit looking. He had the same blue eyes as Vicki Wilkerson and his hair, though cut very short, was the same honey blonde. Her brother perhaps. Dave hadn't said anything about a brother being here.

Emma stepped forward and extended a hand. 'I'm Emma,' she said. 'Dave's other half. Just got here.'

'Oh, right.' He did not seem terribly interested. He was better looking than his sister, but his face was fixed into something of a scowl. He did not take her hand, so she was forced to drop it.

'You're one of the family, are you?'

'You could say that.' His tone was indifferent. 'I'm supposed to be keeping out of the way, at least until supper.'

37

His face softened then, as he eyed her up. She could feel his gaze lingering on her chest. 'I'm Robbie,' he said.

'Robbie. Nice to meet you.' Emma was intrigued. 'Why are you supposed to keep out of the way?'

'Haven't you heard? I'm *persona non grata*. Not supposed to talk to anyone, on pain of death.' His eyes flashed with amusement. 'I was just coming out here for a slash.'

At that, Emma laughed. 'Be my guest,' she said. She lifted up her wash bag. 'I was going to have a shower, but you're welcome to nip in first.'

Robbie shook his head and leaned back against the wall. 'No, you're all right. I'll go out the back.' He turned to the steps but stopped as a voice called out from the other side of the door.

'Robert!' An older man's voice. 'What did we say?' A second figure appeared in the doorway. Again, Emma struggled to make him out in the dim light, but this time the figure reached across and flicked a switch. A second lightbulb, hanging from one of the crossbeams above, now fizzled into life.

Robbie gazed up at the other man with barely disguised contempt. 'I know, I know. Keep out of the way until dinner. Don't blame me. I didn't know there was anyone in here.'

The older man, at a guess, was Giles Wilkerson. He was a portly bloke in his early fifties, balding with glasses and sporting a rather colourful jumper and a pair of red corduroy trousers. Not a man who gave much thought to his appearance, but at that age, it didn't really matter. 'You must be Emma,' he said, stepping carefully down into the room and holding out a hand. 'So nice to meet you.' He wheezed slightly, as if recovering his breath, but his voice was firm and cordial. 'This is my son, Robert. You'll have to forgive his manner. He can be a little abrupt on occasion.'

'Too right,' Robbie muttered.

'I'm sorry I wasn't here to greet you. How was your journey?'

'Not too bad,' Emma said. 'Glad we got here before the weather really hit.'

'Yes, I heard the forecast on the radio. It sounds as if it might be quite severe.' Giles had a distinctly cultivated voice. He looked and sounded like a slightly dishevelled university professor. 'But there's no cause for concern. We're very well provisioned. Although we hadn't expected to have to accommodate quite so many people this weekend.'

'He means me,' Robbie declared, with a grunt. 'I wasn't invited.'

'We weren't expecting him,' Giles put it, smoothly. 'But it's always nice to see him, of course.' The sentiment wasn't entirely convincing. *Those two have got some issues*, Emma thought. But it was none of her business. 'He'll be staying the night. So long as he minds his manners.'

Robbie rolled his eyes.

'That's what we agreed, Robert. This is a special occasion, for your mother and I. It's meant to be a happy time. We've both worked hard for it and I would appreciate it if you didn't do anything to upset her.'

'Course not. Wouldn't dream of it.' Robbie looked across at Emma and gave her a quick wink. She smiled back at him.

'I'll get you some blankets,' Giles said, addressing his son. 'You'd better unpack your things. Just for the one night, though. As we agreed.'

'Yeah, yeah, I get it.' Robbie scratched his head and grinned at Emma again. 'I'd better make myself scarce. I'm the bad penny.' He raised a mocking hand. 'I'll be seeing you later, probably.' With that, he turned his back and disappeared up the steps into the far room.

Giles gazed after him thoughtfully, then returned his attention to Emma. 'I have to apologise for my son. His manners can be a little rough on occasion. We really weren't expecting him this weekend.'

'That's all right,' Emma said. 'The more the merrier, as Dave would say.'

'David, of course.' Giles frowned at the mention of his friend's name. 'I quite forgot. I've been rushed off my feet, organising the beds. Then Robert arrived, and the gendarmes…'

'It's been a busy day,' Emma said.

'I should have been there to greet him, though. It's most remiss of me.'

'Oh, don't worry. He's unpacking the luggage. But he's looking forward to seeing you again. Catching up. You two go way back, I gather.'

'Yes, we've known each other for many years,' Giles agreed. 'He was the best man, at our wedding.'

'Yeah, he told me. Twenty-five years, eh? Congratulations.'

'Twenty five happy years,' Giles said, rather emphatically. He gestured to the living room door. 'Can I get you a drink? Something to warm you up?'

'Maybe in a minute.' Emma lifted her wash bag and jerked a thumb back at the bathroom. 'I was thinking of taking a shower, but it's a bit chilly in here.'

'There is a radiator inside,' Giles said. 'I'm not sure if Marion put it on. But the water's quite hot, if you leave it a minute or so to run through.'

Emma gazed up at the pipe, running along the inside wall. She could see the shower head too, just above the lip of the plywood. 'I'll give it a go,' she said. She'd wait for the water to warm up before she got undressed, though.

'I'll leave you to it, then.'

Emma pulled open the bathroom door. She moved inside, her eyes on the shower head at the far end of the room. It was a pretty rudimentary affair, attached to the living room wall, but with a curtain rail in front and some glass panelling against the plywood. There were tiles on the floor and a ceramic basin to catch the water. Dave had told her the facilities would be primitive, and they were, but she didn't mind. She had been in worse places than this. Some of the toilets in Ibiza...

The shower head was lower down than she had thought, tall enough for her, but likely not for Dave. Actually, with the height of the walls, his head would be visible from the outside when he went for a shower. Emma laughed, picturing his bald dome bobbing up and down from the outside as he lathered himself up.

She pulled back the arms of her jumper and stepped into the

shower. It was tricky, trying to switch it on without getting wet. Ordinarily, you stripped off first, but she'd freeze her tits off if she did that. There was a radiator on the floor, as Giles had said, but it wasn't switched on. It was a bit dodgy, having that in here, with all the water splashing about, but there weren't any exposed elements that she could see. Emma twisted the dial on the shower and stepped back quickly, before the head burst into life. She pulled the curtain closed in front of it, and then looked back at the rest of the bathroom. A toilet and a wash basin, some towels hanging from a rack and opposite the door, above the basin, a mirror. She hadn't really noticed that before. She moved across to it.

The mirror was not in a good state. A jagged crack ran diagonally across the centre, from top to bottom. The damage was recent. There were flecks of glass in the wash basin and some on the floor. Emma stared at her disjointed image in the glass and shivered, as the shower hissed into life.

Chapter Three

Vicki Wilkerson hadn't played ping pong in years. The table tennis set had come with the house, one of many abandoned items in the barn that nobody had touched in decades. There were all sorts of ancient sporting equipment in here. A basketball hoop, tennis rackets, baseball bats. It was the ping pong table that had caught Akash's eye, however. It was enormous, even folded up, and Vicki was happy to help him clear a bit of space and pull it out, to see if it might be usable. They had pulled down the sides and cleared off the cobwebs. Akash found a small box containing a net and a few bats, and once the net was tightened into place everything was set.

Vicki picked one of the bats and started serving. She had been quite good at table tennis as a girl and it came back to her quickly. A bit of exercise out in the barn would help to warm them all up.

Uncle Dave was catching up with dad out in the kitchen. Vicki hadn't had a chance to talk to him yet, not properly; but he had given her a big hug when he first came through the door. His girlfriend, Emma, seemed very nice. She had long, silky black hair, wide brown eyes and a beautiful, disarming smile. 'She's a bit of all right,' Akash had whispered, mischievously, when mum had led them off to show them their rooms. 'Nice figure, too.' Akash was never shy about showing his appreciation for the female sex.

Vicki jabbed him playfully in the stomach. 'You shouldn't be looking.'

'I only have eyes for you, doll. You know that. But Mr Flint knows how to pick them.'

'Nicholas is quite good looking too,' Vicki observed, determined to get her own back. Aunt Betsy's boyfriend had disappeared off to the bathroom, having barely spoken a word to anyone. Nicholas Samoday was the latest in a long line of shy young men who had fallen under Betsy's spell. She had met him at work, apparently. He was about the same age as

Vicki, but looked younger, with a boyish mop of fair hair flopping down and partly obscuring his eyes. The name Samoday was a familiar one, but Vicki couldn't recall where she had heard it before. Her mum had remembered though. 'I went to school with a girl called Mary Samoday,' she said.

Nicholas had been reluctant to join them out in the barn for a game of ping pong. He seemed to be floundering a little, with all these new people, but Vicki was determined to put him at his ease. She would have invited Emma along too, but the older girl had disappeared off somewhere. Vicki put on her best smile for Nicholas and pleaded with him to join them, assuring him it would be good fun. Akash had backed her up and between the two of them they had bamboozled him into coming out to the barn, leaving the older ones to catch up in the living room.

Once he started playing, Nicholas had suddenly come into his own. It turned out he was rather good at table tennis. After a quick three-way knock up, Akash had tactfully bowed out, leaving Vicki and Nicholas to play the first game. To her surprise – and a little annoyance – the young man had beaten her confidently in that first set, eleven-seven.

Akash was strumming his guitar, seated on the moped, paying only a casual interest in the game. Unlike Vicki, he had never been a particularly competitive person. He preferred to sit back and let other people fight it out. The music was soft but insistent. Akash really knew how to play. He knew a lot of songs off by heart; mostly old ones, all of them rock. He was dressed heavily against the cold – a woollen hat covering his curly brown hair – but the woollen gloves on his hands were fingerless, allowing him full rein on the guitar.

Vicki laughed as another ping pong ball whizzed past her head. She had barely had time to lift her bat. 'You really are good at this,' she said. She was feeling a bit chilly, her woollen tights not quite keeping out the cold, though her dress was thick and warm and she had a cardie on top of it. All this activity was helping to warm her up a little, though.

'That's two-one,' Nicholas said, with a shy smile.

She moved across to pick up the ball, which had bounced its

way over to daddy's wine rack in the far corner. Now that Nicholas was starting to relax, Vicki decided it was time to draw him out a little; to get him talking. 'Mum said she knew your mother. They went to school together.' That elicited no response. Vicki returned to the table with the ball. 'Apparently, she used to babysit my brother when he was very little.'

Nicholas shrugged. 'I don't remember. She died when I was very young.'

Vicki frowned. She hadn't realised his mother had died. 'I'm sorry,' she said, throwing the ball across the table to him. 'Did your father bring you up then?'

Nicholas served another hard shot, but this time Vicki got a bat to it and bashed it back across the table. It clipped the corner, an inch away from the waiting bat, and then disappeared.

'Two-all!' Vicki declared. That meant the serve returned to her.

Nicholas squatted down to retrieve the ball. 'I never knew my father,' he said, rising up. 'I don't know anything about him.' He spoke softly and Vicki had to strain to hear him. 'When my mum died, I was put into care. Foster parents, Steven and Angie. But I kept my mum's name.' He placed the ball on the table and set down his bat. 'I have a photograph,' he volunteered, reaching into his trouser pocket.

'Let me see.' Vicki skipped round the table.

Nicholas pulled out his wallet and, from inside, produced a faded photograph of a young woman. She had the same mop of fair hair as her son, partially covering her eyes. She did not look much older than Vicki was now. Or Nicholas. 'She was very pretty,' Vicki declared. She could see where Nicholas had inherited his looks from.

A photograph of any woman was enough to gain Akash's attention. 'Let's have a look.' He set his guitar aside and hopped down from the seat of the moped. 'Nice!' he agreed, coming to a halt next to Vicki and peering across Nicholas's shoulder. 'Really pretty. What did she die of?'

The young man hesitated. 'I don't really know. She had a fall, I think. I was only four at the time.'

44

'Too bad,' Akash said, as Nicholas returned the photo to his wallet.

The game resumed. Nicholas won the next point and recovered the serve. By now, Vicki's mind had wandered just a little. The last time she had played ping pong it had been with her brother, Robbie. She had wanted to invite him out here, to make it a foursome, but dad had told him to keep out of everybody's way. At least he had been allowed to stay the night. The snow was falling heavily now, as the light began to fade. It would soon be night and the temperature would only continue to drop. The barn was getting noticeably colder already. It was certainly no time to be outside. Vicki was glad the two of them had managed to find some common ground. It might only be a temporary truce, but it was a start. This whole business had gone on far too long. Perhaps this weekend would be the start of the healing process. Vicki would do whatever she could to make that happen. She knew mum wanted Robbie back in the fold and she suspected, deep down, that daddy did too.

It wasn't just the past that was worrying her though. When the gendarmes had come knocking, that afternoon, Robbie had immediately bolted from the living room. They were not here for him – it was something to do with a break-in at another farm – but he had thought that they might be. *What has he been up to this time?* She wondered. Had he stolen the moped, like Akash had suggested? It had a French number plate, so the idea could not be ruled out. Vicki loved her brother dearly, but sometimes he could be such an idiot. He never stopped to think of the consequences of his actions.

The gendarmes had been very polite. Vicki had overheard a little of their conversation. Not that she really understood it, but she'd picked out a few of the more obvious words. Mum's French had come on leaps and bounds in the last six months. She was practically fluent now. It was just as well, since dad had never shown the inclination to learn. Giles was more like her, Vicki thought; struggling along, obstinately refusing to take any lessons, preferring to learn a language by speaking to people rather than in a classroom. It hadn't got him very far.

Vicki smiled at the thought. Dad had only caught the end of the conversation, when the two officers were leaving. Aunt Betsy and Uncle Dave had arrived at that point, so there wasn't much time for mum to translate the conversation for him.

It seemed a little strange that the police would call here, just to warn them about a couple of vagrants, even if they had broken in somewhere nearby. Vicki was more concerned, though, about that moped. What would dad say, if he knew Robbie was up to his old tricks again, out here in France? Maybe he already knew. That thought worried her a little. Daddy wouldn't just hand him over to the police, would he? Not out here, in the middle of France? But he would not have allowed Robbie to stay, if there had been any question of him being in trouble with the law.

Robbie had had such a difficult time these last few years. Vicki had worried about him, when he was in prison. What it would do to him. He'd seemed so angry and miserable then. And afterwards, when he went off travelling, there was always the thought that he would get caught up in something horrible. Mum had worried about that too, though she had tried not to show it.

None of that mattered now though. Robbie might not have been invited this weekend, but he was here now and he was safe.

Another ping pong ball flew past Vicki's head, dragging her attention back to the game.

Akash had wandered over to the window. He stared out into the chilly twilight. 'Bloody hell, it must be three inches deep already,' he said. 'All the cars are covered over.' He glanced back at them. 'I don't think anyone's going anywhere for the next few days.'

Vicki smiled as she picked up the ball. As far as she was concerned, that was absolutely fine.

The fire was crackling in the grate, a welcome heat radiating out across the living room. Emma McNamara was sitting at the dinner table, enjoying the warmth and watching the busy bees with some amusement as they moved about the kitchen. Her hair was dry now, thank God. It had been something of an operation, getting in and out of that shower. Not one of her better ideas, she thought. She really had frozen her tits off afterwards, trying to dry herself and get dressed as quickly as she could. She had thrown caution to the wind and flicked on the little radiator, but by then it was too late to do any good. Once she was dressed, she had returned to the living room and had a word with Marion about the bathroom mirror. Nicholas had noticed the damage as well, but he had been too embarrassed to say anything. Marion was in there quickly with a dustpan and brush. Perhaps something had fallen on the mirror from up in the rafters. It was screwed to the wall, so Marion had left the frame in place for the time being.

All hands were now focused on preparing supper. Giles Wilkerson, in his brightly coloured jumper, took it all very seriously and was busily fussing over several boiling pots. Dave Flint was leaning against a nearby work surface, looming over the shorter man, chatting away, taking the piss out of everyone as usual. Giles didn't seem to mind, though his attention was focused mostly on the food.

'I was going to start with a prawn salad,' he declared, looking across at the dining table, where Emma was sitting. 'But in the circumstances, I thought you might appreciate something a little warmer. Tomato soup to start with.' He dipped a spoon into a bubbling pot and took a quick sip.

'The old ones are the best,' Dave declared happily. The two men were chalk and cheese – Giles fussy and meticulous, Dave laid back, not taking anything seriously – but they seemed to get on well enough. Everyone liked Dave – he was that kind of bloke – but it was more than that; he was part of the family; part of the furniture, even. Marion was tactfully manoeuvring around him, opening cupboards and pulling out plates to lay on the table, in between bouts of feeding the log burner. She had to keep washing her hands, as she changed tasks, all the while exchanging pleasantries with the guests.

'He's such a good cook,' Betsy Klineman asserted, as Emma poured out the last of the beer from a bottle. The older woman was drinking a glass of wine. 'I was saying to Marion – wasn't I – you're so lucky to have such a good cook for a husband.' Betsy had the chair closest to the fire and had abandoned her winter clothes for a cobalt blue dress. She had really dressed up for the occasion. Everything was on display. Mind you, she had the figure for it.

Marion was laying out some cutlery. She was short and rather stocky, with reddish brown hair and a lined but characterful face.

'Come and sit down,' Betsy told her, patting the seat next to her. 'She never stands still, this one. Always busy. I keep telling her, she'll wear the floor out.'

'Just for a minute then, dear,' Marion agreed, pulling back a chair. Even in this, she could not quite bring herself to abandon her duties as hostess. She grabbed the wine bottle in front of her and offered Betsy a refill.

Betsy did not need asking twice. 'Is the pope a Catholic?' She guffawed. 'Come on, sit down,' she insisted again, as Marion topped her up. 'You deserve a glass yourself. I was telling Emma here, you never stop moving.'

Marion smiled calmly and seated herself next to her friend. Then she poured herself out a small glass of wine. 'Just the one, I think, dear. I don't drink as much as I used to. I'm trying to cut down. Can I get you another beer?' she asked Emma.

'No, no, I'm fine,' Emma said. She still had half a glass left. They had some whisky here too and she was planning to move onto that after dinner.

Betsy took a slurp of wine. Her teeth flashed a red-stained smile. 'A smashing drop of plonk. I was telling Emma, you never stint on your guests. And this place.' She put down the glass and gestured extravagantly to the house. 'It's got so much potential.'

'It needs a lot of work,' Marion said. 'But we're very pleased with it.'

'You got a bargain, I reckon.' Betsy smiled.

'I gather you've done a lot of work on the place, in the last six months,' Emma said.

'A little bit here and there. It's coming along,' Marion said.

'I've fixed a few holes in the roof. Laid some new floorboards. And got the shower working, almost.'

'It was very nice. Hot, at least.'

'The pressure's not quite there yet. We probably need to shift that tank. But I wanted to get something done before we had guests.'

'It was much appreciated,' Emma said. 'Are there any shops nearby? You must need a car. It's a little bit out of the way here.'

'Duras is only ten minutes away,' Marion said. 'We don't do too badly, dear. And we always stock up well whenever we shop.'

'You don't find it a little quiet?' It might be fun for a long weekend, but being stuck out here for weeks on end with only one other person would drive Emma crackers.

'Not at all. That's one of the attractions, dear.' Marion said, taking a sip of wine. 'The peace and quiet. And, to be honest, there are not enough hours in the day. The time flies by, there's so much to do. And we're not starved of company. We have friends in Duras. There are quite a few ex-pats living out here, and we're getting to know one or two French people too.'

'You've been learning the language?'

'I have lessons twice a week, with Bernard.' Marion pronounced the name the French way. 'He's very good. I'm trying to persuade Giles to take a few lessons too, but he prefers to learn the old-fashioned way.'

'I could never be doing with languages,' Betsy snorted. 'I was saying to Nicholas, before we got on the plane, *"bonjour"* and *"je m'appelle Betsy"* and that's my lot.'

'When the weather picks up,' Marion said, 'I'm going to lay a patio out the front. We should be able to sit out there in the summer. Oh, and I was going to put a radiator out in the back room. I really ought to see to that. We don't want anyone getting chilly when they're going to bed.' She pushed back her chair.

Betsy rolled her eyes. 'Oh, sit yourself down!' she said. 'Finish your drink. She never sits still. What did I tell you?'

Marion pursed her lips and reached for her glass. 'Just for a little, then.' Like Dave and Giles, Marion and Betsy could not have been more different, but it was obvious that they had been friends a long time.

'So what was the weather like when you got married?' Emma asked.

Betsy cut in before Marion could reply. 'It was marvellous! A glorious summer's day. Wasn't it, Marion?'

The other woman smiled slightly. 'It was a little overcast, I think, dear. But warm for April.'

'Well, spring. But I was saying to Nicholas, the other day – we were talking about the wedding. Twenty-five years! Can you believe it? How time flies. But I was telling him, it was such a lovely day.'

Emma had heard a bit about it already. Dave had been the best man and was in charge of organising a lot of it. 'I gather Dave gave a rather good speech.'

Betsy shrieked with laughter, remembering. 'It was so rude! The things he said. And then he got off with one of the bridesmaids. Typical Dave!'

'One of the bridesmaids?' Emma raised an eyebrow.

'Not me!' Betsy laughed again. She had been the maid of honour. 'Not my type. Sorry, lovey!' she called across the room.

'What's that?' Dave was in conversation with Giles and hadn't heard what she said.

Betsy raised her voice even louder. 'I was saying to Emma, you were never my type, even when you had hair!'

'I was gutted,' Dave dead-panned back. 'She was the love of my life and she rejected all my advances.' He spoke with mock regret. 'I've been pining for her for the last twenty-five years.'

Emma chuckled at that. Clearly, neither of them had ever really fancied the other and she was not surprised. Betsy was too much of a chatterbox for Dave's taste.

Betsy was in on the joke. 'He is so naughty,' she sniggered. 'Twenty-five years. Imagine that. It's flown by, hasn't it?' She gripped Marion's arm with her left hand. 'You've done so well, lovey. I can't believe the two of you are still together after all this time.' She chuckled again. 'I barely managed five years with my husband. I was saying to Nicholas, I was glad to get shot of him.'

Marion put down her wine glass. 'I always rather liked him.'

'What, Harry?' Betsy was outraged. 'No, I was well rid of him. Too clingy. No sense of humour. You should have seen him, Emma. Biggest nose you ever saw. Thank God we didn't have kids! Anyway, I've got Nicholas now. Isn't he gorgeous?'

Emma smiled, content to play the feed to the older woman. 'He's a good looking bloke,' she agreed.

Betsy caught the inference. 'I know, I know. I'm a cradle snatcher. But why not? It's a bit of fun for both of us. It's not as if he doesn't get something out of it. He's had a miserable life, the poor thing. In and out of foster homes. I was saying to him, we both of us get something out of it.' That was probably true, Emma thought. Betsy got to play around with a good-looking youngster – not too young, thank God – and he got an education in the ways of the world. Beside, Betsy was still an attractive woman; lots of nice curves which she wasn't shy of showing. Blokes always went for that sort of thing. 'It's not as if I'm the only one,' Betsy said, eyeing up Emma in her turn. 'Dave there, he's – what? – seven years older than I am. And you can't be much more than twenty-five.'

'Twenty-nine,' Emma said. The age gap wasn't quite as great in her case.

Betsy eyed her up and down. 'You look younger, lovey. Doesn't she look younger? He's done well with you.'

'We've both done well,' Emma said, catching Marion's eye and stifling a laugh.

Over in the kitchen, Giles had turned back from the hob. 'The first course is nearly ready,' he said. 'Marion, can you give the others a call?'

His wife was pleased to be given an excuse to rise up from the table. 'You'll have to excuse me for a moment,' she said.

'You'll love this,' Betsy asserted, leaning in to Emma as Giles prepared to spoon out the soup. 'He's a real gourmet, is Giles. A proper chef. I was telling Marion, he could be a professional.'

The news had gone down very well. Vicki had waited until after dessert to make the announcement and there had been a flurry of congratulations. She told them about the baby first and then that they were getting married. Mum seemed particularly pleased, though she was not altogether surprised. 'I thought you'd put on a little weight, dear,' she observed. Akash held Vicki's hand and beamed with pride as she outlined their plans. He was lying next to her now, under a pile of blankets in the upstairs room, fast asleep. He looked so peaceful, his curly hair fanned out across the pillow, the covers pulled high up to his neck. Vicki squeezed him gently and he let out a contented sigh, though he did not wake up.

Akash had made a good impression, joining in with all the chatter over supper. Uncle Dave certainly seemed to like him. The two of them had already established a rapport, Akash calling him "Mr Flint", and Dave telling everyone how awful his homework had been.

Vicki felt herself drifting in and out of sleep, as little moments of the evening flittered back into her mind. There had been a mountain of food. Daddy had done a wonderful job. The wine had flowed. Champagne too, which had been brought out when dad had heard the news about the baby. Vicki only had a small sip. It was better not to drink now she was expecting. The wine Uncle Dave had brought had apparently been very nice, though.

After supper, they had played cards and Akash had sung a few songs on his guitar. Vicki had suggested he play something traditional – her dad didn't really like pop music – and Akash was happy to oblige. She was surprised just how many songs he knew. His singing voice could be very soothing, when he wanted it to be. Vicki watched him with a quiet pride as he entertained the room. *My husband to be and the father of my child.* Even dad seemed impressed.

Giles came over to sit with her by the fire, to discuss the wedding. He offered to pay for it outright, which was kind of him, though Vicki had half expected it. The realisation that he was going to be a grandfather had almost brought a tear to his eye. His little baby girl, all grown up, and about to bring new life into the world. She knew he wasn't altogether keen on Akash, but he said nothing of that tonight. Vicki had made her decision and he respected it. And she could see his point of view. Akash did not have a steady job and she was still studying. Their life was in flux and it was an awkward time to start a family. But that was true whatever stage of life you were at. Dad just wanted her to be settled and safe, which was completely understandable. And she would be, in time, just as her parents were now. Everything would work out well. Vicki was sure of it. She loved Akash with a depth of feeling that was difficult to put into words. He was her life, her soul mate, and whatever the world threw at them, they would get through it, together.

The lights had gone off, down in the living room. Vicki was vaguely aware of voices chatting away. People heading off to bed. She didn't know what time it was now. She and Akash had stayed up until half past eleven, and then crept upstairs. The bedroom was directly above the living room, accessible via a ladder out the back. As soon as they arrived, and made sure the radiator was on, Akash had pulled her under the blankets and the two of them had made love. It was a beautiful moment, the end of a glorious day. They had to be quiet about it, though. People were still up and about and the floorboards did have a tendency to creak. Light and sound travelled all too easily through the open chimney stack, a remnant of the fire place that had once dominated the main room.

The wind outside had quietened a little now, the frame of the window rattling a bit less, as the storm died down for an hour or two. Vicki had peeked out the window, before they had come up to bed. The farm had been transformed into a winter wonderland, a white blanket covering everything as far as the eye could see. It had to be at least six inches, maybe even more. The trees at the far end of the field were swaying under the heavy wind, and the air was thick with ice. If the storm carried on like this, they would be completely cut off by morning. Snuggling up close to Akash, the warmth of his body pressing against her, that did not seem like such a bad thing. A few extra days here would be very welcome. Vicki was not due back at university for a couple of weeks yet. It was the middle of the Easter holidays. There was no worry about food, either. Dad had planned for every eventuality and their small pantry was jam-packed with supplies. Perhaps she was being selfish, though. Other people had lives to go back to, jobs to return to, and the snow would be something of an inconvenience for them.

Not that Uncle Dave would mind too much, she thought, with a smile. It was so nice to see him again. He hadn't changed a bit. It was like stepping back in time. His girlfriend, Emma, was a sparky, good-humoured woman. Very pretty, as Akash had been quick to point out. She had a confidence and a casual charm that Vicki could not help but admire. Nicholas – Aunt Betsy's young man – had retreated into his shell over dinner, though he seemed a little less nervous than he had when he first arrived. Vicki was determined to draw him out over the course of the weekend. He had certainly shown some spirit out in the barn. She still couldn't quite believe he had beaten her at ping pong. After the game, however, he had quietened down. Aunt Betsy had dominated the conversation at her end of the table. It was probably good for him, being with her, Vicki concluded, although Betsy was notorious for the rate at which she got through her young men. Vicki hoped this relationship would last a little longer than the others. It would be an education for Nicholas, if nothing else. She hoped he would enjoy the ride. He had had a difficult life, by all accounts.

That thought brought her back to her brother, Robbie, who had also been at the dinner table.

'Aye, aye!' Uncle Dave had exclaimed, when he had first emerged from the back room. 'The prodigal son returns. Better lock up your valuables.'

Robbie had been on his best behaviour, not scowling or muttering under his breath, and he had taken the teasing in the spirit in which it was given. Everyone knew what Uncle Dave was like. Robbie had kept quiet over dinner, not really saying much. Vicki could tell he did not want to be there, but she was grateful that he made the effort. It was progress of a kind. She was just glad to see him in the same room as her father. It had been such a long time since the two of them had been together, and even longer since they had managed to exchange a civil word.

Robbie had perked up a little when she had made her announcement and had congratulated her on the baby, albeit in a perfunctory way. For all his faults, Robbie had never been one to pass judgement. So long as she was happy, he was happy.

Apart from the initial ribbing, nobody made any mention of the past. They had all been there the last time daddy and Robbie had spoken. Well, in the same house, anyway, when the two of them had had their initial bust up. It had been a family weekend – her birthday, in fact – and lots of friends and family had been there. Robbie had just dropped out of university and asked dad for some money, so he could go off travelling. Dad had refused, they had rowed and, in his anger, Robbie had stolen half a dozen credit cards and caused no end of grief. It had been a stupid thing to do, but he had always been headstrong, prone to rush into things without thinking. Tonight, though, at least for a time, all was forgiven and forgotten.

Vicki snuggled up to Akash under the blanket. He was a heavy sleeper. When they made love, he was considerate and enthusiastic, but as soon as they had finished, he would fall straight to sleep and would be out for the count until morning. She didn't mind that. Vicki liked to have him close to her; to watch him sleep. She felt his warmth against her and her heart soared. They would be married soon and have a family. And, for now, her entire family were together, sleeping under the same roof, sharing in her joy. Despite an awkward start – Vicki shuddered at the memory of the near miss on the road – the day could not have gone better. The reunion, the house warming and her engagement.

To her surprise, the first flickers of daylight were beginning to dance through the far window. Had the night passed already? She had rocked in and out of sleep, without being aware of it, and the hours must have slipped by. There were no curtains on the window, just a wooden shutter, which they had left open when they crawled to bed. A line of snow had built up on the sill. A dimmer light was filtering up through the chimney hole, reflecting off the pipe leading up from the wood burner. Half asleep, Vicki could hear someone moving about in the living room. It was probably mummy, up early, opening the shutters. Her parents had always been early risers. Or perhaps it was dad, preparing a nice breakfast for everyone.

What time is it? Vicki wondered. She lifted her head from the pillow to gaze out of the window. It was well past dawn, by the looks of it, the white of the snow amplifying the daylight as it began to flood through the dusty upper room. Vicki rolled herself sideways and reached out for her bag by the side of the bed. She pulled out her phone and checked the time. It was ten to seven.

The voices downstairs were louder now. She recognised her dad and heard her mum move into the kitchen.

'I don't know, dear,' Marion said. 'I just found it like this. The barn door's open too.'

'It's all over the place.' Giles sounded concerned. 'It can't be an animal, surely?'

Vicki rose up from the bed. 'Daddy?' she called, disentangling herself from the blankets. Akash moaned but did not wake, as she shuffled over to the hole. 'What's going on?' she called down. 'Is everything all right?'

The reply was not reassuring. 'I think we've had visitors, in the night,' Giles Wilkerson said.

Chapter Four

The sofa had been tipped onto its side, the fabric slashed in several places. A bin had been overturned too and its contents spewed across the tiled floor. Even the microwave on the work surface had been toppled over, its door hanging open. Worst of all, so far as Vicki was concerned, was the painting on the wall. It was one of dad's landscapes, hanging between the window and the front door. The canvas had been slashed, viciously, in several places, as if it had been clawed by a bear or some other savage animal.

As soon as she became aware that something was wrong, Vicki had rushed downstairs. She had dressed first – pulling on some leggings, a skirt and a woollen jumper in the freezing upper room. The radiator seemed to have switched itself off during the night. Akash was dead to the world and she left him to his slumber, descending the ladder and moving directly into the living room. The first thing she saw, as she stepped through the door, was her mum and dad lifting the sofa back into an upright position. Then she saw the devastation of the room and her mouth fell open. 'Daddy, what's happened?' she gasped. Chairs were overturned and some of the rubbish from the bin was strewn across the rug.

Her dad stepped back, having righted the sofa, and regarded his daughter. 'You're not to worry, Victoria,' he told her, correcting his glasses, which had dropped slightly onto his nose. 'They're gone now.'

'Gone? Someone's been in here?'

'I'm afraid so. I think they must have broken in during the night.' Giles wiped his hands on the side of his brightly coloured jumper, his expression grim.

'The barn door was wide open,' her mother said. Marion was dressed in her usual dungarees with a thick sweater over the top. Her reddish hair was neatly combed, but her face was creased with concern. 'We think it must have been the vagrants,' she added. The ones the gendarmes had warned them about.

'Why would they come here?' Vicki asked, incredulously.

'They must have thought the house was empty,' her dad replied. He scratched his head and glanced around the room. 'I'm not sure if they've taken anything. It might be that they were just looking for somewhere to sleep. With the weather as it was last night, they must have broken in to the first place they came across. They might not have known there was anyone here.'

Vicki did not like the thought of that at all. The idea of strangers in the house, ransacking the place. 'Oh, daddy, that's awful.'

'Well, they're gone now, dear,' her mum said. 'There's no need to worry.'

'It's wanton vandalism,' Giles declared. 'I can understand people needing to seek shelter. But to do all this, for no reason...' He was at a loss to understand it.

'The barn is even worse,' Marion admitted. 'It's going to take some tidying up. But at least it's stopped snowing now.'

'Should we call the police?' Vicki asked, looking to her dad. 'They might still be around here somewhere.'

Marion did not think that likely. 'I'm sure they must be long gone by now, dear.'

'But to do all this...' Vicki frowned, surveying the damage. 'I didn't hear anything last night. Did you?'

'Not a thing,' Marion admitted. 'Mind you, your father and I were on the other side of the house. You didn't hear anything?'

Vicki shook her head. 'I must have slept through it.' She shuddered at the thought. Strangers ransacking the house, a few feet below where she and Akash had been sleeping.

'They couldn't have made much noise,' Marion thought. 'Although there was quite a storm blowing. Well, anyway, we ought to make a start on clearing up. Vicki's right, dear, we'll have to phone the police.'

'Yes, of course.' Giles nodded. 'Although I doubt they'll be able to do anything much this morning.' It was unlikely the gendarmes would be making house calls today, with the weather as it was. 'We ought to see what they've taken. Assess the extent of the damage.'

'Vicki and I can make a start on that,' Marion said. 'If that's alright with you, dear?' She looked to her daughter. 'Giles, why don't you put some breakfast on? I'm sure we could do with something to eat.'

'Good idea,' he agreed. He moved across to the hob and grabbed a frying pan.

'We should start out in the barn,' Marion suggested, returning her attention to Vicki. 'It's in quite a state, I'm afraid.' The barn doors were banging against the outer walls. One of them must have come loose. 'We'll get the doors closed first.'

Vicki followed her mum across the living room towards the barn. There were some coat hooks near the corner, but all the clothing was in a heap on the floor. Marion reached down to grab a coat and Vicki did likewise.

Meantime, Giles poured some oil into the frying pan and switched on the gas. He moved to the fridge, to retrieve a pack of bacon, and let out an exclamation of surprise when he opened the door.

Vicki was putting an arm through the sleeve of her coat. 'Daddy, what is it?'

'The electricity's off.' Giles frowned. He closed the fridge door and looked through the gap behind it to see if it was plugged in. It was. He tried the kettle, flicking on the switch, but nothing happened. 'It looks like there's been a power cut.'

Marion had finished putting on her coat. 'The line must have come down during the night.'

'I wondered why the radiator wasn't on,' Vicki said.

'And the hot water,' her mum agreed. 'We'll have to get the fire stoked up. It's just as well I got all the wood in yesterday afternoon. But we can do that after we've cleared up the barn.'

'At least the gas is still on,' Giles said. There was nothing to stop him preparing some food. 'I'll put some water in the pan.'

Marion nodded and looked to Vicki. 'Let's make a start, shall we, dear?'

Vicki followed her down the steps into the barn.

The exterior doors were wide open and the brilliant white of the snow was a dazzling sight. A small mountain had formed in the doorway, where the snow had tumbled through. 'Careful, dear,' her mum warned. 'It's a little slippy.'

Vicki stepped onto the floor and skirted around the ice. Outside, the snow looked to be two or three feet high. She shivered, feeling the cold air as it wafted through the doors. The wind was still howling, although not as much as it had last night. The snow had stopped falling, however.

Marion clambered up the snow to survey the exterior. Vicki smiled, watching her scrabbling forward on her hands and knees. Mum was never afraid to get her hands dirty. She had a pair of gloves on, but she sank a little into the snow as she stood up.

'What can you see?' Vicki asked.

'An awful lot of snow. There are no footprints. Whoever it was, they must have left the house some time ago.'

Vicki was still puzzling over the lack of noise. 'I did hear *something* last night,' she recalled, trying to remember. 'The odd footsteps, when I was half asleep. Maybe a whisper. A voice. I...I thought it must have been someone going to the loo.'

'There was quite a gale blowing. It's hardly surprising you didn't hear much.' The wind had certainly been battering the windows when Vicki had gone to bed, but it had died down for a while after that. 'This door is wedged hard,' Marion observed. One of the barn doors had stuck fast in the snow. The doors could be opened either way. The second door was hanging loose and was flapping about on the inside. 'There should be a spade in here somewhere.' She pointed back across the barn. 'Just by the wall there.'

Vicki went to find it. There was quite a clutter of equipment piled up near the wall, just this side of the ping pong table; sporting equipment closer to the stairs, and garden implements a little further along. Most of them had been knocked over and carelessly scattered about. Yesterday afternoon, everything had been neatly propped up against the wall. Vicki dipped down to grab a spade and a trowel, and then turned back to her mother.

Marion was on her hands and knees once again, digging out the snow with her gloved hands. Vicki could not help but smile at that.

'Here you are, mum,' she said.

Marion pulled herself up, but took the shovel rather than the trowel Vicki had offered. 'Thank you, dear. Will you prop something against that other door, to stop it flapping?'

Vicki nodded and grabbed a small toolbox, which was on its side. She wedged it against the base of the door.

Marion had already set to work clearing the mountain of snow from inside the barn. 'To the left,' she suggested, digging into the pile with her shovel and then offloading it outside. Vicki helped out as best she could, marvelling at her mother's energy. Marion was a small, solid woman, but what she lacked in height she made up for in grit and determination.

After a couple of minutes, she stopped to catch her breath, but then was at it again, before Vicki could even offer to take over. Five minutes later, the floor had been cleared sufficiently that Vicki was able to remove the toolbox and close up the first of the two doors. The second proved a little more tricky, as it had been partially buried, but a few more minutes work – Vicki helping out with the trowel – soon managed to get it free; and finally they were able to shut the doors and close off the outside world.

While she was digging, Marion had come across the broken lock. It was buried in several inches of snow; dumped when the barn doors had been forced open. It was beyond repair. They would have to find some other way to lock the place up.

With the doors closed, Marion and Vicki turned their attention to the interior of the barn. Now that the place was shut up, it was dark and gloomy. Vicki flicked the light switch, but nothing happened. The electricity was off, of course. She had forgotten that. The holes in the roof had been covered over with snow. The only light available was from a small window to the right of the double doors. Icy water dripped down in places onto the concrete floor.

Slowly, Vicki's eyes adjusted to the darkness. 'Look at Robbie's bike!' she exclaimed. She had been so intent on clearing away the snow that she hadn't noticed the battered looking moped, lying on its side. It had been turned around in the night, so that the front was facing the barn doors. The leather seat had been slashed and so had the tyres. Vicki shivered at the sight of it. 'Why would anyone do that?'

Marion didn't know. 'They must have been trying to steal it, dear.'

'They wouldn't have been able to ride it. Not during a blizzard. I suppose they might have tried to walk it out.'

'That possible,' her mum agreed. 'Until they realised it was broken.' Her eye caught on the sofa, which was just behind the moped. She let out a gentle tut. That too had been toppled over. 'Give me a hand, will you, dear?'

'Of course.' It was the matter of a moment for the pair of them to right the settee. The cover was lying on the ground. Vicki reached to pick it up. Her eyes were now accustomed to the dark. She placed the cover back on the sofa.

'They must be young, whoever they were,' Marion said, stepping back. 'An adult wouldn't be spiteful like this. All this hooliganism.'

'It's awful,' Vicki agreed.

'But they're gone now, dear,' Marion reassured her. 'That's the main thing.'

Emma McNamara stretched out her arms and arched her back. Her long black hair was fanned out across the pillow and, as her body shifted, the bedsheets crinkled beneath her. She opened her eyes and let out an enormous yawn. Light was flickering in through a gap in the curtains. *Definitely morning*, Emma realised, rubbing her eyes and pulling herself up. There was no sign of Dave. She sat up and the cold air hit her at once. *Blimey.* She glanced over the edge of the bed. The electric fire was off. That was strange. She couldn't remember switching it off. Perhaps it was on a timer. The bed was nice and springy, though, and the blankets had kept her toasty during the night, even in just a t-shirt and a pair of pants. It felt a bit odd, though, lying here without Dave. Emma was used to sleeping alone – she had her own flat, which she shared with a couple of girl friends, and usually only hooked up with Dave at the weekends

– but on a cold night, there was nothing quite like a hefty bloke to warm up your bed; especially out here, in the middle of nowhere. *Honestly, he invites me over to France for a dirty weekend and he doesn't even come to bed.* She chuckled. *I must be losing my touch!* Perhaps he had been and gone; but there was no sign of that. The far side of the bed was cold and the bedsheets had not been disturbed. Dave had a habit of messing things up and Emma would know if he had been there.

She had come to bed at about midnight, leaving Dave by the fire talking to Giles. The two of them hadn't got much of a look-in over dinner, what with Betsy Klineman jabbering away, and Dave deserved a bit of quality time with his old friend. What was the point of coming all the way out here if you couldn't spend a few hours talking bollocks with a mate, whilst getting quietly stewed? All the same, Emma had assumed he would follow her to bed eventually, probably in the early hours, when she was fast asleep. She could just picture him, creeping into the bedroom in the dead of night, the great balding lump, trying desperately not to wake her up but in the process banging and bumping and thudding into just about everything. Dave could not move quietly to save his life. He was all arms and legs. It would be a miracle if he survived the weekend without knocking himself out on one of the wooden beams.

He must have stayed up the whole night through. That was unusual, for him. He liked a drink and a chat as much as the next bloke, but Dave usually knew when to call it quits. *Perhaps he dozed off in front of the fire*, she thought. It wouldn't be the first time. He had been known to nod off in front of the TV on occasion. Or perhaps he couldn't face having to creep through the other bedroom in the early hours, with Betsy and her bloke probably at it like rabbits in there. Emma smiled at that thought. It was always the quiet ones. Nicholas, not Betsy. No, Dave had probably grabbed a blanket and settled down in front of the fire, rather than risk waking up the entire household.

Christ, it's cold. Emma pulled the blanket up to her shoulders. The bedroom was absolutely freezing. She'd have to switch the fire on again, if she could work out how to do it.

Getting dressed was going to be a mission and a half. *I wonder how bad the snow was.* She glanced at the curtains. The blizzard had died down a bit in the night but there had been a pretty heavy fall before she had gone to bed. She sat back, pressing her head against the pillow. It was far too cold to get up and look. Nicer just to lie here under the warm blankets. She sighed theatrically. *I suppose ought to go and see where he is. Make sure he hasn't passed out on the floor or something.*

She pulled back the blankets and swung her legs over the side of the mattress. The rug was cold to the touch, but probably less so than the stone floor beneath it. Hurriedly, Emma reached across to a chair to grab her clothes from last night. She pulled on a pair of trousers and grabbed a top and a sweater; then sat back on the bed and put on a pair of socks. The clothes made very little difference. It was still bloody cold. She could see her breath in the air.

The electric heater looked like it had seen better days. Emma was pretty sure she hadn't switched it off. It had probably blown a fuse.

She slipped on a pair of shoes and moved over to the window, drawing back the curtains. *Blimey,* she thought, shielding her eyes from the white glare. The snow was almost up to the window. They'd have a job getting out the front door, with the snow at that height. It looked like they really were stuck here. She chuckled at the thought. Dave had said it would be a memorable weekend, but even he hadn't realised how memorable. *I hope they're well stocked up with food.*

Hopefully, it would be a bit warmer in the living room. She moved across to the door. Betsy and her bloke were bunking down in the middle bedroom. Emma opened the door just a crack. The other room was in darkness. The two lovebirds were still asleep. *Bless.* She could see the two lumps spread out across the bed, barely visible under a pile of blankets.

Emma had to fight not to laugh, as she tip-toed silently across the room. She wasn't much better at moving quietly than Dave. She stopped midway, almost bumping into a chair in front of the dressing table. There was a bit of light coming in around the edges of the curtains and she took a moment to let her eyes adjust to the dark.

Betsy Klineman's head was poking out the top of the blanket. She was lying on her back, snoring gently. Not quite a beached whale – actually, she had a nice figure – but a sizeable presence nonetheless. A silk blindfold covered her eyes and she had earplugs sticking out of each ear. Emma smiled at that. Betsy had a luxurious mane of dark brown hair, tucked neatly behind her on the pillow, but she did look faintly ridiculous, with that mask on. It only needed some curlers in her hair and a bit of face cream and the image would be complete.

Nicholas Samoday was lying ramrod straight on the other side of the bed. He was awake, Emma realised abruptly, his eyes poking out over the top of the blanket, looking at her, though they were partially obscured by the mop of blond hair. Emma waved at him and mouthed a silent 'hello', pointing a finger at the far door by way of explanation. Nicholas lowered the blanket slightly and gave her a half-smile in return.

The living room greeted her with a pleasant domestic scene. Giles Wilkerson was at the hob, cooking breakfast. He looked to be in his element, his portly frame and balding head clashing with his brightly coloured jumper, but his face relaxed in the business of cooking. The pleasant smell of bacon and eggs wafted across the room and Emma felt her stomach begin to rumble.

'Good morning!' she called, as she closed up the door behind her.

The daughter, Vicki Wilkerson, was sweeping the floor with a broom. She looked up and smiled a greeting in return. Her mother, Marion, was busily putting some logs into the burner. She echoed the greeting and lobbed another piece of wood onto the fire.

Giles flipped over a rasher of bacon. 'Did you sleep well?' he asked, as Emma stepped forward towards the sofa.

'Like a log,' she said. 'The bed's really comfy. And I had it all to myself. You haven't seen Dave, have you?'

'No. Not this morning,' Giles said.

Marion peered at her curiously from over at the fireplace. 'Was he not with you, dear?' she asked.

Emma frowned. 'No, he didn't come to bed last night. I thought...' She stopped, her eyes catching suddenly on a rather large rip in the fabric of one of the armchairs. There was a tear across the sofa as well. Her gaze swept left, to the painting on the wall. That too had been slashed in several places. 'What's happened?' she asked, in surprise. Now that she looked closely, there were a lot of things that seemed to be out of kilter.

'It's awful,' Vicki said, stopping for a moment and propping herself up on the top of the broom handle. 'We had a break-in last night.' She wiped a strand of honey blonde hair from her eyes.

'A break-in?' Emma blinked. She hadn't heard anything.

'While we were asleep.'

'They caused a lot of damage,' Giles added, from over by the hob.

'The barn doors were open this morning,' Marion explained. 'They smashed the lock and started turning over all the furniture.'

'Christ,' Emma said. 'Was anything taken?'

'Not that we know of, dear. But we think it must have been the same people who broke into that other farm a few days ago.'

Emma's eyes widened at that suggestion. 'You mean, the ones the gendarmes told you about?'

'We think so.' Marion nodded. 'The odd thing is, dear, they didn't actually take anything. It doesn't seem to have been a burglary, as such.'

Giles Wilkerson moved the frying pan from the hob. 'We think they might have been looking for some shelter from the storm. But there's no excuse for this.' He gestured to the damaged furniture. 'It's sheer vandalism.'

'Have you called the police?'

'Not yet,' he said. 'They won't be able to come out in this weather. We thought we'd have a bit of breakfast first.' It would help to settle their nerves. Giles lifted up the frying pan and shovelled the bacon and eggs onto a plate. He looked across at Emma. 'You say David didn't come to bed last night?' He lifted the plate and carried it across to the dining table. He indicated for her to sit down. He sounded more surprised than worried.

'No, not a peep,' Emma replied, taking the proffered chair. Giles laid the food down in front of her. 'Thanks.' A knife and fork had already been set out. 'I thought he must have stayed up chatting with you.' The last time she had seen him, Dave had been polishing off a bottle of wine. Giles was still up then, and Betsy and her bloke were just heading off to bed. Marion had also been on the point of calling it a night.

'Yes, we had a long talk,' Giles admitted. 'We finished off the bottle. There's some coffee on the boil, if you want it?'

'Yes, please.' Emma lifted up the knife and fork and made a start on the food.

'We must have stayed up until about half past one, I think.' There was a coffee pot on the kitchen work surface, with several cups and saucers already laid out. Giles grabbed the pot and thought for a moment. 'Not much later than that.' He poured out the steaming liquid into a cup. 'Do you take milk?'

'No, just black. No sugar, thanks.'

'We finished the wine. He went off to the bathroom. Then I went in there, and he came back out here. That was the last time I saw him.' Giles put down the pot and stirred the cup, then carried it across to the table.

'Thanks,' Emma said, as he placed it down in front of her.

Giles hovered for a moment, perplexed. 'You're sure he didn't come to bed? He couldn't have slipped in and out of the room, while you were asleep?'

Emma swallowed a mouthful of egg. 'No. I don't think so.'

Vicki Wilkerson was on her knees, with a dustpan and brush, clearing up the pile of rubbish. She looked up. 'What about the side door?' she asked. The internal door between Emma's bedroom and the workshop at the back.

Marion pulled up a chair. 'No, that's been locked for months,' she said, seating herself next to Emma. 'There is so much junk piled up in front of it, you couldn't get through there even if you wanted to.'

Emma took a slurp of coffee. 'That's true. I tried it yesterday. And he wouldn't have gone out the front door. Not in this weather.' She put down her cup, a little worried now. 'No, if he'd come to bed, I'd know about it. He's such a fidget. Even if I was half asleep, I'd know he was there. And the bed was cold too. His half, I mean. It definitely hadn't been slept in.'

'That is peculiar.' Marion frowned. 'He definitely hasn't come through here this morning. I wonder where he could have got to.'

'The heater's off,' Emma remembered suddenly. 'The whole room was pretty chilly this morning.'

Giles brought across a second cup of coffee, which he placed in front of his wife. 'They're all off, I'm afraid. The electricity is down. One of the cables must have blown over in the night.'

'Thank you, dear.' Marion took the cup. 'It's lucky we have a gas cooker. Otherwise we wouldn't even have hot water.'

Emma sipped her coffee. This was getting really odd. Where the hell could he be? A horrible thought struck her. Could he have been up and about, when those people broke in? Maybe he had caught them trashing the house and had tried to chase them off. *God, I hope not. Not in this weather.* 'You don't think he might have gone outside, do you?' If Dave wasn't in the living room or the bedroom, where else could he be?

Marion did not think that likely. 'He couldn't have gone out the front door,' she said. A small avalanche of snow would have fallen through onto the mat. 'He might have gone out through the barn, I suppose. The doors were open. But it doesn't seem very likely, dear. Not in this weather.'

'No, it doesn't,' Emma agreed. Even with Dave's long legs, he'd be lucky to get more than ten metres in snow this thick. She looked down at the half eaten bacon and eggs in front of her. Suddenly, she did not feel very hungry. 'He must be in the house somewhere.' She pushed back the plate. 'I should go and look. Do you think he might have crashed out in the barn?' That place was like a small aircraft hangar. If he was lying down somewhere there, amid all the junk, it would be easy enough to miss him.

'Vicki and I have just been cleaning up in there,' Marion said. 'I think we would have seen him. I can't imagine where he could be.'

Emma slid back her chair and rose to her feet. If there really had been intruders in here, ransacking the house, then anything might have happened. She was starting to get really worried now. 'I might just take a look out the back, if that's okay.' She could not think where else he might be. 'Thanks for that.' She gestured to the abandoned plate.

'You're welcome,' Giles said. He was already back at the hob, cooking another round.

'I'll come with you, dear,' Marion said, rising up. 'There's a torch in the sideboard. We'll need a light.' She strode over to the unit and pulled open a drawer, which was full of bric-a-brac. She flicked on the small torch, to make sure it was working. 'It always pays to be prepared. We used these a lot out the back, before the wiring was put in. We have some candles too, somewhere.' She made for the door. 'Mind the drop,' she warned, stepping down into the utility room. She turned back and flipped the beam of the torch down so that Emma could see her feet as she followed her into the room. 'I'll have to put one of these in the bathroom, if the power doesn't come back on soon.'

Emma's mind was on other things. 'I'm just hoping he hasn't gone outside,' she said, as the door swung shut behind her. 'In this weather…'

'We'll check the workshop first,' Marion suggested, moving across the room. She turned back and flashed the torch once again, so Emma could follow her. As she did so, the light briefly illuminated the ladder to her left.

At the top of the ladder, a face popped into view, a mass of curly hair framing a handsome puppy dog appearance. Akash Antonelli gave a wide yawn. 'Morning all!' He waved a hand cheerfully. There was no wall on this side of the upper room, just the ladder and a sheer drop. Health and safety would have a nightmare. 'Hey, what time is it?' he asked.

'A little after seven, dear,' Marion said. 'Did you sleep well?'

'Yeah, not bad. Is that bacon?' The smell of food was permeating the air. It was probably drifting up through the space where the old chimney had been.

'Yes, Giles is just cooking some breakfast.'

Akash's face lit up. 'Aww, nice! I could just do with some of that.'

'Come down and help yourself,' Marion suggested.

'Better put some clothes on first.' Akash shivered. 'It's freezing this morning. Vick must have switched the radiator off.'

'It's the electricity,' Emma said, peering up at him. 'It's all off. It's freezing in my room too. I'd grab a coat, if I were you.'

Akash nodded and disappeared from view.

'Be careful on the ladder, dear,' Marion called up to him. 'Emma, will you grab another torch from that drawer? I don't want Akash doing himself a mischief.'

'Yes, sure.' Emma moved back into the living room and pulled another torch from the sideboard. When she returned, Marion was halfway up the ladder, handing the first torch over to Akash. Emma suppressed a smile. Marion really was the practical one of the family. She flicked on her own torch and guided Marion back onto level ground; then the two women moved through to the workshop.

This was another hangar-like space, almost as big as the barn. It was piled high with junk; some of it useful, some of it less so. A few prickles of light filtered in through the glass panels in a set of doors at the far end. They provided just enough light to see by without the torch. Emma switched off the flash light. There was no sign of Dave in here.

'Giles and I are up there,' Marion said, indicating a home-made wooden staircase at the far end of the hangar. A door on the first floor led through to an upstairs bedroom. 'We came down here a little before seven. There was no sign of anyone. It was only when I went into the living room that we realised anything was amiss.'

Beneath the staircase, at ground level, was the inside door Vicki had mentioned. Boxes were piled up in front of it, and all sorts of other odds and ends. *Our bedroom must must be on the other side of that*, Emma realised. It was taking her a while to work out the geography of the house. Upstairs, there was also a

70

middle bedroom. This was an open wall affair, like the one where Akash was sleeping. A sheer drop, with a precarious looking A frame the only access.

Emma picked her way around a couple of small tables and what looked like some industrial machinery, towards the glass doors at the far end. 'It doesn't look like he came through here,' she said, gazing at the cardboard boxes and the magazines stacked up against the wall.

'Not with all that piled up,' Marion agreed, regarding all the mess with mild exasperation. 'Giles keeps promising to sort out his junk. It does tend to build up rather. But there's always so much else to do.' She gazed out of the windows, at the winter scene beyond. 'We had those doors open for a while, last year, when we first arrived. Airing the place.' A small desk was blocking the way now, covered in dust. Nobody could have entered or left the house that way. 'It's very unsettling,' Marion said. 'Having strangers in the house. Causing all this damage.'

'It's not very nice. You don't think Dave might have seen them? Gone after them or something?'

'I don't know,' Marion answered honestly.

Emma could just picture the great lump, playing the hero. Dave could be pretty tough, when he needed to be. But what if they had been armed? Not guns, obviously. They would have heard that. But a knife or a cosh. She lifted a hand to her head. *Better not to think about it*. Dave was probably fine. Had too much to drink and passed out somewhere. 'Is there anywhere else he could be? In the house, I mean?'

Marion shook her head. 'Not that I can think of, dear. We've looked everywhere.'

'Isn't there a hayloft? Out in the barn?' Emma remembered somebody mentioning it. *I should have thought of that before.* 'Could he have climbed up there and crashed out?'

'I don't think so,' Marion said. 'I'll be honest, I haven't actually looked, but he wouldn't have been able to get up there. We borrowed the ladder yesterday for Robbie's room.' She gestured to the A frame up against the wall.

'Oy!' a male voice called out abruptly. The man himself. 'Keep the noise down, will you! Some of us are trying to

71

sleep!'

Marion pursed her lips.

Emma smiled, looking up at the open middle room. The prodigal son. She had wondered where he was. 'You haven't seen Dave, have you?' she called up.

The reply was unhelpful. 'No, I haven't. Why would I have done?'

'He seems to have gone walkabout,' Emma explained.

'Good luck to him!' Robbie snorted.

Marion shot an apologetic look at Emma, but she just shrugged. Robbie was clearly not a morning person.

'We'll have another look in the barn,' Marion suggested.

Vicki did not feel at all hungry. Ordinarily, she could not get enough of her dad's fried bread, but after all that had happened this morning, she no longer felt like eating anything. Uncle Dave was missing. They had searched the building from top to bottom – even checking the barn a second time, at Emma's insistence – but there was no sign of him anywhere. It wasn't like him, just to disappear like this. Surely he hadn't gone outside in the middle of the night? But if he wasn't in here, then he must have done. He might have slipped and hurt himself, in all that snow. What with that and the break-in, Vicki could not help but worry. The thought of him, out there in the ice and the cold. He might catch his death. They would have to go out and look.

Dad had tried to put a call through to the police, but the land line was not working. 'It's out of order,' he muttered, tapping the top of the phone and holding the receiver to his ear. 'The line must have come down during the night.'

Vicki tried her mobile, but that wasn't working either. The battery was fully charged, but there was no signal. And that meant they were completely cut off. It was no wonder her appetite had disappeared.

Akash was tucking into a plate of bacon and eggs. His appetite at least had not been affected. 'He'll be all right, doll,' he said, trying to reassure her. 'Probably went out for a fag and got a bit lost.'

'He doesn't smoke any more. Oh, Akash, he might have hurt himself. He could be lying out there, unconscious, in the freezing cold.'

Emma had come to the same conclusion. She was staring out of the window at the snow covered fields. 'I'm going to go and look for him,' she said. 'He's got to be out there somewhere.'

'He can't have got far,' Akash thought. He took a last mouthful of egg and pushed back his plate. 'I don't mind popping out and having a look with you.' He grabbed his phone from the table top. He had not been able to get a signal either. 'Maybe we could head up the hill. Get a better view from there. We might be able to get a signal and phone for help.'

Vicki did not like the idea of Akash heading out in such awful conditions. 'It's a long way to go in this,' she said. 'The snow looks really deep.'

'We have to do something,' Emma insisted.

'It'll be all right, doll,' Akash said. 'It's not snowing now. It might be a bit of a slog, but it's broad daylight and we'll be in sight of the house. It's worth a shot, isn't it?'

Vicki nodded. If they were going to find Uncle Dave, it was probably the only way.

'If he *is* out there,' Emma said, peering out of the window once again, 'I don't think he could have got very far.'

'There were no footsteps,' Vicki recalled. 'Outside the barn, I mean, when the door was open.'

'If he went out in the night, they might have been covered over by now,' Emma thought. 'Who lives in the other farmhouses?'

'There's a French couple next door, in the first house,' Vicki said. 'But mum says they're hardly ever here.'

'They live in Bordeaux,' her dad interjected. He knew more about this than she did. 'And come down for the odd weekend. I don't think they're here at the moment, though.'

'What about the other houses?' Emma asked.

'The building on the other side is unoccupied,' Giles said. 'It's been empty for some time.'

'Well, there you go.' Akash pushed back his chair and

grinned at Vicki. 'Perhaps he got a bit lost and dossed down over there for the night.'

'Don't be silly,' Vicki scolded him, gently.

Akash shrugged. 'Just a thought. If there's an empty building going begging, it's a wonder them people didn't break in there first. Hey, maybe that's where they ended up. They must have found somewhere to kip, if they're not here now.'

That was not a happy thought.

The far door opened and Vicki's mum bustled in from the utility room. 'Mrs Pavan,' she said, apropos of nothing. She was carrying a basket of fruit, which she placed down on the table in front of them. 'The electricity must be down there too.'

'Who's Mrs Pavan?' Emma asked.

Vicki had the answer to that. 'She lives in the house at the far end of the lane.' Vicki had never met the woman. She was Italian, apparently.

'Please help yourself to fruit,' Marion said, indicating the basket. 'Her husband died a couple of months ago. Hilda's in her seventies. She'll be there all on her own. I ought to give her a ring and see if she's all right.' She moved over to the telephone, which was on top of the corner cabinet.

'I'm afraid it isn't working,' Giles said, as she picked up the receiver. 'We just checked.'

Marion grimaced and returned the phone to its cradle. 'So you didn't call the police?'

'No, we haven't been able to.'

'My mobile's not working either,' Vicki said.

Her mum let out a sigh. 'Well, then. I will have to go and check to see if she's all right. We ought to go out anyway. If Dave isn't in the house, he must be out there somewhere. He might be hurt.'

Akash scratched his nose. 'Yeah, we were just saying that.'

'I think we should go now,' Emma said, pulling back from the window. 'While the weather's calm. I don't suppose you've got a pair of boots I could borrow?'

'Of course, dear,' Marion said. 'By the door there. I think we have something that will fit you.'

Akash was raring to go. 'I reckon we should check out the

74

place next door first. See if that's been broken into.'

Giles would have been happy to go with him, but Marion would not allow it. 'You're not going anywhere, dear,' she told her husband, firmly. 'Not with that leg. Emma and I can look in next door, once we've made sure that Hilda is all right. If that's all right with you?' She looked to Emma, who nodded her agreement. 'And if there's any sign of Dave, we will find him.'

Vicki didn't like the idea of her mother trudging out through the snow. 'What about the vagrants?' she asked. The thought of them still being out there somewhere was rather troubling. 'What if they're still around? In this weather, they can't have got far either.'

'Don't worry, dear. I can take care of myself. And they're probably long gone.'

'There'll be two of us,' Emma pointed out. She reached down into the pocket of her jeans. 'I'll take my rape alarm. If we do get into any trouble, you'll be the first to know.'

'That settles it, then,' Marion concluded. 'Your feet are about the same size as mine. Those Wellingtons should suit you. You'd better grab a coat too.'

The two women moved over to the corner to get dressed.

Akash was still intent on having his own adventure. 'If those two are heading downhill, I reckon we should head the other way. See if we can't get up to the road and phone someone. Get some help. You want to come, doll?'

Vicki considered for a moment. She did not like the idea of Akash going off on his own; but if Uncle Dave really was in trouble then it made sense to look everywhere. The more people who went out, the greater the chance they had of finding him. They wouldn't get lost now, in broad daylight. 'All right,' she agreed tentatively. 'We should give it a try. I'm not sure how far we'll get though.'

'As far as we need to. A bit of snow never hurt anyone.'

Giles was reluctant to let the pair of them go. 'I'm not sure it's a good idea, Victoria. Not in your condition.'

Vicki dismissed that with a wave of her hand. She pushed back her chair and stood up. 'Honestly, daddy, I'm perfectly fit. I haven't even got a bump yet. Akash will look after me.'

Giles bit his lip. 'All right, darling. But be careful. And wrap yourself up warm.' He adjusted his spectacles. 'I might take a look around the outside of the house, while you're gone. David might be much closer than you imagine.'

'If you're sure, daddy,' Vicki said, eyeing up his leg.

'I'm not an invalid either,' he shot back. 'And you, young man.' He addressed Akash. 'You take care of my daughter.'

'No worries. You've no idea how precious this girl is to me.' He extended an arm and squeezed Vicki around the waist.

She kissed him gently. 'And you to me.' She pulled away. 'I'll see what I can find upstairs.' They had packed plenty of warm things, including a pair of hiking boots. Vicki disappeared into the back room and quickly ascended the ladder.

'So what do you reckon?' Akash asked her dad, down below. Vicki could hear his voice through the gap in the floor. 'Do you think something serious has happened to Dave?'

'I'm afraid it's a real possibility,' Giles Wilkerson said.

Blimey, this is hard work. Emma was trudging awkwardly through the snow, well behind the other woman. Marion was wrapped up well, with a woollen hat over her reddish brown hair and a thick scarf around her neck. She was carrying two hiking sticks. These were not designed for snow but they were still surprisingly useful. Emma had a couple as well, but it took a bit of time to get used to them: digging each one into the ice, pulling yourself forward, extracting the last one and then pushing it out again. The snow was almost waist deep but it had compacted enough over the last couple of hours to take some of their weight. Emma wasn't actually disappearing into it, even if a foot occasionally vanished underneath her. She was also well protected from the cold, with a sand coloured fleece, thick socks and a set of woollen tights underneath her trousers. Not to mention the obligatory daft hat. All told, there was barely an inch of her visible except her nose and her eyes. She was used to being well wrapped up – in motorcycle leathers and a helmet – but this was ridiculous.

It took them a few minutes to walk the length of the house, after they had scrambled out of the barn doors. Marion had quickly found her feet, Emma less so, as they set off into wilderness. Marion was well ahead of her now but she stopped periodically and turned back with a smile, giving Emma time to catch up.

'How are you doing, dear?' she asked.

'Well, I haven't fallen on my arse yet.' Emma chuckled and then promptly lost her footing and fell over. She laughed as Marion trudged back to give her a hand up. 'Me and my big mouth. This is more difficult than it looks. I don't know how you do it.'

'I do a lot of walking,' Marion explained. 'It helps to keep me fit. Although not usually in weather like this.' She had better boots on too, walking boots rather than Wellingtons.

Emma retrieved her sticks and gazed around her for a moment. 'It's a real wonderland, isn't it?' she breathed. 'In April.' It was madness. Apart from the houses, and the fir trees at the bottom of the field, there was nothing in sight but snow in any direction. Their footprints were the only tangible signs of life. Even the cars in the driveway were completely buried. That made Emma smile. She had always loved the outdoors – the open road – and there was nothing like a bit of snow to brighten up a landscape. *Covering up a multitude of sins,* she thought.

If she had not been so worried about Dave, she would probably have enjoyed all this. He would have loved it. She could just picture him, in his gloves and a muffler, grabbing great handfuls of snow and lobbing them at her. It was perfect weather for a snowball fight. Emma would have got her own back, though, pushing him over and half burying him. There had been a bit of a snowfall back in England, just before Christmas. Nothing like this, but heavy for them. They had gone out to the park together and hurled snowballs at each other like little kids. It was such a laugh. But Emma had never seen snow like this in England. Three feet, for Christ's sake. If this was Canada it would be understandable, but *France*? It beggared belief.

'Shall we get on, dear?' Marion asked, already moving off.

Emma followed on as best she could. It crossed her mind to pick up some snow and throw it, but she didn't think the older woman would appreciate a snowball in the back. Dave would have thrown one anyway. *I hope to God he's okay*. She hit another soft spot in the snow and her leg disappeared abruptly beneath her. 'Oh, hell!'

'Are you all right, dear?' Marion looked back.

'Yes, fine,' Emma said, struggling to pull her leg back up, with the help of the walking stick. The next patch of snow was a little bit firmer, thankfully.

'Nearly there,' Marion said, as they drew close to the first house. This was a little smaller than the Wilkersons' residence. No barn here that she could see; the same rough stone walls though and the tiled roofing. Not that you could see any of the tiles just now.

One last push, Emma thought, *and I'll be there*. It was hard work and her energy was beginning to flag. *And I thought I was fit*. Marion Wilkerson, who had to be a good fifteen years older than she was, was putting her to shame. It was the concentration that used up most of her energy. Perhaps she could bridge the last few yards in one quick burst, using her momentum to carry her through. It didn't work. Emma tripped up again and this time went flying through the air, crashing down hard onto the solidly packed snow just in front of the wall. Her heavy clothing deadened the impact a little, but Emma's face smacked into the snow and, as she pulled herself away, she found herself covered in the stuff. 'Not exactly graceful,' she laughed, as Marion gave her another hand up. Emma pressed a glove against the wall to steady herself and then brushed off some of the snow.

'All right, dear?' Marion asked, for the umpteenth time.

'Fine,' she said, brushing herself down. The whole of her front was now covered over. She was a walking snowman. She must look a right sight. She glanced back the way they had come. Between the pair of them, they had worked an impressive furrow between the two houses, with bigger dips where Emma had fallen on her arse, dotted each side with small holes from the walking sticks. The distance, however, was miniscule; barely more than a hundred metres.

Two figures were heading out from the Wilkerson farm in the opposite direction. Vicki and her boyfriend Akash were aiming for the house closest to the main road, but they had not got very far. *Blimey, they're even slower than we are.* The distance was less but the youngsters had barely got halfway. They had a slight upward slope to contend with, however, and that probably wasn't helping. Vicki, in particular, was struggling, and Akash was hanging back to help her out.

At least I'm not the only one falling arse over tit.

Marion was already moving around the side of the house, using the wall as a support. She found a window and brushed off some of the snow with her glove; then she peered inside. 'I can't see any sign of life,' she called back, as Emma moved to join her. 'There doesn't seem to be anyone in there. Hello!' Marion called out. '*Bonjour! Ça va?*'

The front door was just a little way along. Marion shuffled towards it and pulled at the latch, but the door was locked.

'No joy?' Emma asked.

'No. I don't think anyone's been in here for a while.'

'No sign of Dave?'

'I'm afraid not, dear. Or our young hooligans.'

Emma growled in frustration; but it had had always been a long shot. It seemed unlikely that Dave would have got this far in any case, not at night, in this weather. Then again, the snow would have been a lot less deep in the early hours. There had been at least two separate snowfalls, one late in the evening and then another just before dawn, according to Marion. That later fall would have covered over any footprints. If Dave had gone out before then, he might have got this far.

'I wish they had broken in here rather than our house,' Marion said.

'They might not have had much choice,' Emma thought. 'Just went for wherever was closer. I don't think Dave came this way, though.'

'No, it doesn't look like it,' Marion agreed. 'Let's hope Vicki and Akash have more luck. I'm going to carry on to the far house over there, to see if Hilda is all right. There's a chance she might have heard something. Last night, I mean. Depending on which direction they came from. But if you'd prefer to go back...'

Emma shook her head. 'Better to stick together, Marion.' They had trudged this far and it was unlikely the others would be reporting back any time soon.

'As you wish, dear.'

'Just give me a minute.' One of her socks had become twisted in the bottom of her left boot. Emma had borrowed these as well as the Wellingtons and they were a little bit loose on her. She steadied herself against the wall and thrust a hand down into the boot, to try to pull it up.

Marion propped herself up against the window sill. 'Don't worry, dear. We'll find him,' she said. 'Wherever he is. Giles would never forgive me if anything happened to Dave.'

Emma wiggled the sock up and shifted the boot on the snow. 'They've been friends for a long time?'

Marion nodded. 'Since they were children. They went to the same school, though they weren't in the same year. They were in business together too, for a short while. This was before Dave retrained as a teacher.'

Emma knew the story, or some of it all least. Dave and Giles had set up their own company. 'Something to do with printing, wasn't it?' she asked, pulling herself back up.

'That's right, dear. They started it together. Both of them invested quite a bit of money, but I'm afraid it didn't do very well. It was the timing, you see. There was a bit of a downturn in the economy. Dave was worried, if the business folded, that he would lose everything. It wasn't a limited company, you see. So he pulled out as soon as he could. That was when he decided to become a teacher. To retrain.'

'And what happened with the business?'

'It very nearly went under. But Giles persevered. He can be a stubborn man when he wants to be. And eventually, things picked up. In the end, it became quite a success.'

'Enough to buy a farm in the south of France?'

'More than enough. We sold the business eighteen months

ago. It was a good decision, I think. We have enough now to see to our needs.'

'Early retirement?'

'Effectively,' Marion agreed. Very early retirement, in her case. She was in her mid forties. According to Dave, they had made several million quid selling the company.

'So if he'd held his nerve – Dave, I mean – he'd have been a millionaire too,' Emma guessed.

'Possibly, dear. It's difficult to say. Who knows what would have happened? I'm not sure Dave has a head for business. And he seems content with his lot these days. Akash tells me he was a very good teacher. No, it was his decision and it was probably right for him at the time. There was never any bad feeling about it. Well, you know Dave.'

'Yes, he doesn't bear grudges,' Emma agreed.

Marion lifted herself up from the window sill. 'All ready, dear? Shall we carry on?'

'Why not?' Emma smiled. She glanced back at the Wilkerson farm. Giles was outside now, making his way around the edge of the house, as he had said he would, looking for any signs of life closer to home. He was probably keeping an eye on Marion too, across the fields, concerned for her safety. But they were in no danger. There wasn't a hint of any other life on this side of the valley.

Fifteen minutes later, they reached Mrs Pavan's house. This building looked to be in a much better state than the middle one; and there was definitely somebody in residence. Smoke was creeping out of a snow-covered chimney pot.

'It looks like she's got a fire going,' Emma observed.

'Hilda!' Marion called out, as they drew close to the building. 'It's only me! It's Marion. I thought I'd come and see how you were.'

Emma heard a bolt being drawn back. The front door opened slowly.

There was a crack in the glass. That was the first thing Vicki noticed, as they approached the house. You couldn't see it from the side, only when you looked at the window from the front. There was a small hole in the centre pane, with cracks splintering out from it.

'Someone's definitely been here,' Akash breathed, examining the crack at close quarters. His curly hair was covered over with a woolly hat but his cheeks were red with cold. 'Looks like someone's lobbed a stone through it. A little one, anyway.'

Vicki suppressed a shudder. So the vandals had been here too. She looked up and down the front of the building. 'You don't think they might still be around?'

'Nah, I don't reckon so.' Akash grabbed her shoulder with his hand and gave it a reassuring squeeze. 'Don't worry, doll. I'll look after you.'

'I'm perfectly fine,' she said, a little irritably. Her mum had offered them a walking stick each, but Akash had turned down the offer. As a result, Vicki had been slipping and sliding all over the place. Now she was covered in snow. Akash had managed much better, of course. If he hadn't been here to help her out she would probably have stuck fast long before now. 'Just a little out of breath,' she added, leaning across and kissing his cheek.

Akash lifted a hand to his eyes and peered in through the fractured glass. 'If I was going to break in and doss down somewhere, this is the place I would choose,' he said. 'Nice gaff.' It was quite unlike the Wilkerson farm. A sizeable chunk of the exterior wall had been replaced with glass. Inside, the building was modern and sparsely furnished, with a polished floor and a spiral staircase leading up to an opened-out landing. It had all the modern conveniences too: a wide screen TV, a games console, elegant but minimal furniture. It looked more like an apartment than a farmhouse. A lot of money had obviously been thrown at it. There was no sign of life, however. 'Doesn't look like anyone's been inside.'

'The window, though,' Vicki said, eyeing the crack once again. 'They obviously came this way.'

'It looks like it. Where are the owners?'

'In Bordeaux, I think. That's what mum said. We'll have to

call them, when the phone's back on. She has their number, in case of emergencies.' Vicki stamped her feet for a moment. The cold was really beginning to bite and it was worse when they stood still for any length of time. Vicki had borrowed a pair of trousers, to put on over her tights – a skirt wasn't practical out here – but when she fell over, a lot of the snow had gone up her trouser leg. The tights were now wet through.

'Feeling a bit chilly?' Akash asked, sympathetically. He put his arm around her. 'Do you want my scarf?'

'No, I'm fine. I just need to keep moving.'

Akash dropped his arm and nodded. 'Right. Up the hill then. See if we can get a signal. The sky's beginning to clear,' he observed happily. 'With any luck, the sun'll be peeping through in a minute. Warm us both up, eh?' He grinned, and gestured for Vicki to lead the way. It was easier for him to help her, if he was bringing up the rear. He was thoughtful like that.

Vicki was sceptical whether the phones would work, even at the top of the hill. She peered ahead, at the main road. There was no traffic that she could see. Mind you, she could not actually see the road itself, only the crest of the hill and a few snow covered bushes. She had tried to phone yesterday from the car, but hadn't been able to get a signal. It was worth a second try, however, and a higher viewpoint might prove useful in their search for Uncle Dave. There was certainly no sign of him down here. Vicki was trying hard not to think the worst, but with every awkward step she was becoming more and more concerned. In the daytime, it was just about bearable out here, with the right clothes on. But if Dave had come out here at night... Vicki shook herself. She did not want to think about that.

'Hey look!' Akash called, coming to a halt in front of the far window. Vicki glanced back at him. 'They've got a phone in there!' He gestured to the window. 'A land line.'

Vicki shuffled back and peered inside. Sure enough, on a coffee table, there was an old fashioned telephone. 'Do you think it might be working?' she wondered.

'I don't know. It might be. What do you reckon, doll? Shall we give it a go? Go in and have a try.'

'How do we get in?' Vicki asked.

'We could break in,' Akash suggested.

She gave him a look.

'It *is* an emergency.' He scratched his nose, which was even redder than his cheeks. 'Or we could go round the side, see if there's anything open? If the phone's working, we could call for help.'

Vicki was sceptical. 'I don't think it's likely to be connected, if ours isn't. They're bound to be on the same line.'

'Probably. But we might as well have a look and see if we can get in. It'll save us a trek up the hill.'

'All right,' Vicki agreed reluctantly. A quick circuit of the house.

Akash grinned. They could cover the whole area in just a few minutes. It was easier to walk if you had the side of a house to support you. Maybe there would be an open door somewhere, or a loose window. Vicki had a vague memory of a spare key. Her mum had mentioned it once. Maybe they could get hold of that, if the worst came to the worst. But it would take too long to head home and fetch it. Better to have a quick look around first.

There was an old barn to the rear of the building. Unlike the Wilkerson house, this was a separate structure, set back from the main house. The doors were chain locked – Akash had already hopped across to have a look – but there was no sign that anyone had got inside. A particularly high mound of snow encased a pile of wood directly in front of it. Akash wiped some of it away with his gloves. 'How often do they come here, the owners?' he asked.

'Just once or twice a month, mum says. I've only met them once. He's an artist or a lecturer or something. Dad says he's very good, although I don't think it's really his taste. Lots of half naked women.'

Akash's eyes lit up. 'That sounds all right. What about the missus?'

'I don't know what she does.'

'But they live in Bordeaux most of the time?'

Vicki nodded.

'They must be minted.'

'I think they're quite well off.'

'Just like your mum and dad,' Akash teased.

'*Our* mum and dad,' she corrected gently. 'You're part of the family, now. Besides, they're not *that* rich.'

He smiled. 'Of course not.' He reached forward, pulling hard on the chain locking the barn door. 'You know your dad thinks I'm a gold digger, don't you?'

'Akash, he thinks nothing of the kind.'

'I don't blame him, doll.' He found a window and peered into the barn. 'I'd think the same in his shoes. He doesn't know what we've got, you and me.'

'He's just a little old fashioned,' Vicki said. 'But he was very pleased about the baby.'

Akash moved back from the window and pulled her to him. 'And me making an honest woman of you.'

'That too.' It was a little awkward, cuddling up, with all the layers of clothing between them, but she pushed her head forward and kissed him gently. 'Your lips are so cold!'

'So are yours!' He chuckled. 'Come on. Let's try round the back.'

The back of the farmhouse was much less developed than the front. The original stonework was more in evidence here. There was a small patio, though, to catch the evening sun and a set of glass doors with snow piled up against them. Akash tried the handle but these too were locked. Nothing seemed to be out of place inside.

'What do you reckon?' he asked, looking back. 'Break a window, then?'

'No, Akash. We can't.'

'We could pay for the damage. I'm sure they won't mind.'

Vicki was insistent. 'No,' she said firmly. There was no justification for breaking and entering. Not when they could just as easily pop home and get the key; and certainly not on the off-chance that the phone might be working.

Akash shrugged. 'All right, doll. You're the boss.'

She smiled at him then, as best she could. 'I'll hold you to that.'

'Here, there's some steps round there.' Akash pointed to the corner. A mound of snow led upwards, around the far side of the house. 'What do you reckon? Another patio?'

'I think so. Oh, they've got a pool,' Vicki remembered suddenly. 'Mum said they put it in last year.'

Akash's eyes lit up. 'A swimming pool?'

'A plunge pool, I think.'

He whistled his appreciation. 'Nice. So it's not just your parents who are loaded.' He gestured her to take the lead. 'Fancy a swim?'

Vicki could not quite laugh – her teeth were chattering too much – but she smiled again. 'Not today. But you're welcome, if you like. I don't think it will have any water in at the moment,' she added, more seriously.

'Shame.' He chuckled again, as they shuffled towards the steps. 'Worth a look, anyway. See how the other half lives.'

The steps were completely buried, though a low wall provided an outline of the path, which disappeared up and around the corner.

'It looks a bit slippy. Careful how you go.'

Akash took her hand and the two of them made their way up, feeling for each step as their legs sank slowly into the snow. The ice was not quite as firmly packed here as it had been elsewhere, or as smooth. Vicki kept to the wall of the house, while Akash ran his gloved fingers over the top of the supporting wall. He misjudged his footing, though, as they moved around the corner and this time it was Vicki who had to support him. 'Careful,' she said.

Above them, the sky was continuing to clear and for an instant sunlight beamed down on them, before disappearing once again behind the clouds.

The far side of the house had a low walled patio, perhaps a metre and a half higher than the surrounding terrain. In this weather, it was difficult to judge exactly. There was another set of glass doors to their left, plus the outlines of several chairs and a table. It was the large bump, however, spread out to the right, that really drew their eye.

'Is that the pool?' Akash asked, gazing at the circular mound of snow, which was slightly higher than the rest of the patio.

'I think so,' Vicki said. It looked to be about four metres across, ovoid rather than circular. A short metal ladder protruded at one end. 'It must have a cover on.' That was the only way the snow could have built up on top of it like that.

Akash took it all in, with a wide smile. 'Very nice,' he said, shuffling forward. 'I reckon there must still be some water in there, underneath.'

'If there is, it'll be frozen over.'

'Yeah, probably.' A small metal pole was poking up to one side. 'There's some sort of winch here.' It had a small handle on the side, covered over with a light dusting of snow. 'Must be for the cover,' Akash guessed, grabbing hold of it. The handle could be wound and unwound as required.

'It must be quite sturdy,' Vicki thought. There was a lot of snow there.

'All weather. How the other half lives, eh?'

She nodded. The snowfall on the rest of the patio was not as even as they had seen elsewhere. Vicki gazed back at the steps, curving downwards to the rear. The same was true there; not quite as level as she would have expected. 'I think someone's been up here already,' she said, abruptly. 'I mean, recently.'

'What makes you say that?'

'I don't know. It's just a feeling. As if…as if things are out of place, somehow.'

Akash scratched the edge of his woolly hat. 'Looks all right to me.'

Vicki shook herself. 'I'm probably imagining it.' She surveyed the ground quickly. No, she wasn't imagining it. The snow dipped about all over the place. Not exactly footprints; at least, not any more, but it looked like somebody had been up here in the night, walking around. Then more snow had fallen and partially covered it over. Vicki shuddered. 'No, I'm sure. Akash, somebody's definitely been here.'

'Maybe.' By now, Akash had wandered around to the far side of the pool. The sun appeared briefly once again and cut across his face. 'There *is* water in here,' he said, looking down. 'Ice water. The cover's not on properly.' He got down onto his knees and wiped some of the snow from the top of it. 'There's about thirty centimetres clear...' He stopped, surprised, and pulled back momentarily.

'What is it?' Vicki asked, her eyes fixed on him.

'There's something under there.'

'What is it?'

'I don't know. Give that handle a pull, will you?' He gestured to the roller.

Vicki did as she was told. She grabbed the handle and began to unwind the cover.

'Other way,' Akash said. 'That's it. Just a little...oh.' He sat back on his haunches. 'Bloody hell.'

'What is it?'

He waved a hand. 'You stay there, doll. You don't want to see this.'

Vicki was already making her way around the pool towards him. 'What is it?' she asked again.

'I wouldn't if I were you...'

But it was too late. Vicki had already come to a rest beside him. She crouched down and stared into the icy water. The cover had moved back a metre or so and the sunlight was glistening off the water, which was only partially frozen. It was the sight beneath the water that caught her attention, however.

Vicki lifted a hand to her mouth and let out a silent scream.

Looking up at her, with his eyes wide open, staring vacantly, was her Uncle Dave. It looked like he had been dead for some time.

Chapter Five

It was her own stupid fault, Emma reflected bitterly. She had insisted on coming out here to see him. She had not been prepared to believe he was dead until she saw it with her own eyes; and now she would never get the image out of her head.

Dave Flint was lying face up in the icy water, the crown of his head rubbing against the edge of the pool. The cover had been pulled back, revealing most of the body, the arms and legs tangled up in semi-frozen plates of water shuffling across the surface. It was a horrible sight. The straggly hair beneath the bald dome, and the vacant eyeballs staring sightlessly upwards. That was the worst part. Emma had seen dead bodies before. Mostly animals, at the clinic, but the odd person too. Her grandad, who had died in his armchair in front of the telly. But this was different. It was obscene. She shuddered but she couldn't draw her eyes away. Dave Flint, one of the nicest, kindest, funniest men she had ever met, dead. All that life, all that energy, just gone. Emma couldn't get her head around it. It wasn't possible. It just wasn't. *I think I'm going to be sick.*

She felt a hand on her shoulder, the reassuring hand of Marion Wilkerson. Marion had known Dave for far longer than Emma had. Decades probably.

She was the one who had got them all organised. Emma hadn't wanted to believe it, when Vicki and Akash had returned to the house to break the news. How could he be dead? Her Dave, the great lump, so full of life. She had insisted on coming out here to get him – they couldn't just leave him lying in the pool – and Marion had backed her up. Now, though, Emma was regretting coming out at all.

'We can manage, dear,' Marion said. 'You don't have to do this.'

Emma shook her head. 'No. No, I do.' She had no intention of leaving Dave in the water and she couldn't expect everyone else to do all the dirty work for her. It was unpleasant, but if they all mucked in together they could get it done more quickly.

There was a time factor involved. The clouds were starting to thicken again and more snow was on the way. Emma had heard the forecast. Mrs Pavan – the old woman at the far house – had had a portable radio, tuned to the BBC. The signal had crackled and popped, the voice fading in and out, but the forecast was clear: an unseasonal blast from Siberia had covered England, France and Belgium in a thick carpet of snow and there was more on the way. The announcer recommended people wrap up warm and stay inside.

Chance would be a fine thing, Emma had thought at the time. But now it gave them an added impetus. They needed to retrieve Dave from the plunge pool while the weather was still in abeyance.

Robbie Wilkerson hadn't wanted to come out at all. He was standing on the opposite side of the pool; a tall, strong looking bloke in his mid twenties, with light blue eyes and honey blonde hair. No hat on his head, but he did have a pair of gloves on and a scarf wound around his neck. He had only just surfaced when the news broke, back at the farm. His sister Vicki was in floods of tears, clinging to her dad. That was no surprise. Her favourite uncle, dead. Robbie thought it was a bad idea, recovering the body. 'If someone's done him in, we should leave him where he is. The police will do their nut if we start tampering with the evidence.'

The police weren't likely to come any time soon, however. The farmhouse could pick up Radio 4 all the way from London but they couldn't get a mobile connection for love nor money. Marion had checked the land line next door. She'd brought the spare key with her and let herself in, but the neighbour's phone was as dead as all the others. If the telephone had been working, if the police had been on their way, that would be a different matter. But there was no help coming today and Emma was damned if she was going to leave her boyfriend lying at the bottom of a swimming pool. Vicki had agreed with her and persuaded her brother to accompany them.

Emma was under no illusions about how easy this was going to be. It was bloody freezing out here and the plunge pool was half frozen. They would need all the muscle they could manage. Akash had come too, to help out with any heavy lifting. He was a bit torn, thinking maybe he ought to stay home and comfort his bride to be, but Vicki had insisted he go.

Robbie moved over to the winch and started turning the handle, drawing the cover back.

Akash was standing to his right, looking skinny even under all those layers, the mop of curly hair peeping out from underneath a woollen hat. He had brought a broom with him – Marion's idea – and was using it to dislodge the snow from the top of the cover as it inched open. He looked ridiculous, stretching out over the edge of the pool, shuffling the snow out of the way. But he was doing his bit, for a man he barely knew, and Emma was grateful.

Once the pool was fully open, the two men shifted around the edge, to where Dave's legs were floating, some distance away. Robbie pulled off his gloves and threw them across onto one of the snow covered chairs. Akash was already crouching down, brushing away some of the snow from the edge. He lifted the broom again and extended it across the surface, using the handle to hook onto the half frozen legs.

'Careful, dear,' Marion called across, as he began to pull the lower half of the body towards him.

Emma watched in horrified fascination as the legs drifted slowly to the edge of the pool, the ice crackling around them as they did so. When one of the feet was close enough to grab, Akash abandoned his broom and plunged a hand into the icy water. Robbie followed suit, both men grabbing an ankle and beginning to pull the body towards them. The water crackled again, thin shards of ice shattering as the hefty figure shifted its position. Swiftly, the boys lifted the feet out of the water and over the lip of the pool.

Emma and Marion went over to join them, as the lower half of the body was dragged slowly onto the shore. Emma removed her gloves and, crouching down beside Akash, she reached forward to grab an arm. *Jesus*, she thought. She had to work hard not to gag as she plunged her hand into the freezing cold water and took hold of a limb. The fabric of Dave's coat was wet and slippery to the touch, the arm stiff and unmoving inside. Emma found it difficult to focus, to dismiss the horror of the situation and get on with the job.

Marion grabbed the other arm and, as Robbie and Akash moved slowly backwards with the legs, the two women lifted the top half of the body out of the water. Dave's head flopped backwards, crunching against a patch of ice, as the water poured off him; but together they managed to raise him above the surface and helped to shuffle the body back onto the land. It was not easy. Dave wasn't exactly light at the best of times. The icy cold didn't help, as they manoeuvred him away from the edge. Finally, they laid the body out on the ground, just in front of the patio doors. That done, they took a moment to catch their breaths.

Emma wiped the ice from her hands while Robbie recovered his gloves from the chair. Akash spoke for them all, as they gazed down at Dave's body, spread out across the snow. 'Poor bugger,' he breathed. 'What the hell happened?'

It was obvious what had happened, that was the worst thing. Emma shuddered as her eyes caught the wound on the back of his head. The frozen blood. That only confirmed it. Dave must have confronted the intruders last night, when they were ransacking the building. Perhaps he had been out in the bathroom for five minutes, or poking about in the workshop in the early hours. Like Giles, Dave did have a tendency to potter around. And then he had heard or seen them. Maybe scared them off. Either way, he must have followed them out into the night. Mrs Pavan – the woman in the far cottage – had actually seen it happen; or seen something. She had been up in the early hours, trying to fix some shutters which were banging in the wind. She had seen a light moving about outside the Wilkersons' barn. This was at about two or three in the morning, she said. That must have been when it happened. Dave had gone out – with a torch, or maybe using the light on his phone – and then...and then they had hit him with something. And that was that.

Emma felt a silent rage boiling up inside her. 'How could they do it?' she breathed. 'How could they do that to him?' Clubbing him to death, out in the cold and the snow. 'He was no bloody threat to them. And then…and then this.' That was the most horrible part. It wasn't enough that they had killed him. They had to dump him in the pool as well, like so much rubbish to be disposed of. Oh, she understood the reason. Covering their tracks. Delaying the discovery of what they had done. But that didn't excuse it. 'If I get my hands on them…' Emma shook with rage, surprised at the extent of her own anger. She took a moment to calm herself. This wasn't like her at all. What was the point of getting angry? It didn't change anything. It wouldn't bring Dave back.

She crouched down and moved a strand of semi frozen hair from his eyes. *You stupid great lump. Why did you have to follow them out here? Why did you have to go and get yourself killed?* But she couldn't blame him for doing it. Dave would never think about the consequences of an action, that was his trouble. He just reacted instinctively. She had loved him. She really had. It wasn't romantic love, none of that teenage rubbish. They were not soul mates. It was more like a meeting of minds, two friends, first and foremost. One of the best friends Emma had ever had. The thought that she would never see that smile again, never laugh at one of his useless jokes, never feel his body close to her, the bristle of his beard against her face, or tease him about those great long legs of his. It was too much to bear. She reached across and tried to close his eyes, but the lids were frozen and she couldn't do it. It was so stupid. She couldn't even do that for him. Emma let out a low sob and felt the tears begin to stream down her cheek.

Marion placed a hand on her shoulder and gave it a squeeze. Everyone else was looking away politely, as Emma gave way briefly to despair. *Oh, Christ,* she thought, her body trembling, as she struggled to recover herself. This was ridiculous. She wiped the cheek and rocked back onto her heels. There was no point crying. They had a job to do. It was bloody freezing out here and it was starting to snow again. 'Let's just finish this, shall we?' she said, rising to her feet. 'Before the snow really starts to come down.'

'We'll take a leg each, shall we?' Marion suggested.

Emma nodded, wiping her hands against her coat and

putting her gloves back on. Then she bent down and grabbed the arm a second time.

They lifted the corpse and carried it over to the stairs. This was the tricky bit, but they were careful. Their footsteps had already ploughed a useful furrow, providing a makeshift path for them to navigate. The snow was starting to fall heavily now, but it was a relatively short hop back across to the farm.

The barn doors were wide open, inviting them in. The lights were on too. The electricity must have come back on. Giles and Nicholas were waiting to greet them. Betsy's young man looked as white as a sheet, as they manoeuvred the body onto the concrete floor of the barn. He had probably never seen a dead body before.

Giles came forward to help, but Marion waved him out of the way. They had all the muscle they needed. They carried the body past the moped and placed it down in front of the sofa. Dave's bald head cracked unpleasantly against the concrete.

Nicholas turned away to the wall and started to retch.

Once the body was laid out, Marion grabbed hold of the dust cover from the sofa. 'Would you mind, dear?'

Emma nodded and helped to drape it over the top of him. Dave was wet through, the snow and ice melting and forming a small pool around him, but the blanket would at least provide some dignity.

She took a breath and wiped another tear from her eye.

Vicki Wilkerson had already retreated to one of the bedrooms. Dad had told her that the others were on their way back and she did not want to see them, struggling with the body of Uncle Dave, as they brought him into the barn. One glimpse of those horrible, sightless eyes staring up at her from the pool was already too much. She had almost fainted when she saw him. Instead, she had cried out and stumbled backwards. If Akash had not been there, she would have lost her footing altogether. It wasn't even the fact that he was dead that had shocked her, though that was terrible enough. Before they set out, she had feared that he might have got lost in the snow and died of exposure. But that someone had done this to him, deliberately; that Vicki could not even begin to understand. Even in her worst nightmares, she would never have considered such a possibility. But it was true: somebody had slid his body into that plunge pool and deliberately drawn the cover over the top. They had killed him and tried to cover it up; the people who had broken into the house. It was horrible, so horrible. Why would anyone do such a thing?

The minutes following the discovery were now little more than a blur. Akash did his best to comfort her – she remembered his arms, his body against her, as the tears poured out – but the journey back to the farmhouse was a fog. How she managed to put one foot in front of another, she had no idea. Akash must have half carried her. At the house, she ran straight into the arms of her father.

Now, Vicki sat back on the bed. The radiator was glowing on the wall opposite. The electricity was back on now. She had changed out of her wet clothes and hung them up to dry.

'There you are, lovey. Nice and toasty,' Aunt Betsy said, seating herself on the blanket next to her.

Vicki wiped a tear from her eye. She had managed to hold herself together, briefly, while she was changing her clothes, but the news that the others had arrived back had set her off again. No matter how hard she tried, she could not hold back the tears.

Betsy had a box of tissues by the side of the bed. This was her bedroom, on the ground floor. She pulled out a tissue and handed it to Vicki. 'Give it a good blow,' she advised.

Vicki did as she was told, then wiped the end of her nose and deposited the tissue in a small wicker bin by the side of the bed. She shuffled back onto the blanket.

'I can't believe he's gone,' she said. It hadn't even begun to sink in, even now. Uncle Dave, dead. It was unimaginable. 'I can't believe...I can't believe anyone would do that to him.' Aside from her father, Dave had been the loveliest man she had ever known. Vicki felt numb, exhausted with grief. For a moment, it felt like there were no tears left in her; but then she sobbed again, as an ever deeper well of sorrow bubbled up inside her.

Betsy reached out and pulled Vicki's head gently against her bosom. 'I know, lovey. I know.' Betsy had always been a comforting presence, a large, bosomy woman with thick brown hair and blue eyes, invariably accentuated by heavy make up. Vicki clung tightly to her, as Betsy stroked her hair. 'What a horrible day. I've never known anything like it.' She sighed. 'I said to your father, if it's not one thing it's another. All that snow falling, then the break-in. And then him going missing, and you finding him. It doesn't stop, does it?'

'I didn't know what to do,' Vicki stuttered. 'I didn't know how to tell anyone.' She remembered the faces around the dining table – Betsy, Nicholas, Robbie and her dad – the horror and the disbelief, as they passed on the news. Emma and her mum were just as appalled when they got back from Mrs Pavan's, though Emma had been much calmer than Vicki. There were no tears from the older woman, just disbelief that her boyfriend was dead and lots of urgent questions.

Mum took charge, as always, organising a party to go across and gather the body. Vicki was in no fit state to go out again, but Akash volunteered and she did not try to stop him. Even so, she could not help but worry, watching her brother and the father of her child venturing out into the cold. The people who had killed her uncle were still out there somewhere.

'You did the best you could,' Betsy assured her. She pressed Vicki's head tightly against her. 'You were always his favourite, you know. He used to bounce you on his knee, and you should have seen the smile on his face. 'Course, I haven't seen him so much in recent years. Not since he moved away. I said to Nicholas, it'll be nice to see everyone again.'

'Daddy's going to blame himself, for inviting him here.'

'I don't think so, lovey. Why would he blame himself? He wasn't to know what would happen, was he?'

Vicki screwed her eyes shut. 'It was meant to be such a happy occasion.'

'And it was. He was on good form last night. I said to Nicholas, he doesn't change. Just like I always remembered him.'

96

Vicki nodded numbly. 'Were the two of you close when you were younger?' she asked, out of curiosity.

Betsy considered for a moment. 'I wouldn't say close exactly. I didn't know him like your father did, from when we were kids. But he was always laughing and joking. He could be a bit frisky.' She chuckled at the memory. 'One for the ladies, if you know what I mean.' She cackled, her bosom heaving in time with the laugh. 'Not my type, though. But he could be quite a wild one, when he'd had a few drinks. Life and soul. Did your dad ever tell you about his stag do, the week before the wedding?'

Vicki shook her head, pulling back and lifting herself up. 'No, what happened?'

Betsy was about to reply, but then thought better of it. 'Probably not the right time for that. Bit of a mix up that day. He tried it on with me a few times, you know. I was saying to Nicholas, he has good taste! But I wasn't having it. No, we were none of us saints in them days. We all did a lot of daft things. I certainly did. Me and your dad!' She chuckled again.

Vicki knew that story all too well, though it had happened long before she was born. Aunt Betsy and her mum had been best friends at school. Dad had been going out with mum for a few months and then Betsy had waltzed in and briefly turned his head. Dad should have known better, but he quickly realised his mistake. Marion was not quite as dazzling as Betsy, but she was a much better match for the sober, artistic Giles Wilkerson. They had got back together, and eventually Betsy had been forgiven. The fact that she had been the maid of honour at the wedding was proof of that. And by that time, mum was already pregnant with Robbie.

'It all worked out in the end though, didn't it?' Betsy said. 'It always does. I was telling Nicholas, things always work out.'

'Not for Uncle Dave,' Vicki pointed out miserably. She buried her head once again in her aunt's breast. 'Oh Aunt Betsy, what are we going to do?'

There was a knock on the plywood door. 'You all right in there?'

Emma had been lost in thought, staring at the bathroom wall. A single electric lightbulb illuminated the interior. She had thought a quick wash and brush up would do her some good. Getting the tangle out of her hair and drying herself off. A bit of routine to help her get her head together. But in the end, she had just sat down on the loo, fully clothed, staring into space. The voice at the door startled her out of her reverie and brought her back into the moment. It was Robbie Wilkerson. 'I'm fine,' she called back. 'I'll just be a moment.'

He was probably wanting a wash too. They all needed a change of clothes, after that nightmare expedition. Emma didn't think her hands would ever be warm again.

'Don't worry,' he said, through the door. 'I'm not looking to go.'

Emma got up and moved over to the sink. She glanced at herself in the mirror. The fractured image made her smile momentarily. *The mirror never lies,* she thought. Bits of her all over the place. *That's exactly what I feel like.* One part of her brain felt like it was frozen, unable to think; another wanted to scream and shout and kick the door in. It was the pointlessness of it all, that was what was really getting to her. There was no reason for it. No reason for Dave to die. Why did he have to go outside and confront them? She grimaced. *Oh, sod it.* This wasn't achieving anything. *Pull yourself together, girl.*

She unlocked the bathroom door and stepped out into the relative darkness of the utility room. Robbie was gone. He must have sneaked off somewhere. To her right, out in the living room, she could hear signs of activity. Giles was cooking lunch; putting on a brave face. Like as not, Robbie had headed in the opposite direction. Perhaps he had gone up to his room.

Emma moved into the workshop. Robbie was standing at the far end of the barn-like structure, holding up a large, square piece of wood. He must have heard her coming as he glanced around and lifted it up to show her. 'What do you think?'

Emma came over and took a look. 'What is it for?'

'The window, up there.' He gestured to the A frame ladder,

98

which led up to his bedroom. 'At the front. There's no glass in it. The wind whistles right through. It's bloody freezing.' It was cold in the barn, too – there was no heating in here – but at least there was no breeze.

'That can't be much fun,' Emma thought.

'No. Serves me right for turning up without an invitation.' He grinned sourly. 'You all right?' he asked, as Emma hovered in front of him. It was a grudging display of concern, but from Robbie that was practically an invitation.

'No, not really,' she admitted. She peered up at his bedroom. 'You've got blankets, though?'

'Yeah, a couple. And mum put a sheet over the window. Didn't do any good, though.' He placed the wooden panel against the wall. 'If I've got to stay here for another night, I might as well try and make myself comfortable.'

'You can kip down in my room, if you like,' Emma suggested. 'I could do with the company.' She didn't fancy sleeping on her own again, not after last night. 'There's an electric fire in there.'

'Kip down with *you*?' His eyes gleamed mischievously.

'On the floor, I mean,' she told him firmly. The dirty sod. 'You're not having the bed. But you can bring the mattress down and lay it on the floor, if you want. There's plenty of room.'

Robbie considered this. 'I might take you up on that.' He grabbed an upside down chair from against the wall and righted it. 'God, I can't believe I've got to spend another night in this dump.' He shook his head. 'I'd be out of here right now if I could.' Sadly, that was not an option. Once again, snow was piling up against the exterior doors. Robbie plonked himself down on the chair. 'This family. I think we must be cursed. The whole bloody lot of us.' He pulled out a packet of cigarettes and opened the lid. He proffered the pack to Emma. 'You want one?'

'I'd better not,' she said. There was a second chair nearby. Emma pulled it up and sat down next to him.

Robbie drew out a cigarette and lit it quickly. 'You do smoke?'

She nodded, settling herself in the chair. 'For years. But I gave it up a few months ago. I don't want to start again.'

Robbie shrugged. 'Please yourself.' He took a quick drag and stretched out his legs in front of the chair. He didn't seem to notice the cold. Emma had taken off her outdoor coat but still had several layers on. Robbie appeared to be wearing only a jumper and a shirt. The fag would probably warm him up a little. 'It's all such a mess. No one wanted me to come out here, you know,' he said, warming to his theme. He seemed to want to talk and Emma was happy to let him. She could use the distraction just now. 'I'm such an idiot,' he added.

Emma didn't know the ins and outs of what had happened to make Robbie so bitter towards his dad. It was something to do with stolen credit cards, apparently. Something daft like that. 'Your mum was pleased to see you,' she pointed out.

'Maybe.'

'How are things with your dad? You haven't made it up with him yet?' That was the point of him coming here, as far as Emma understood things.

Robbie took another puff of his cigarette. 'We've talked a bit, come to an understanding, of sorts. He didn't have much choice.' Robbie banged his hand down on his knee. 'God, this family. Everything's such a mess.'

'Your mum and dad seem to get on all right,' Emma said.

Robbie scoffed at that. 'Oh sure, they present a nice image. But that's all it is. An image. They're chalk and cheese, them two. I don't know how they've stuck together so long.'

'Perhaps they complement each other.'

That got a laugh. 'You must be joking.' He gestured to the walls. 'This place doesn't help. Away from all their friends back home. I can't see them sticking it out, in this dump. It drives mum up the wall.' He smiled to himself. 'She getting rather friendly with her French teacher, so I hear.'

Emma stifled a laugh at that suggestion. The idea of Marion Wilkerson indulging in a torrid affair seemed ludicrous. *But I suppose you never know.*

'Not that I'd blame her,' Robbie said, seriously. 'This family.'

'Your sister Vicki seems all right.'

'Oh, she's okay. The little princess, living in her own little world. She hasn't got a clue what's going on. Don't get me wrong, I love her to bits.' He took another drag of his cigarette. 'She's the only one who stood by me. Kept in touch, no matter where I was. She always tries to think the best of everyone. Even me.' He laughed. 'More fool her. She has no idea what people are really like. The world we live in.'

'She's seen some of it today,' Emma suggested. 'We all have.'

'Yeah.'

'I'd be a lot happier if the phone was working. If we could just call someone.'

'What, the police?' Robbie was dismissive. 'They can't do anything. Snooping all over the place. A waste of time.'

Emma regarded him thoughtfully for a moment. 'Dave told me you'd been in prison.'

'Did he now?' Robbie grunted.

'Nothing serious. Credit cards or something?'

Robbie tapped out a bit of ash from the end of his cigarette. 'Yeah, something like that.'

'But that's done and dusted, isn't it? You've served your time.'

'Yeah. For that, anyway.' He met her eye briefly. 'But once a criminal, always a criminal, isn't that what they say?'

'You've stolen something else, have you?' Emma couldn't help but ask. More credit cards, perhaps?

'Let's just say I'm not planning to hang around, when the ice thaws.'

She smiled. 'You mean, when the police come knocking?'

'You got it. Mind you, a French prison would probably suit me. It'd make a nice change.'

Emma wasn't sure if he was joking or not. 'Was it the moped?' she asked. 'Is that what you're worried about?' He didn't reply. 'You nicked it, didn't you?'

'Yeah. I picked it up in Calais,' he admitted, with a half smile. 'Some prat had left the keys in it.'

'You were lucky not to get caught. CCTV, they might easily

101

have picked you up. The number plates and all that.'

Robbie shook his head. 'Not as much of that in France as there is back home. Anyway, I stuck to the back roads. Plenty of places without cameras.'

'How did you know where to come? You've not been here before, have you?'

'No, I haven't. But Vicki gave me the address, when they first moved out here. It wasn't difficult to find it. Sort of. Just head to Bordeaux, then Bergerac, then Duras. Took me a couple of days, coming down here. Had to sleep rough.' He banged his knee again. 'I must have been mad. What the hell was I thinking? I thought we could talk it out. Me and my dad, you know. And we did. God, did we talk. But I should have known it would all go tits up. Why couldn't...' Robbie closed his eyes and drew in a heavy breath. 'Listen to me, banging on, feeling sorry for myself. You must be feeling worse than I am.'

'I've had better days,' Emma admitted. 'I can't believe he's gone. It's just...he was just there, you know...and then...'

'Yeah, I know.'

'You knew him a lot longer than I did.'

'Since I was a nipper, yeah.'

'He always spoke fondly of you.'

Robbie was dismissive. 'Vicki was his favourite. She thought the sun shined out of his arse. He could always put on the charm.' He took a final puff of his cigarette and then stubbed it out on the floor. 'Have you ever broken the law?' he asked, abruptly.

Emma laughed. 'Yes. I was arrested for shop lifting once.' She didn't mind telling him that. It wasn't a big secret. 'I must have been fourteen.' She smiled at the memory. 'There was this skirt I really, really wanted and I couldn't afford it.'

Robbie grinned. 'We've all been there. Well, maybe not a skirt.'

'I wouldn't do it now though. I'm a respectable girl.'

'Course you are.' His eyes gleamed. 'Actually, you're all right, you are.' He gazed across at her thoughtfully for a moment. 'I can see what he saw in you. Dave I mean.' He leaned forward. 'But you made a mistake, coming here. We're not nice people. Seriously. I think there's something dark at the heart of this family.' His expression was deadly serious. 'If I were you, I wouldn't hang around. I'd head straight out the door the first chance you get and never look back.'

Chapter Six

It was only midday, but it felt like a lot later. Giles had prepared a light meal for them all: bread, ham, cheese, fish paste and a bit of salad. Emma had joined the rest of the group at the dinner table. She was surprised at how hungry she felt. All of that exertion this morning had taken its toll. She needed a bit of feeding up; and the dinner table was a welcome distraction.

Betsy Klineman – who had not been outside at all – was wolfing down the bread, forgoing the hot coffee on offer in favour of a large glass of wine. Akash, who was sitting next to her, had quite an appetite too. He was as skinny as a rake, but you wouldn't have guessed it from the amount he put away. Mind you, he deserved it, after all the hard work he had put in this morning.

The Wilkersons had a radio plugged into the wall, a smart chrome model much more up to date than the one Mrs Pavan had. The reception was not great, however, and the news was mixed. Airports were closed, across Britain and Northern Europe. Ferries had been grounded. In England, most of the schools were off – which would please the kids – but there had been quite a few deaths on the road.

Outside, the clouds had thickened to an ominous black and the snowfall was heavy. Marion put on the lights, but the bulb hanging above the dining room table was flickering like a demented moth. 'Aye, aye,' Akash said, eyeing it up with a half smile. 'Here we go again.' The light went out for a moment, then flicked back on and gradually stabilized. It was anybody's guess how long the power supply would last. The wind was battering the side of the house and the windows were rattling hard in their frames. The good news, though, was that the storm was likely to blow itself out in the early hours of Sunday morning. A slightly warmer front was beginning to make its way across Western Europe. In a little more than twelve hours, it would all be over. *Not before time*, Emma thought. Mind you, another two or three feet of snow could still fall in that time.

Come morning, they'd be lucky if they could get the doors open. But at least some sort of end was in sight. The airports would reopen in due course, so they were not going to be stranded out here forever. The phone lines would come on again. Emma would be able to call home, talk to her flatmates and the people at work, come Monday. It would be nice to hear some familiar voices.

Marion and Giles were doing their best to normalise the situation. They had resumed their roles as hosts. Marion was cutting up some more bread, while Giles was brewing up a further round of teas and coffees, to keep them all warm. The wood burner was doing a decent enough job, but there was nothing like a nice cuppa. A hot meal would have to wait until this evening, however. Giles had apologised about that. He had not had time to prepare anything, he said. He was being modest, though. There was plenty of cold grub available.

At any other time, it might have been quite fun, the eight of them huddling together in the warm like this while a storm raged outside. At a casual glance, you wouldn't have known anything was wrong. But everyone was wrapped up in their own thoughts, keeping themselves to themselves. Vicki Wilkerson looked pale and distracted. Nicholas Samoday wasn't eating anything. He was probably still in shock. Robbie Wilkerson was eating, but he wasn't talking. The scowl on his face said everything he needed to say.

The conversation Emma had had with him had been a bit odd. Robbie had opened up to her a little, which she hadn't been expecting. He had filled in a lot of interesting details; but he had seemed strangely adamant that she should get away. What was all that about? Emma didn't have a clue. In circumstances like this, you would have thought the family would have been pulling together, supporting each other. That would have been the natural thing to do. But it wasn't happening. Giles and Marion were trying desperately to paper over the cracks, but the tension was palpable. *Perhaps I'm imagining it,* Emma thought. How well did she really know any of these people? Could she really have any idea what they were thinking?

Betsy was doing her best to cheer everyone up, babbling away as if nothing had happened. Emma couldn't help but smile at that. It was a good strategy, carrying on regardless. 'I've never known anything like it,' the woman exclaimed, in between mouthfuls of pork. She was sticking to the subject of the weather, which couldn't possibly upset anyone. 'Not in April. I was saying to Nicholas, we'll be lucky to get home at all. Mind you, we had some pretty severe winters when I was a girl. Do you remember, Marion, when that tree fell down at school? It broke the roof of the gymnasium. You should have seen it.' Betsy cackled. 'The whole roof was shattered. Well, of course, the school was closed, so we went out to the park – you remember, Marion? – with that tea tray, and went tobogganing.'

'I remember,' Marion said, sawing at the bread.

Emma reached forward and grabbed a chunk. 'Dave always liked the snow. He said it purified everything. And then, the next minute he'd be throwing a snowball at me.' The mention of Dave briefly stopped everyone in their tracks.

Akash put down his fork. 'It feels wrong, don't it?' he said. 'Sitting down for dinner when he's lying out there in the cold.' Akash had been having a cigarette out in the barn when Giles had called to tell them lunch was ready. He couldn't pop outside for a fag – the snow was falling too heavily – so he had stood at the open barn door, watching the snow fall, trying to ignore the body lying underneath the sheet a little way inside. Emma had been tempted to join him, but the last thing she needed now was to start smoking again. Besides, judging by the smell, Akash wasn't smoking an ordinary cigarette.

An unexpected voice broke the momentary silence. 'I only met him yesterday,' Nicholas said. The young man looked up sadly. 'I barely spoke a dozen words to him. But he…he seemed so full of life.' He swallowed with sudden embarrassment, as the attention of the table focused upon him. Nicholas was pale and rather fey looking at the best of times, the hair partially covering his eyes only adding to the sense of awkwardness.

'He was lovely,' Betsy agreed, putting a hand on Nicholas's

106

arm. 'He was always such a laugh. Well, you saw at dinner last night. I was telling Emma about his speech at the wedding. It brought the house down. You remember, Giles?'

The head of the household adjusted his spectacles and nodded. 'It was very well judged and quite touching, too. He was a good friend.' Giles lifted the kettle and poured out some hot water into a coffee percolator.

'He was a pretty good teacher, inall,' Akash volunteered, with a scratch of his nose. He slid an arm across the table. Vicki was sitting opposite him. He grabbed her hand and cupped it gently. 'You should have seen him, doll. In front of the class, had us in fits. The woman before, Miss Bansley, she would just drone on and on, you'd struggle to keep awake. But then off she went on maternity leave, and Mr Flint came along.' He smiled at the memory. 'And you used to look forward to the lessons. I'm not sure if we learnt much, but he was such a laugh.' Akash released his grip and sat back in his chair. 'He had us in stitches. It was a shame when Miss Bansley came back. Then it was back to afternoon nap time.'

'I remember him in his suit, at the wedding,' Marion put in. She had finished cutting up the bread and had now resumed her seat. It seemed that everyone was chipping in with a memory. 'He was so tall, he had to order it especially. It cost him quite a bit of money.'

'He's still got that suit,' Emma said. She frowned. 'I mean, he did have.'

'It never quite suited him,' Marion recalled. 'He was never a smart man. He didn't like dressing up. But he made the effort that day.'

'One of my first memories of him,' Vicki said, softly. 'He was wearing shorts. I remember his hairy knees. Back when he had hair. He was lifting me up and spinning me around. Round and around. I thought I was going to take off. He had such energy. And he was always so kind.'

'Broad minded too,' Emma chipped in. She stifled a laugh as she remembered an incident from a year or two ago. They had been going out together for about six months. They were at a party and some guy had started hitting on her. He was quite good looking but not her type. She told him she was with Dave, and he suggested the three of them go off together for the night. Jokingly, she had passed on the suggestion to Dave, and she was gobsmacked when he said it might be a good laugh. And so they had gone off and spent the night together, the two of them and some random bloke. She couldn't remember his name. It was strictly a one off – it wasn't the sort of thing she would normally do – but, all the same, it had been fun. Dave had been on particularly good form that night. God, the energy. He would have put a bloke half his age to shame. Emma caught Vicki's eye – innocent young Vicki; and her mother and her softly spoken but authoritarian father. *Best not to tell them that one*, she thought.

Robbie pushed back his plate, uninterested in the conversation. 'I'm done,' he said.

'Have some more salad,' Giles suggested, returning to the table.

'I said, I'm done.' Robbie pushed back his chair.

Marion cut in, to smooth any ruffled feathers. 'I'll put some more wood on the fire,' she said.

It helped a little, to remember him; to talk about Uncle Dave at lunch. Vicki hadn't eaten much, but it was good to have her family around her, everyone getting along as they always had. Mum was keeping busy, barely sitting down for more than a couple of minutes at a time, laying things out and clearing them up as soon as anyone was finished. Vicki wished she was able to keep so calm; but the tears kept on coming. It was years since she cried as much as this, but the events of this morning had shocked her beyond anything she had ever experienced. It felt like at any moment, she would collapse under the weight of her grief. It wasn't just that Uncle Dave was dead. That was horrible enough. It was the fact that someone had killed him. That someone had deliberately…Vicki could not even finish the thought. Akash was doing his best to comfort her, but there was only so much he could do. They talked a bit after lunch and she had had another good cry. He cuddled her then and stroked her honey blonde hair. 'Your mum's got the right idea,' he suggested, soothingly. 'You need to take your mind off it, doll. Try to keep yourself busy.' But that was easier said than done.

Marion was filling up the washing machine in the utility room. Vicki had helped her with the washing up, when she came back downstairs, and together they had stoked the fire in the living room. That helped a little. For the time being, Vicki was managing to keep the despair under control.

'Will you fetch the powder, dear?' her mum asked, looking up. She lifted a mound of clothing from the plastic basket and plunged it into the machine. 'It's in the cupboard there at the bottom.'

Vicki moved across the room to fetch it.

The washing machine was in an awkward position, just beneath the ladder leading up to the first bedroom. The glass door opened out sideways and Marion was crouching down in the space between it and the steps leading back into the living room. They had left that door open, to help with the light and to let in a little heat. The radiator was on in the bathroom, too, and that helped to take the edge off the cold. Vicki was dressed up well in any case, in fresh woollen tights, a knee length skirt and a thick sweater. She had a pair of boots on too and some fingerless mittens to keep her hands warm. Marion was in her usual dungarees, with a cardigan over the top. Her mum didn't tend to feel the cold as much. She closed up the door of the washing machine and pulled out the tray. Vicki handed her the box and Marion scooped out some of the powder.

'I ought to see to Robbie's room next,' Marion said. Robbie had already disappeared upstairs, out in the workshop. 'He'll need a bit of help to fix that cover over the window. We don't want the wind blowing through there all night again.'

Vicki leaned back against the wall, as her mum pressed the button and the washing machine vibrated into life. 'I was talking to Aunt Betsy earlier on,' she said. All that talk at lunch had brought the conversation back into her mind. 'She was telling me about daddy's stag do, before the wedding. She said something happened that day. Something odd. With Uncle Dave, I mean. But she wouldn't say what.'

Marion stiffened visibly. She lifted up the empty basket and placed it on top of the machine. 'It was a long time ago, dear.'

'I can't help wondering, though. If something happened – I mean, something bad – why has nobody ever mentioned it?'

It was an honest question, but Marion seemed reluctant to talk about it. 'It wasn't anything *bad*, dear. Well, not really.' She glanced across at the living room door. 'I suppose there's no harm in you knowing.' She kept her voice low. 'It was your father's do. As you know, your Uncle Dave was best man at the wedding, so it was his job to organise it.'

'The stag do?'

'That's right, dear. He organised the entertainment.' Marion pursed her lips, before adding, 'I gather there was a young woman involved.'

Vicki's eyes widened. 'You mean, a stripper?'

'I believe so. Well, that's what happens at these kind of events. Dave had booked this young woman and, by all accounts, she was very good looking. As she would be, of course. And your uncle always had an eye for a pretty face.'

'He still does,' Vicki said. 'I mean, he did. Emma is very pretty.'

'Yes, isn't she? Anyway, as I understand it, your Uncle Dave was quite taken with this particular young woman.' Marion frowned. 'I suppose there must have been a few crossed wires. He thought she was interested in him too, but it turned out that she wasn't. He...may have overstepped the mark slightly.'

Vicki was horrified. 'Uncle *Dave*?'

'I'm sure it was a misunderstanding,' her mum asserted hastily. 'Mixed signals. It happens all the time. Unfortunately, this young woman took umbrage and called the police. Nothing ever came of it. It was all a fuss over nothing. In those days, Dave could sometimes be a little over-friendly on occasion. It was just the way people were back then. He was a young man and he drank a lot more. Not that that excuses it. But I'm sure it was blown out of all proportion.'

'And what happened with the wedding?'

'That all went ahead as planned. The parties were held a

week before the big day. I insisted on that. Which worked out well, as it transpired. But it's all a long time ago, dear.' She gave Vicki a reassuring smile. 'Your Uncle Dave was a lovely man. I'm sure it was all just a misunderstanding.'

'Yes. Yes, it must have been,' Vicki agreed.

'Your Aunt Betsy should know better than to rake over old memories like that. Some things are best forgotten. You know what men can be like, on their own. And not just the men, of course.'

'Was there a hen do too?'

'Well, of course, dear. Your Aunt Betsy organised that.' Marion smiled tightly. 'And the less said about *that* the better.'

There was somebody in the bedroom. Emma caught a flicker of movement as she pushed open the door. She stopped, unconcerned, as she recognised the mop of curly hair from behind; but she had no idea what he was doing in her bedroom. Akash was crouched down in front of a chest of drawers, over by the window. The bottom drawer was open and Akash was rifling through the contents.

'What are you doing?' Emma asked, stepping further into the room. She tried not to make the question sound critical. It was a little odd, him being in here, but it wasn't her house and she didn't want to make an issue out of it.

'Hey, Emma.' Akash looked back, without embarrassment. He raised a hand. 'I was trying to find some candles. Giles said there were some in the drawers in here. I thought, if the power cuts out again, we could do with a few for this evening.'

'Good idea,' Emma agreed. She moved across to the bed and perched herself on the end. Something of a torpor had settled over the household after lunch. Giles had drooped into an armchair with a hardback book. Marion and Vicki had done all the washing up – Emma had offered to help out, but Marion wouldn't hear of it – and then they had disappeared out back to do some chores. Keeping themselves busy. Robbie had disappeared up to his room, to get away from everyone. Betsy had organised a game of cards, with Akash and Nicholas, to cheer everyone up, but that had soon fizzled out. Emma had settled on the sofa with yet another cup of coffee and flicked back through her phone, looking at some old photos. But that had only made her angry, so she had turned her mind to more practical matters. Like sorting out Dave's things.

She would need to get in touch with his family, as soon as she could. They had a right to know exactly what had happened to him. Dave's mother was still alive, but she was in a home. Emma doubted she would understand anything. But there was a brother too. Nice bloke, a lot quieter than Dave. Emma had only met him once. He would have to sort out the funeral, as the next of kin. Emma would help him out as best she could. The flat would need to be cleared too. There were so many practicalities; so many loose ends, when someone died. It helped, in a way, having things like that to think about. Focus on the details and ignore the bigger picture. But Emma had never been much of a one for details. *I don't even know if he left a will.* Probably not. Dave had not been much of a one for practicalities either.

Thoughts of the funeral led her back to his body, lying out in the barn. How would they get him home? He didn't have any insurance. Dave didn't think they'd need it, just coming to the South of France. Sure, they had those little cards that entitled them to emergency medical treatment. But getting a body back home, that was a whole different kettle of fish. Once the police had finished with him, of course. She would have to speak to his brother about it. What was his name? Steven? No, Stefan. God, how was she going to break it to him? How was she going to tell him that his brother had been murdered?

Even now, Emma could not get her head around it. The sheer callousness of it. It made her blood boil. Those sick bastards. And the fact that it had happened here, out in the middle of nowhere. Everyone was pretending he had just died, that it had been some sort of accident, but they all knew better than that. Murder by persons or persons unknown. It was the sort of thing you read about in the papers or saw on TV. It was not something you ever expected to happen to you.

Better to focus on a few practical things. Emma kept trying

to get a signal on her phone, but it was a waste of time. She wasn't going to be able to contact anyone for at least another day. Part of her just wanted to jump on a bike, get out on the road and disappear off into the wide beyond; but that was not possible either and she hated herself for thinking it.

She had come back to the bedroom, before lunch, to grab a change of clothes. The room had seemed empty then, desolate. Dave was gone and nothing was going to bring him back. Now at least there was a bit of activity.

'Here we are!' Akash exclaimed triumphantly. He pulled a couple of candles out of the bottom drawer. They were long and purple in colour. 'Looks like they're scented.' He grimaced theatrically. 'These are going to stink the house out.'

Emma regarded him with amusement. 'Hopefully we won't need them.'

Akash placed the candles on top of the unit and returned to the drawer. 'Hey, there are some matches in here, too. That'll save my lighter.' He dragged himself upright and placed the box, with a couple of other things, next to the candles. He turned back to Emma, leaning himself against the unit. 'How are you doing?' he asked, sympathetically.

'I'm okay,' she said.

'Vicki's not so great. She's taken it hard. Not surprising really. She loved the old sod, she really did.' He glanced across the room, at the luggage on the near side of the bed. 'Hey, do you want me to pack up his things? If you don't want to do it.'

'No, I'll manage. But thanks anyway.' Emma smiled. It was decent of him to offer. 'She's found a good one in you, your Vicki.'

'That's what I keep telling her.' Akash grinned. 'No, I'm the lucky one,' he said, seriously. 'She's a diamond, that girl. Twenty-four carat. One in a million.' He turned back to the drawer and bent down to close it up. 'Oh, I found a key as well,' he said, nodding to the top of the unit. 'You might be able to use that.' A rusted metal key was lying next to the matches and the candles. 'I reckon it must be for the front door.'

'I don't think so,' Emma said. That door – leading out of the house – was on a latch. Besides, it had a modern looking Yale lock, whereas the key Akash had found was long and skinny. 'It might be for the other one,' she thought. The doorway that connected the bedroom with the workshop. That hadn't been opened in years, according to Marion. Emma stood up and reached for the key, thinking to give it a try. She stopped abruptly, noticing an odd, acrid smell in the air. 'What's that?'

'What's what?' Akash met her eye.

'That smell. It's like…it's like something's burning.' Emma gazed across at the door in surprise. Something *was* burning. It was then she noticed the smoke beginning to creep under the bottom of it.

Chapter Seven

The scene that greeted Vicki Wilkerson was one of utter confusion. She had been sleeping fitfully upstairs, on the mattress. She'd had a bit of a headache and decided to have a lie down. Before she knew it, she had nodded off. Her dreams had been unsettling: images of Uncle Dave and of masked men carrying knives and guns; and then blood, and a body bursting into flames. 'Fire!' someone was calling out. 'The whole thing's gone up!' It took her a moment to realise the voices were real. Her eyes flicked open. Vicki could hear shouts and confusion from downstairs. Her dad was issuing instructions, ordering somebody out to the barn to fetch a fire extinguisher. In alarm, Vicki pushed back the blankets and lifted herself up, almost banging her head on the slanted beam above her. A fire! She struggled to contain her panic, as the enormity of the fact hit home. The house was a tinderbox. There was wood everywhere. It took her a few moments to clear the sleep from her mind. Vicki hadn't bothered to undress when she had come upstairs, and it was the work of a moment to find her shoes. She struggled into them, as the voices continued to cry out, before heading for the ladder. The odd thing was, she couldn't smell any smoke. If there was a fire, it had to be a small one. She gripped onto that reassuring thought as she backed herself onto the ladder and made her way down to the utility room. She was in such a rush, however, that her foot missed a step and she almost fell.

A hand grabbed her from below. 'Careful!' Nicholas was standing near the bottom and he helped her to steady herself, before raising his other hand to guide her down the last few steps.

'Nicholas, what's happening?'

'There's a fire,' he said, his eyes as wide as hers. He gestured through into the workshop. 'It's caught on some of the wood. They're trying to put it out.'

Vicki followed him quickly across to the doorway, but they had to step back as her mum appeared in front of them, blocking the way.

Marion was holding the end of a hosepipe. 'Nicholas, be a dear and attach the end of this to the tap in the bathroom sink.' Her tone was urgent but calm, as she handed him the end of the pipe. 'Turn it on as full as you can.'

Nicholas nodded and stumbled back across the room. The plywood walls wobbled as he pulled open the bathroom door.

'Mummy what's happening?' Vicki asked.

'It's all right, dear,' she said. Even with a fire blazing, Marion was not about to lose her cool. 'I think we can get it under control.'

Vicki looked past her, through the doorway and across the workshop. Smoke was starting to billow towards them. She could smell it now. Flames were crackling underneath the stairs at the far end, beneath her parents' bedroom.

Emma was wielding a fire extinguisher. The dark-haired girl was right in the thick of it, trying to smother some of the wood. Akash was there too. Vicki gasped as she saw her fiancé grab the edge of a burning table top and pull it away from the rest of the pile. *Be careful*, she thought, bringing a hand up to her mouth but not wanting to cry out in case she distracted him at a critical moment. It was obvious what he was trying to do – detach a few bits and pieces from the pile, so they could be dealt with individually – but it was still very dangerous. That was Akash all over; brave but very foolish. Luckily, her dad was on hand to help out with a second fire extinguisher. Giles had one hand clamped to his mouth to stop himself from choking, while letting the foam loose with the other. Aunt Betsy was observing the scene from the sidelines.

Vicki held her breath for a moment, watching the events unfold; then a wave of dizziness threatened to overpower her and she took a gulp of air, shooting out a hand to steady herself on the edge of the door.

Marion was busily unspooling the hosepipe. She glanced back at her daughter. 'Vicki! Will you go and help Nicholas, please?'

The authority in her mother's voice jilted her back to her senses. She tore her eyes from Akash, and moved back across

116

the utility room, almost tripping over an empty wash basket as she headed for the bathroom door.

Nicholas was inside, by the sink, trying to attach the hosepipe to the tap. 'I can't get it to stay on,' he mumbled.

Vicki squeezed in next to him. 'Let me have a look,' she said, grateful to have something practical to think about. There was a hook on the end of the pipe and a metal wedge that had to be turned. She shoved the hole firmly over the end of the tap. 'Hold it there,' she said. Nicholas nodded and Vicki adjusted the widget, clasping the end in place. She smiled at the boy, who dropped his hand; then she gave the pipe a quick tug, to make sure it was secure. They exchanged a brief look of relief, then Vicki turned on the tap, rotating it as far as it would go. 'Mummy! It's coming through!' she called out. She just hoped the pressure would be enough.

'Is there anything else I can do?' Nicholas asked.

'I don't know,' Vicki said. 'Mum will take care of it. It'll be fine.' But her words sounded unconvincing even to her own ears. She checked the seal on the pipe one last time and then followed Nicholas out of the bathroom, making sure there were no snags in the line.

A fire in the house. How had it happened? Could it have been an accident? A stray cigarette? Daddy kept telling people not to smoke indoors, but Robbie was unlikely to have paid any attention to that. Or could it be – she shuddered at the thought – that someone had started the fire deliberately? Much as she wanted to, Vicki could not dismiss the idea; not after all that had happened today.

Akash was still in the thick of things, over in the workshop. Vicki swallowed hard, trying to contain her anxiety as she watched him kicking out some of the embers with his shoes. He took such silly risks sometimes. But it looked like the fire was gradually coming under control. The water was now flowing through the hosepipe and mum was using it to smother the worst of the flames. A lot of things had already been lost, however; all daddy's books, under the stairs. He had spent years collecting them.

This surely couldn't have been an accident, she thought.

Those people last night who had trashed the house, it had to be them. Vicki clenched her hands together in horror. They had killed Uncle Dave and now they were back, to finish the job. *This is a nightmare,* she thought, her body shaking uncontrollably. *Please let me be dreaming. Please let me wake up.* But she knew in her heart that everything she was seeing was real.

Emma had not been fully prepared for the sight that greeted her on the other side of the bedroom door. The handle was barely even warm. She had inserted the rusty key and pulled it open, not quite sure what to expect. Smoke had billowed out from the workshop and, behind it, there was a wall of flame. Emma had no choice but to step back, as the sudden heat engulfed her.

Akash spoke for both of them. 'Bloody hell!'

The flames were flickering upwards, from a heavy pile of junk bundled up on the other side of the door – bits of furniture, books, canvases, magazines – and most of it had already caught light. It looked like the fire had only just got going, however – the early whoosh as the big bits caught – but even so, just the sight of the flames, visible through the smoke, was enough to render the two of them momentarily speechless. After a second, however, common sense prevailed and Emma jumped forward to slam the door shut. 'We'd better tell the others,' she said.

'Fire!' The single word shattered the quiet lethargy of the living room. 'There's a fire in the workshop!'

Giles looked up sharply from his book. 'A fire?'

Marion was at the dining table, mending a pair of shoes. She was quicker to grasp the danger than her husband. 'In the workshop?' She laid the shoes aside.

Emma nodded. 'We saw some smoke coming under the bedroom door. We opened it up, and everything's burning. It's a small bonfire already.'

'Underneath the stairs?' Marion asked, in alarm.

'Yes.'

Giles adjusted his spectacles and rose up from his armchair. 'Good God.'

Marion was already on her feet. 'We'll need the fire extinguishers,' she said.

'There's one in the utility room,' Giles replied. 'And one out in the barn.'

Akash was on the case. 'I'll get the one in the barn.' He moved across to the door.

'At the far end,' Giles called after him. 'Just next to the tennis table.'

'Righty-ho.'

Several chairs were now scraping back from the table. Betsy and Nicholas, who had been sitting opposite Marion, were climbing to their feet. The mismatched couple exchanged glances. It was Marion who took charge, however. 'Betsy, be a dear. There's a bucket under the sink.'

The larger woman nodded, circling the dining table. 'Don't worry, I'll fill it up. A fire.' Betsy shook her head in disbelief. 'How bad is it?'

'It's bad,' Emma said, moving past her towards the far door. Marion was already there and Giles was following behind.

They located the fire extinguisher in the utility room. Giles handed it to his wife, who barrelled across to the workshop.

'Oh, my goodness!' she exclaimed, catching sight of the fire.

Emma was only just behind her.

The flames were concentrated in the far corner of the workshop. Actually, from this side, it didn't look quite so bad. A bonfire, sure, with a lot of smoke, but not quite an inferno yet. The flames were licking up from the bric-a-brac to the wooden landing just above it.

Giles came to a halt beside Emma. 'How could it have happened?' he breathed, gazing in disbelief at the burning boxes.

'Search me.' Emma shrugged. How the hell were they going to put it out? That was the more important question.

Marion had already threaded her way through the jumble of equipment and was letting loose with the fire extinguisher. Emma came up behind her. The foam had an immediate effect, dampening down the flames a little, but it was not nearly enough. Emma could feel the heat of the fire up close now. It was scorching. The smoke was becoming a problem too. She pulled her jumper up to cover her mouth and gazed once again at the staircase, looming over the fire. 'If that catches, the whole house will go up!' she said.

Marion was focusing her energies on the base of the stairs. A table top was lying propped against an old sideboard. Both were alight. It looked like several blank canvases and a bundle of old papers had been stacked up in front of the door. 'Giles's paintings!' Marion observed, over the crackle of the flames. 'And his magazines.' The pile had already been reduced to a blackened mess. 'That must have been what caught light.' A stray spark, perhaps smouldering for a little, and then whoosh, a fire had spread upwards and engulfed the sideboard and the table top. Marion coughed and wiped the sweat from her forehead.

'Here, let me have a go,' Emma said. It was difficult to breathe with this much smoke about. It was easier if they took turns. She pulled her jumper further up, over her nose.

Marion was not the only one coughing. Somebody upstairs was also in trouble. Emma gazed upwards in surprise, as she took hold of the extinguisher. A dusty figure was peering over the ledge of the middle bedroom, the one without a wall. Smoke was billowing up in his direction and spreading through into the open bedroom.

'What the hell's going on?' Robbie Wilkerson coughed.

Giles was closest to him. He regarded his son in alarm. 'Stay where you are, Robert! For goodness sake.'

Robbie wasn't going anywhere. 'I can't get down!' he said. The A frame ladder had toppled over and there was no other exit.

Marion had a solution. 'Go to the window,' she called. 'Stay there. We'll have everything sorted out in a jiffy.' Robbie nodded numbly and disappeared. It was a good idea. The window would keep the air clear for him; and if the worst came to the worst, he could always jump out into the snow.

Emma returned her attention to the sideboard, which was now white hot. *Bloody hell.* She sprayed at it like mad, but the extinguisher was having little effect. The flames were now licking against the bedroom door on the other side.

All at once, the door opened. Emma had to stifle a laugh as Akash appeared on the far side, his curly hair glowing in the light of the fire. He was carrying the second extinguisher, which he had grabbed from the barn. 'How you doing?' he called through, with a grin. He was enjoying this, she could tell.

'Careful!' she warned him.

He took in the bonfire, assessing the scale of the problem with a youthful eye. 'We've got to get this lot away from the door!' he reckoned, gesturing to the pile of furniture standing between them. They didn't want the door itself catching light. 'Stand back, Emma!' he said. So saying, he turned the nozzle onto the fire and then thrust out a foot to kick against some of the burning wood. That done, the idiot launched himself right into the middle of it – an acrobat leaping through a flaming hoop – kicking as hard as he could, knocking over part of the table and the sideboard next to it. Emma would have laughed had it not been so bloody dangerous. But she could see what he was up to: using brute force and his own momentum to shift the fire away from the door.

Akash wasn't the only one doing something useful. Marion had discovered a hosepipe ferreted away behind another workbench. 'We might be able to use this,' she suggested, lifting the end of the pipe and unspooling it quickly.

By now, Betsy Klineman had arrived from the kitchen, armed with a full bucket of water. Akash was on the nearside of the inferno. He handed Giles the extinguisher and grabbed the bucket from Betsy. In one quick burst, he threw the water over the sideboard. Betsy stood back to watch.

Giles, meantime, had joined Emma at the coal face, with the second extinguisher. She met his eyes with a brief, ironic smile and together they set about the blazing table top, which Akash had kicked over onto the floor.

The furniture was not the only flammable thing here. There were all those books lighting up too. Akash handed the bucket back to Betsy and then, covering his mouth with the rim of his sweater, he resumed his attack, kicking away at the various bits of wood, breaking them up into smaller piles. His trousers caught a few embers, though, and he had to pull back for a moment, to damp himself down.

'Anyone got any blankets?' he asked.

'There are some upstairs.' Emma gestured to the middle room. Akash had succeeded in spreading out the fire a little bit, so a cover or two might come in useful. 'Robbie! Can you throw down some blankets?'

'What?' a puzzled voice called back, from the depths of the upper room.

'Blankets!' Emma repeated, louder this time.

Robbie popped back into view, a hand covering his streaming eyes. 'What you going on about?'

'Blankets! You've got some bedding up there.'

He shrugged. 'Yeah, so what? Oh, right.' He saw what she was getting at and disappeared off to grab them.

Marion returned from the utility room, with the end of the hose. Someone had turned on the taps and the water began to flow. At first, it was a gentle trickle. 'I really ought to sort out the pressure in that bathroom,' she reflected, dryly. A few seconds later, however, the pressure began to increase, and Marion moved into action. There was no nozzle on the end of the pipe, but she put her thumb over the hole and aimed the water directly at the heart of the fire.

'All together now!' Akash said.

Emma and Giles expended the last of the extinguisher fluid, while Marion moved in between them with a jet of water. The pressure had upped considerably and, at last, it was beginning to have an effect. The flames were flickering and dying. The smoke was still a bit of a problem, but the hosepipe was doing its job.

'And over here!' Akash directed. A second, smaller fire needed to be contained, and then a third. At this point, Emma's extinguisher gave up the ghost.

'Look out below!' Robbie was back at the ledge, hurling down a bundle of blankets. Akash hopped across to recover them.

'Thanks, mate!' he said. But Robbie had already retreated from view.

Akash grabbed the blankets and set to work, smothering the remnants of each little fire as best he could.

It took another five or six minutes – and a few more gallons of water – but at last the blaze was brought under control. They had done it. They had stopped the damned thing from spreading. For a moment, Emma stood back, surveying the sooty mess, steam still rising from it but no longer ablaze. She started to shiver, as the bitter cold of the workshop reasserted itself. She didn't care about that, though. For a moment, she joined the others in a relieved silence. The only sound, apart from the wind outside, was the gentle chug of water forming large puddles on the concrete floor as it spilt out from the end of the hose pipe.

Marion looked back at her daughter, who was now standing in the doorway behind her. 'You can turn the tap off now, dear,' she said.

'It couldn't have been anyone from outside,' Akash said, with a shake of his head. Vicki had brought him a cup of tea as he sat out in the workshop, surveying the smouldering ruins. The blackened mound in front of the door was a testament to all the damage done, but the landing above it was untouched. 'Look at it, doll. All the doors are locked.' He gestured to the glass windows on the other side of the room. 'You can see the snow piled up against them. No one came in through there, did they? And if anyone had come in through the barn, we'd have seen them.'

Vicki nodded and snuggled up next to him on the bench. Akash was right. Of course he was. In the heat of the moment, she had let her imagination run away with her. The fire had nothing to do with those horrible people who had broken in last night. It had been a terrible accident. Just one more awful thing, to add to all the others.

'It was that brother of yours,' Akash asserted, with a grin, 'having a crafty cigarette.' Robbie had admitted as much, when he eventually clambered down from his bedroom. Akash had righted the ladder for him. A stray cigarette butt had been left

123

out here, before lunch, smouldering away. It must have caught on some of the magazines. It was lucky Emma and Akash had seen it when they did. If the alarm had been raised a few minutes later, they might not have been able to contain the fire.

'I'm so proud of you,' Vicki said, gazing at her fiancé as he took a slurp of tea. Akash was the hero of the hour. He had leapt in without a thought for his own safety and he had saved the day. 'I do wish you wouldn't take such risks, though.' Her heart had been in her stomach when she had seen the flames catching on his trouser legs.

Akash grinned again. 'Someone had to do it.' He put down the steaming mug and scratched his head. 'Mind you, didn't think I'd be kicking through a flaming door this afternoon. I was just looking for some candles.'

'I should have done more to help,' Vicki said. 'I just couldn't think.' She had frozen, for a moment, in the doorway.

'Better to keep well out of it. That smoke, in your condition. Not a good idea.' Akash pulled her head close to his breast. She could feel the warmth of him, even through the heavy sweater. 'And you got the hosepipe going, didn't you? That helped.'

'I suppose so.'

'Don't worry about it. It's all done and dusted.'

Vicki peered across at the blackened doorway. 'Dad's not happy, though.'

'You can hardly blame him. All those books of his, gone up in smoke.'

'Some of his paintings too.' They had been piled up against the sideboard. 'It's such a waste.'

'I wouldn't want to be in Robbie's shoes right now,' Akash admitted.

Robbie had been listening to music on his phone upstairs when the fire had broken out. For some reason, he hadn't noticed the smoke until the last minute. Knowing Robbie, he was probably at the window, having another cigarette. After they had put out the fire, he had come down from the bedroom and dad had rounded on him. He had not raised his voice – Giles never did – but he still demanded to know if Robbie had been smoking in the workshop. Robbie did not deny it. It looked like he had kicked one of the dog-ends under the bric-a-brac and it had smouldered there while they were having lunch. 'Why didn't he just go outside?' Vicki wondered. 'Like you did?' Akash enjoyed the occasional cigarette too, but he went to the barn door when he wanted to smoke; and he made sure the cigarette was properly extinguished, in the snow.

'It *is* bloody cold outside,' Akash pointed out. 'And windy. Still, no harm done. We got it all sorted, didn't we?'

It had been a close run thing. Robbie could have been killed. The fumes might easily have overpowered him. Vicki didn't want to dwell on that possibility too much. With the ladder lying on its side, Robbie would not have been able to get down. No-one knew how the ladder had come to fall over; but the thing was rickety at the best of times. It was possible he had clipped the top of it as he hopped up into the room. With his headphones on, he might not have noticed it falling over. The main thing was, he was all right. 'Thanks to you,' Vicki said, nuzzling closer to Akash. 'If you hadn't got here in time...'

'It was pure luck, finding that key in the drawer when I did.' Akash reached down for his mug and took another slurp of tea. 'It's been a strange old couple of days, hasn't it?'

'It was supposed to be such a happy time. The anniversary. The baby. The house warming.'

'Well, we certainly warmed the house up.' Akash chuckled. He gazed at his fingernails, which were clogged with soot. 'I think I might need a wash.'

'Finish your tea first.'

Akash took another sip. 'I reckon we're through the worst of it, anyway. It looks like the snow's easing off a bit too.' He kissed Vicki gently on the head. 'It's going to be all right, doll. You'll see.' He slid his free hand down to her belly. 'For all three of us.'

'I hope so, Akash.' Vicki nodded. 'I really hope so.'

Emma could have done with a cigarette, but she wasn't going to give in to temptation. The smell of smoke lingered in the air, though there was no sign of burning in here, in her bedroom.

Emma had finished packing away Dave's things and was lying flat on her back, on top of the bed, staring up at the ceiling. She wasn't ready to go back to the living room just yet. The atmosphere was a bit odd in there at the moment. Nobody quite knew what to say. Betsy, the perennial life and soul, was attempting to paper over the cracks, chatting everyone into submission, but the fire had spooked them all. Robbie had taken the fall for it, but Emma had been with him in the workshop, before lunch. He had dropped the end of the cigarette onto the floor and stubbed it out with his foot. She had seen him do it, but she hadn't seen him kick it under the sideboard and he couldn't remember doing that either. That didn't mean it hadn't happened. It would have been the obvious thing to do, a reflex action, to get rid of the evidence. And it wasn't completely crazy to suppose it had festered there and then caught on those old magazines. It wasn't terribly clever, piling all that junk up in the corner like that. But the thing of it was, it must have been a good two hours between that and the moment Emma had called the alarm. Could a single dog-end really have bubbled away for that long? Emma wasn't sure she believed it; and she wasn't sure if anyone else did either.

The other possibility, which no-one had dared to suggest – not out loud anyway – was that Robbie had started the fire deliberately. There was a definite streak of nihilism in him; and he certainly had reason to want to kick out against his family. He had the opportunity too. He had a lighter and he was in the area, after lunch. Emma grimaced, considering the idea. Surely even Robbie wasn't that much of an idiot? Resorting to arson, in the middle of a snowstorm, when he had nowhere else to go? The bloke might have issues with his dad, but he wasn't a complete idiot. And besides, if he had started it, why would he clamber up into his room afterwards and knock over the only means of escape? Did he have a death wish?

It was this business with the step ladder that really bothered her. Nobody else seemed that fussed about it, but Emma could not get her head around the idea. How could Robbie have knocked it over without noticing? Sure, the ground was uneven, and it might have tottered for a bit before it fell; but without

Robbie hearing it? It was made of metal, for God's sake. Even with his headphones on, he was bound to hear something. But if he *hadn't* knocked it over, even accidentally, and it hadn't crashed loudly enough for him to hear it when it fell, then how on earth had it ended up on its side? Had somebody set it down, deliberately? That was a bizarre thought. If it had been the people from last night, she could believe it easily enough, but those bastards were long gone. Giles had checked all the doors and no-one had broken into the house since breakfast time. But maybe, she thought, not all of them had left. Was that possible? Could some ragged stranger be hiding away somewhere, biding his time? Emma shook her head. No, that was just potty. A stranger wouldn't be able to sneak around this place in broad daylight, not without somebody clocking them. The fact remained, however: the ladder *had* been overturned, and if a stranger hadn't done it and Robbie hadn't done it, then logically it had to be another member of the household; someone here who had a grudge against him. And if that was the case, then it meant the fire had been started deliberately.

Was someone trying to kill him? Emma's eyes widened at the idea. Surely not. Maybe they were just trying to frighten him. But for the ladder, Emma would have dismissed the idea out of hand. Okay, she thought: say someone did do it deliberately, who could it be? There weren't that many of them in the house, and any one of the group could have slipped away from the living room at any time. People were always nipping out to go to the loo. It wouldn't be hard to tip-toe through the workshop on the quiet and set light to something with a match or two.

The thought of matches brought her back to her bedroom. There had been a box of matches in the drawer over there, alongside the candles. Emma tilted her head and gazed across at the chest of drawers, and then over to the workshop door. The key was still in the lock, where she had left it. Could somebody have nipped in through there to get to the workshop, rather than creeping through the utility room? That would be a much simpler way of doing things, if they wanted to start a fire. Grab the key, open the door, set things going. But they would have had to know the key was there in the first place.

Akash knew. He had been in here, rummaging around after lunch. He had found the key in the bottom drawer. Could he have had something to do with it? Emma didn't think so. He wasn't the type; and it was thanks to him that they managed to put the fire out as quickly as they did. Although, come to think of it, he had rather enjoyed the whole thing. Could it have been some sort of practical joke, that got out of hand? No, not on a day like this. The truth was, though, Emma barely knew him, and she could not rule anything out.

Anyone who did come in here would have to pass through the other bedroom. Betsy Klineman's room. Emma gazed across at the door. Betsy would have had access to this room, any time she liked, as would that young bloke of hers. Nicholas Samoday was an unknown quantity. Chronically shy. Never met anyone's eye. He had withdrawn into himself even more, since Dave had been brought back from outside, though he had apparently helped out with the hosepipe. Did Nicholas have something to hide, or was he just out of his depth, like everyone else?

Emma pulled herself up and swung her legs over the side of the bed. She was probably overthinking things. Occam's razor. The simplest explanation. The fire was an accident, not a conspiracy; a dog-end festering quietly and then flaring up. It could be that. It probably was that. Emma stood up, slipping on her shoes and moving around the electric fire to the workshop door. She pulled on the handle briefly and opened it up. The smell of ash was still strong on the other side, but there was no-one in the workshop just now.

She closed the door and shook her head, glancing back across the bedroom. There was something odd about it. This room – her room – it looked different somehow, from when she had first arrived. It wasn't just the smell. It felt like something was missing. Not Dave, not his things. Something else. She had felt the same sensation earlier on, when she had found Akash skulking about in here.

Her eyes settled on the wall behind the bed. There was a slight discolouration in the paint a few feet above the headboard. And then it struck her. Yesterday, when she had first got here, there had been a painting hanging on the wall, just above the bed. One of Giles Wilkerson's landscapes, like the ones that had been lost in the fire. Like the one that had been slashed in the living room. But there was no painting there now. Somebody had moved it.

Chapter Eight

It seemed like the right thing to do. Every time Vicki closed her eyes, all she could see was the image of Uncle Dave in the plunge pool, his eyes staring blankly up at her. She did not want that to be her last memory of him. She wanted to remember him how he had always been, a broad smile, full of life. 'He looks peaceful now, out in the barn,' Akash told her. 'Like he's just asleep.' That had tipped the balance for Vicki. She had been avoiding the place since lunch, but perhaps it was time to confront her fears; and to pay her respects. An image of peace to remember him by, rather than an image of violence. Akash offered to come with her, but she wanted a moment on her own. She had gathered a candle and some matches, put on a coat over her sweater, and headed down into the barn. She almost changed her mind as she caught sight of the body from the top of the steps. Dave Flint was laid out in front of the sofa, covered over with a sheet, his boots sticking out of one end. Vicki let out a sob and looked away, but then steeled herself, turning back on the step and closing the kitchen door behind her, but leaving the bolts open. Carefully, she made her way down into the barn. It was gloomy and even colder than the workshop, but a small sliver of daylight was peaking in through the front window, allowing her to see her way.

Robbie's moped was lying where it had been left, blocking her path; and just beyond that was Uncle Dave. Vicki hesitated before moving in. His legs were so long, they had needed more than the dust sheet from the sofa to cover him over with. She swallowed hard and circled the moped, moving around the body and grabbing a cushion from the sofa behind him. She placed the pillow down on the hard concrete next to her uncle's covered head, then knelt down, her knees on the cushion, and placed the candlestick holder on the floor, with the candle in it. Then she leaned forward gently and with her gloved hands pulled back the sheet, revealing his head. Vicki forced herself to look at him, her uncle, lying there, the silent face, eyes closed, the forehead less wrinkled than she remembered. She let out a deep sigh. Akash was right. It looked like he was just sleeping. She leaned forward and kissed his forehead. It was freezing to the touch and her own cold breath momentarily enveloped him. She tried hard not to flinch, as she caught sight of the bruising on the back of his skull. She looked away, her hands trembling, and fumbled in her coat pocket for the matches. She wanted to light a candle for him, for Dave, to see him on his way.

Vicki was not particularly religious. She believed in God, but she didn't go to church and she rarely prayed. She did believe that there was something after death, however, some part of you that carried on. Her uncle's spirit existed somewhere, in some form, she was sure of that. Tears began to trickle down her cheeks as she struck the match and lit the candle. A candle for Uncle Dave.

'I'm so sorry,' she breathed, clearing her throat and gazing down at him once again, as she gently wiped her eyes. 'I'm so sorry this happened to you.' She hesitated, feeling suddenly self-conscious. Her voice sounded thin and reedy in the enormous space of the barn, but she felt sure that her uncle could hear her, that he was here in some form and would take comfort from her words. 'I'm sorry we couldn't find somewhere nicer to…to lay you out…' She stifled another sob and closed her eyes, taking a moment to gather her wits. 'I wish you hadn't come,' she said, abruptly. 'I wish you had never been caught up in all this.' She shuddered, picturing the scene in her mind's eye from the night before, when Dave had confronted the intruders. 'You shouldn't have followed them outside. Those horrible, horrible people. What did they do to you?' She clenched her hands together, the fingerless gloves as cold as the rest of her. 'We'll find them. I promise you. When the police come. We'll make sure they…they are held to account.' The sentiment was poorly phrased, but Vicki meant it all the same. There would be justice for her uncle, somehow. She would make sure of it.

'Don't make promises you can't keep,' a voice rang out loudly from behind her.

Vicki stiffened. 'Robbie!' She whirled her head around.

'You frightened the life out of me. Where are you?' She peered awkwardly into the gloom, searching for him.

'Over here.' Her brother was sitting at the far end of the barn, beneath the hayloft. There was an old garden bench there, set against the wall. It was hardly surprising that she hadn't seen him.

'What are you doing, sitting there in the dark?' she called across.

Robbie shrugged. 'Same as you, probably. Getting away from it all.'

Vicki was suddenly embarrassed, realising he had been watching her, and a little annoyed too. 'You shouldn't have been listening. You should have told me you were there.'

'I just did, didn't I?' he said. 'I wanted to see what you were up to. Paying your respects to the old sod, eh?' Robbie did not sound impressed.

'Don't talk about him like that,' Vicki snapped back, her irritation mounting. It wasn't right, talking that way, not with their uncle lying there in front of them. 'Not even in jest,' she added. Vicki turned back and carefully pulled the dust sheet over his head. That done, she rose up from the cushion, patted down her skirt and turned to face her brother. Her annoyance began to dissipate as she made her way across the barn to join him. 'Oh, Robbie,' she sighed, circling the ping pong table. 'You shouldn't sit out on your own like this. Not today. Not at a time like this. We should all be together.'

'I don't want to be together,' Robbie growled, as she approached the bench. 'I want to be on my own. And I couldn't exactly go back to my room now, could I? I don't want to be burnt alive.'

'It was an accident,' Vicki said, pushing aside a coil of old rope and groping in the dark for the edge of the bench. She sat herself next to him. The wooden slats were freezing beneath her. She could feel them through the fabric of her skirt.

'I could have been choked to death up there,' Robbie grumbled.

'That was your own fault.' Vicki could hear her mother's tone in her voice. 'You shouldn't have been smoking in the workshop.'

'I've got to do it somewhere, haven't I? Anyway, it's none of your business. I don't need you telling me off. I've had enough of that from dad.' Robbie pushed his back against the bench and cricked his neck. He had a coat on too and a Canadian style hat on his head, with large flaps covering his ears. That was one of dad's multi-coloured "lumberjack" hats. In better times, Vicki might have teased him for wearing it. 'Anyway, I'm not the only one starting fires, by the look of things.' Robbie gestured across at the lighted candle on the other side of the tennis table. He grimaced, catching sight of the body beyond it. Vicki could only see the outline of her brother's face, but she could tell he was not happy. 'You think the police are going to find them?' he asked. 'The ones who killed him?'

'I hope so,' she said. 'Dad will make sure they do.'

Robbie had his hands stuffed into his pockets to keep them warm. 'You know he thinks I started the fire? Deliberately. Just to get at him.'

'Did you?' she asked. 'Robbie, please tell me you didn't!'

'Of course I didn't, you dozy mare. If I wanted to burn the house down, I wouldn't do it in the workshop, would I?' He scoffed. 'It might never catch. Much better to do it out here.' He gestured to the hayloft, directly above their heads. 'Lob one of your candles up there and the whole place would be up in minutes. You'd never be able to put it out.' Robbie shook his head. 'But why the hell would I want to do that? There's a blizzard going on out there, in case you hadn't noticed. I don't exactly have anywhere else to go.'

'Mum said some of daddy's paintings were burnt. They were stacked up against the wall.'

'They're no great loss.' He snorted. 'Hardly worth the effort to burn them.'

Vicki gazed at him in exasperation. She hated it when he was like this. 'Why did you come here, Robbie?'

'I told you why. I thought you were pleased to see me.'

'I am. Of course I am,' Vicki said. And she meant it. She always worried about Robbie when he wasn't around. But sometimes her brother could be infuriating and Vicki wasn't sure if she could deal with that right now. 'I love you Robbie. I always will, no matter what you do. I just...I just wish...' She grimaced, aware that her face was stained with tears. 'I just wish you would try harder. Mum and dad really care about you. You know they do. They worry so much.'

'With good reason.' Robbie grunted.

'They're trying to make a life for themselves here. Why can't you be happy for them?'

'They don't care what I think. And you don't really believe *they're* happy, do you?'

'Of course they are. Until today, anyway. It was their dream to come out here. To own a farmhouse. To start a vineyard.'

'It was dad's dream. A comfortable retirement, away from the cares of the world.'

'Well, exactly. Daddy's always been a romantic at heart.'

'But it wasn't mum's dream, was it? You think she's happy out here, in the middle of nowhere, with no-one to talk to?'

'She always keeps herself busy. And she has lots of people to talk to. There's the French couple next door. And Mrs Pavan. And the people she knows in Duras.'

'Oh, yeah. That French teacher of hers.' Robbie smirked.

Vicki frowned, not quite understanding. 'What do you mean?'

He sucked in his breath. 'Dad thinks she's getting rather too friendly with him, so I hear.'

'Robbie, that's ridiculous.' Vicki was outraged. 'Mum would never get involved with anyone like that. Not in that way.'

Robbie shrugged, 'I wouldn't blame her if she did. Look Vick, you're a great girl, but you don't understand people. You always try to see the best in everyone.'

'I...'

'In the real world, people aren't black and white. They're complicated. One minute, they can be as nice as pie and the next...it's as if you don't really know them at all.'

Vicki peered at her brother, not quite sure what he was getting at. 'Who do you mean?'

134

'Anyone, everyone. Anyway, look, I'm not planning on sticking around. You're right, it was a mistake coming here. As soon as the weather clears, I'm out. Getting as far away from this place as possible.'

'Where will you go?'

'I don't know.' He shrugged again. 'Back to England. Hitch-hike, probably. I wish that bloody moped was still working. That's your fault, riding me off the road.'

'You were the one driving on the wrong side,' she shot back. But she could hear the teasing in his voice and she didn't mind. She shifted uncomfortably on the bench. It really was very cold, the edge rubbing against her woollen tights. 'Did you really steal it?' she asked. 'The moped?'

'Course I did.' He grinned half-heartedly. 'Might see if I can find another one somewhere. There's always some idiot leaving the keys in.'

'Oh, Robbie...'

He bumped his shoulder against her, but she could tell his heart was not really in it. 'Don't worry about me, Vick. Everything will be fine. And you've got nothing to worry about. You've got everything sorted. A good looking guy, Akash. He'll look after you. He thinks the sun shines out of your arse.'

'We love each other very much,' she told him, primly. But then her face fell. 'Daddy doesn't like him, though.'

'Daddy doesn't like the colour of his skin.'

'Robbie! That's a horrible thing to say.'

'It's true, though. He'd never say it, but you know it's true.'

'That's nonsense.' Vicki was appalled. It wasn't true at all. It couldn't be. Daddy wasn't like that. 'He just worries that... well, we're both very young. We're just starting out in the world. He's worried how we'll support ourselves.'

Robbie looked away. 'If that's what you want to believe.' He let out a heavy sigh. 'You live in a fantasy world, Vick. You always have. You think everyone is kind and well meaning, that the world is a fair and honest place.'

'No, I don't,' she insisted. 'The world isn't fair. I know that, Robbie. I'm not a child. I just think that the more people who

135

act as if it is, the more people who are kind and honest, the better it is for everyone.'

'If you say so.'

'Akash is the father of my child. I'm going to have a baby, Robbie. You should be happy for us. You should be happy for me.'

Robbie glanced across at her. 'I am happy for you, Vick. Don't get me wrong. You know I am. And I don't dislike Akash. He seems all right. Plays a mean guitar. Bit of a wastrel, but then who am I to talk? He thinks the world of you, that much I do know.'

'He loves me.'

Robbie scratched the side of his face. 'Yeah, probably. More fool him. Promise me one thing, though.' He pointed a finger at her belly. 'When that little bugger's born, make it a clean slate. Keep him away from all this.'

'If it's a boy...'

'Boy or girl. Let him make his own mistakes. Don't judge him too harshly, no matter what he does.'

'Oh, Robbie...'

'And when he's older and acting like a tosser, just listen to him sometimes, eh? Don't dismiss him out of hand.'

'I would never...I'll listen. I always do. I've always listened to you, Robbie.'

'Yeah, I suppose. Just promise me one thing, though, Vick.' There was the ghost of a smile on Robbie's face. 'For Christ's sake, don't name the little bastard after me.'

'You're right, dear,' Marion Wilkerson agreed, peering up at the blank space above the headboard. 'There *was* a painting there. It was that church in Little Hodcombe, near where Giles grew up. We brought it down with us from England.' The red-haired woman looked back at Emma and frowned. 'Where on earth could it have gone?'

'I'm pretty sure it was there this morning,' Emma said. 'When I woke up. But it wasn't there at lunchtime. At least, I don't think it was.' She flicked a strand of hair away from her face. 'You know what it's like. You come into a room and something seems off, but you can't put your finger on what it is.'

'Yes, dear, I know exactly what you mean.' Marion stepped closer to the bed, to examine the mark on the wall. She was a short, stocky woman, but the bed was low to the ground and the discolouration was not difficult to see. 'The hook's been removed too.'

'Unless it fell down the back,' Emma suggested. 'Behind the headboard.'

'That's always possible.' Marion moved the electric heater out of the way and knelt down on the mat. Bobbing her head low, she reached out an arm, probing the area beneath the frame of the bed. 'Yes, here it is.' Her hand grasped the little metal hook and pulled it out. Then she lifted herself back onto her feet and raised the hook to her face. 'I always lift a painting up before I move it,' she said, 'to make sure the string is clear of the upward tick.' There spoke the voice of experience. 'Otherwise, you can end up pulling some of the plaster away from the wall, and afterwards the hook won't stay in properly.'

'But why would anyone want to move it?' Emma asked.

'I'm afraid I don't know, dear.'

'And where could it have gone?' Emma gestured to the middle door, leading through to the master bedroom. 'If anyone had walked it through there, we'd have seen it.'

'It's a mystery,' the other woman admitted. She moved round the bed and over to the chest of drawers. Outside, the snow was falling as heavily as ever. The window ledge was piled high with the stuff. Marion paused for a moment, gazing down at the chest, with its doily and the empty glass bowl on top, then shifted across to examine the exterior door. This was a heavy oak affair, with a metal latch. 'You haven't been outside, have you?' she asked. 'Through here, I mean.'

'No, not today,' Emma said. It was almost a rhetorical question. If the outside door had been opened, even for a second, there would now be a huge pile of snow on the mat, or at the very least a sizeable puddle. 'Dave opened it yesterday, to have a look out. But not since then, as far as I know.' Emma was more interested in the third door, the entrance to the workshop. 'That's a more likely bet, don't you think?' She indicated the door she meant. 'You said it hadn't been opened in a while?'

'Not since we first arrived,' Marion confirmed. 'Although we had a key for it, in the drawer.'

'Who else would have known about that? The key being here?'

'Well, Giles, of course. Vicki. She slept in this room the last time she was here. It's not a secret, dear.'

'And anyone could have rifled through a few drawers.' Emma returned to the bed and sat herself on the mattress. 'Something strange is going on here, Marion.' She looked up. 'Don't you think?'

The woman came to sit next to her. 'It does all seem a little peculiar.'

'What happened to the picture in the living room? The one that was slashed.'

'I took it down. I didn't want to leave it there in that state. Actually, there were a couple of paintings in there that were damaged. I piled them up in the workshop with the others.'

'And they were burnt in the fire?'

'Yes. It's such a pity. Giles is planning…was planning to do some more painting, as soon as the weather picked up. He had a few spare canvases. They're gone too now. It's such a waste. All that work. Giles is heartbroken.' She gazed up at the wall. 'And you think the painting there might have been added to the pile?'

'It looks likely, doesn't it?' Emma said. 'And if someone took it deliberately and added it to the bonfire, before the fire even started…' She let her voice trail off, but then followed up with the obvious thought. 'Then the fire must have been started deliberately.'

Marion closed her eyes. 'I think you may be right,' she admitted, reluctantly. 'Though why anyone would want to start a fire here, I couldn't begin to imagine. We might all have been killed.'

'You don't think…' Emma hesitated. 'I mean, your son…?'

Marion stiffened, the mattress shifting under her weight. 'No,' she asserted, firmly. 'Robbie wouldn't do that. He has his problems, of course, but he would never hurt anyone. Not physically.'

'Not even to get back at his dad?'

'Not even for that. He wouldn't do it, dear, believe me. It's just not in his nature. Oh, I grant you, he has done a lot of foolish things. Things he regrets, things we all regret. But he wouldn't put our lives at risk. He simply wouldn't.'

Emma wasn't so sure. She agreed about the fire, though. 'It does seem a bit unlikely.' She remembered the ladder and the sight of Robbie in his room choking on the fumes. 'But if it wasn't him, then who could it have been? You do think it was started deliberately?'

'Yes, dear, I do.' Marion's expression was grim. 'And not just because of the paintings.' She took a moment to collect her thoughts. 'I was clearing up after the fire, you see. We have a lawn mower, tucked away at the back of the workshop. I like to keep the grass under control, especially when we have guests. When I saw the fire, I thought of the petrol in the fuel tank. I was worried it might catch light. Not just in the mower. There's a can of petrol there too, a plastic container, which we use to top it up when we need to. I was moving that out of the way, when I found the hose pipe.'

Emma nodded. 'I remember.'

'The odd thing was, the lid wasn't properly screwed on. Of the can, I mean. It almost came off when I lifted it clear.' She frowned again. 'I would never have left it unscrewed like that.'

'You think someone opened it? You mean…someone might have used it to get the fire going?'

'It's a possibility, dear. I suppose Giles might have unscrewed it, at some point. He can be quite forgetful sometimes. He might not have put the lid back on properly.'

'Did you ask him?'

'I didn't want to worry him, what with everything else that was going on.'

Emma bit her lip, considering the matter. It did make a kind of sense, she supposed. 'If you wanted to burn the house down, that's probably what you'd do. Douse everything in petrol. The sideboard, the paintings, the books. I don't remember smelling any petrol though. And what about the staircase? You'd douse that too, wouldn't you, if you really wanted to get it going?' The steps up to the bedroom had not caught fire, thank goodness. If they had been saturated with petrol, they would have gone up straight away.

'The can was quite full, when I moved it,' Marion said. 'I don't think much of it can have been used, if any.'

'So maybe someone just put a dab on the newspapers, to get the thing started?'

'That's possible, I suppose.'

'And if the painting in here was added to the pile, that suggests that the fire wasn't just someone kicking out randomly. They were deliberately targetting your husband. Getting back at Giles for some reason. One of us. Somebody here.'

The older woman grimaced, but she could not deny the logic. 'That does seem rather likely.' She paused for a moment, as if wondering whether to say anything more. 'I haven't mentioned this to anyone else, but the truth is, dear, I've been uneasy for some time.'

'Uneasy?'

'Yes. Since before the fire started. There have been so many odd little events, this past day or so. The truth is, I've been feeling rather unsettled since, well...since before we even realised that Dave was missing. There are so many things which don't seem to add up. I've been struggling to make sense of it all.'

'Like what?' Emma asked.

'Well, the break-in last night, for example. The hooligans or whoever they were. I spoke to the gendarmes yesterday. When they broke into the farm – the other farm, I mean – nothing was damaged, they said, and nothing valuable was taken.'

Emma shrugged. 'Nothing was taken here, was it?'

'No, you misunderstand me, dear. The house they broke into, over the hill, it's owned by a British couple, like us. A Mr and Mrs Hughes. I've spoken to them once or twice in Duras. A very pleasant couple. Steve and Lottie. They use the farm as a holiday home. They only come down a couple of times a year, usually in the summer. According to the gendarmes, the people who broke into their house set up home there for a few days. Made use of the facilities. The oven, the washing machine, the beds.'

'So they were more like squatters than burglars?'

'Yes, that's exactly it. Now eventually, somebody saw the lights, someone who knew Steve and Lottie and knew for a fact that they were in England, and naturally they reported the matter to the police. But whoever the squatters were, they were gone before the authorities arrived.'

'And the gendarmes came here to warn you?'

'Yes. They wanted me to keep an eye out, to watch the other houses, the ones on this side of the hill, in case they should try to break into one of them.'

'But you didn't expect them to break in here?'

'Well, no, but it wasn't so much that, dear. Although you would have thought they would have seen the smoke from the chimney and realised the place was occupied. But no, it was the way they left things here this morning. The damage to the barn and the living room. It didn't strike me as the act of a vagrant, or a family of vagrants, looking for somewhere to sleep. It was wilful destruction.'

Emma nodded. Now she was beginning to understand. 'Maybe they were upset, when they realised there were people here, and they'd have to head back out into the snow.'

'Perhaps. But why come here at all? Why choose this house? Surely next door would have been much more suitable?' A house which was obviously empty.

'Maybe they couldn't get in. That French couple, there was a broken window in their place, do you remember? Perhaps they tried to get in there, but couldn't find a way in.'

'They managed to break the lock on the barn door easily enough. If they could do that, I'm sure they could break into any of the houses. It wasn't just that, though.' Marion grimaced. 'Everything this morning, the whole business, it seemed…staged, somehow. I don't know quite how else to put it. Not real. Do you know what I mean, dear?'

Emma nodded.

'And then, when we found Dave...' Marion shook her head. 'The more I think about it, the less sense it seems to make. All this business in the night. He was the last one to go to bed and I suppose he might have been out in the bathroom when they forced their way in through the barn door.'

That was a reasonable suggestion. 'He came out into the kitchen,' Emma suggested, 'heard the noise, and stumbled across them when they were throwing things about.'

'That was my first thought. But for him to chase them out, in the middle of the night, in a snowstorm. Why would he take the risk? There must have been more of them than him. Why would he not just shout and wake us all up?'

'That's a point,' Emma agreed. She had wondered about that herself. 'And why didn't anyone hear them?' Vicki and Akash had been sleeping in the room directly above; and Nicholas and Betsy were just next door. They both wore earplugs in bed, of course, but even so: why had nobody heard anything?

'I suppose most of it might have happened out in the barn,' Marion suggested. 'The stone wall would cut off a lot of the noise. But even then, all the damage in the living room...' Could you go on a rampage quietly?

'Yes. It is difficult to make sense of that,' Emma said.

'And the damage itself. That's the most peculiar thing. The squatters left the other place pretty much as they found it, aside from a broken lock on the door. But the people last night were quite different, don't you see? They were feral creatures, tearing the place up simply for the joy of it. And if that was the case, then why did they do so little actual damage? I mean, proper structural damage, rather than just slashing a few paintings? If I were drunk and wanting to "trash" a place, if that's the right word, I imagine I would do more than overturn a sofa and damage a couple of paintings.'

'You'd think so,' Emma agreed. 'You haven't said anything about this to anyone else?'

'No, dear. What could I say? I may be misreading the situation entirely. Things could well be just as they appear to

142

be. After all, nobody here would have laid a finger on Dave. We all had the greatest respect for him.'

That wasn't entirely true, Emma thought, but she kept that opinion to herself. 'If the fire *was* deliberate, though, it couldn't have had anything to do with the squatters. They're long gone now. It had to be one of us who started it.'

'Not necessarily, dear.'

'Nobody else could have got into the workshop this afternoon without being seen. Your husband checked all the doors. There are no broken windows here. Nobody could have got in without someone noticing.'

'Perhaps not.' Marion let out a short sigh. 'But, all the same, I have a nasty suspicion there may be somebody else hiding here somewhere. Somebody we don't know anything about.'

'But…'

'And I believe one of us may be protecting them…'

Giles Wilkerson grabbed the towel from the stand and wiped his face. He fumbled for his glasses on the table and peered at himself in the mirror. His eyes looked puffy and strained. In the circumstances, that was hardly surprising. In all his fifty three years, Giles could not recall a worse day than this. He shuddered, thinking back over the events of the last few hours. The body being laid out in the barn, then the fire. It was all too much. Had it really been an accident? He was not sure he believed it. His son had admitted having a cigarette, down in the workshop, but was that all he had done? Giles could not be sure. Emotions were running high. Might he have set fire to the place deliberately, his anger getting the better of him? Robert had denied it and Giles wanted to believe him. But the truth was, he no longer knew what his son was capable of. It was his own fault. He realised that. If only he had listened to him more, if only he had taken the time to understand. And now it was too late.

He gazed across at the haggard image in the mirror. His hair was looking a little straggly, what little there was of it beneath the bald dome. Even the beard, usually so neatly groomed, looked a little ruffled and out of place. He had put on a new shirt, with red and yellow stripes. The old one stank of smoke, so he had needed a change. He pursed his lips unhappily and stepped back from the dressing table, dipping his head to avoid the slanted beams of the roof as the floorboard creaked under him. The whole room smelt of soot. It would take days to get rid of the smell. The room wasn't damaged, but even if he opened the windows – which was not a good idea at the moment – the odour was likely to linger.

Giles grabbed a jumper from the top of the clothes rack – another brightly coloured top, suitably thick – and pulled it on, over his portly belly. There was no point wasting time worrying about it. There were things to do. The dinner would need to go on shortly. A warm meal would prove a welcome distraction for all of them. Giles had prepared a nice vegetable soup and had already tenderised the beef for the main course. He just needed to put the pots on and it would be done in no time. Marion had the right idea. When the world was falling apart, the best thing was just to keep yourself busy.

He moved across to the bedroom door and stepped out onto the landing, overlooking the workshop. He grimaced for a moment, a familiar spasm of pain running through his left leg. He had grown used to it now, but it could still surprise him on occasion. It was almost three years since he'd had the accident. It had seemed like a good idea at the time. A parachute jump, for charity. But he had landed badly and ended up in hospital. The leg had improved, gradually, but Marion was always fussing, telling him to take it easy. He could still be a bit wobbly – especially on the stairs – but it was nowhere near the impediment his wife seemed to think.

He grimaced again, as he placed a hand on the wall and began to shuffle down the stairs. He had not behaved well towards his wife of late. They had had a few sharp words, in the run up to this weekend. About that French fellow, Bernard, her language teacher. It all seemed so trivial now. Giles had not accused her of anything outright, but the inference had been there. Marion had taken offence and, in hindsight, she had been right to do so. Of course she wasn't having an affair. It was absurd. Just because Bernard was young and good looking, Giles had assumed the worst. But it wasn't true. He knew it wasn't. It all seemed so petty now.

His leg wobbled slightly again; and the image of David Flint swam back into his mind. He could not get the picture out of his head. That vision of his old friend lying there dead. Even now, he could not believe it had happened. The terrible wound on the back of his head, so visible when they had laid him out. It made him sick just to think about it. The way the head had lolled, lifelessly. A horrible, shocking end. The two of them had grown up together. They were practically brothers. It offended Giles that David could have met his end in such a way. *If you can't protect the ones you love...*

He reached the bottom of the stairs and paused. It would have been better if there had been no reunion at all. The whole thing had been his idea. He was worried that Marion might be feeling a little lonely out here, away from England. He had thought it might serve to cheer her up, having her family and friends around her. They didn't usually celebrate birthdays or anniversaries but this was a special occasion and it seemed right to mark it in some way.

Robert had not been invited and it would have been preferable if he had not come. Granted, there had been a rapprochement of sorts, and Giles was glad of that, but even so. When the gendarmes had come calling, yesterday lunchtime, his first thought was that they must be coming for Robert. He had hidden the boy out of the way, for his own safety. What else could he do? He wasn't about to send his own son back to prison. And then, while his wife was conversing with the police, the two of them had talked. Properly talked. It was a conversation that was long overdue, a painful but necessary catharsis for both of them. Mistakes were admitted, confessions made. Robert had confessed to stealing the moped out in the barn; but, as it transpired, the gendarmes were not there because of that. And then, of course...

He took a moment to gaze around the workshop. Marion had cleared up a little, but the signs of the fire were everywhere. The smell of ash was stronger down here, at the bottom of the

145

stairs. The blackened walls were a testament to everything that had been lost. The books, the paintings. Was it deliberate? He wondered again, in bafflement. Had somebody destroyed all this just to get at him? His son, perhaps. He could not rule out that possibility, though he hoped it was not true, and Robert had denied it, of course. But who else could have done it? It was not as if…

He sighed. *Pull yourself together, Wilkerson.* There was no point dwelling on things that could not be changed. He had a dinner to cook and arrangements to make. As soon as the phone came back on, they would contact the authorities. Until then, it was best just to keep busy. *Take a leaf out of Marion's book*, he thought, making his way across the workshop.

Briskly, he headed through the utility room to the bathroom. The plywood door swung shut behind him and he flicked on the light. The mirror above the sink had been removed, but Marion had found a small shaving mirror to replace it with. This time, Giles ignored his reflection and moved straight across to the loo.

He did not hear the door open, as he lifted the lid and unbuttoned his flies. He had not thought to lock it behind him. The first he knew that anyone else was about was when a hand clamped him abruptly across the mouth. Giles was so surprised, he did not even think to struggle. A sudden stabbing pain cut through him, not in his leg this time but in his belly. He rocked backwards, trying to free himself from his assailant's grip. He had been stabbed from behind. His mind could barely begin to grasp the idea, but he could feel the blood oozing from his back. He wanted to cry out, the pain was so overwhelming. The knife cut into him again and again, slashing away. His vision began to blur. Then he felt the edge of the blade pressing against his throat. Just for a moment, in the small mirror above the washbasin, he caught sight of his attacker, a face blazing with hatred. Then the knife cut across his neck and blood spurted from the wound. With a silent yelp, Giles Wilkerson crumpled to the floor, dead.

Chapter Nine

The crackle of the fire on the far side of the room grew ever more reassuring as the light began to fade. Vicki wasn't sure if it was actually getting dark or whether it was just the snow and the clouds. Dusk was still some way off, according to the clock on the wall. Akash was sitting on the sofa, next to Emma, quietly strumming his guitar. The chords had a soothing, hypnotic quality. Vicki loved to see him like that, absorbed in his own world. Emma was looking at something on her phone. Mum was busily laying the table for dinner. Dad had not come down yet. He was taking rather a long time, changing his clothes. The food had already been prepared, in various pots, and it would not take long to warm it up. Vicki was feeling quite hungry now, much to her surprise. She received a few nods, when she asked if anyone wanted a tea or coffee, so she put the kettle on. A head of steam was now erupting from the spout.

Marion looked up from the table. 'There's a bottle of whisky in the cupboard, dear,' she said. 'If anyone wants a small tot, to warm them up?'

Aunt Betsy's face lit up at the mention of alcohol. 'I could do with a nice strong drink,' she declared. 'I was just saying to Nicholas – wasn't I? – if it gets any colder, I think I'm going to need a few extra layers.'

Nicholas, who was sitting to her left, nodded quietly. 'It is cold.' He had a grey sweatshirt on over the top of his jumper. 'I don't think I've ever been so cold.' The heat from the wood burner did tend to spread itself a little unevenly. Nicholas pushed back his chair and moved across to the open grate, to warm himself up.

Vicki spooned out some coffee into the mugs and poured in the hot water. Instant would do, this time. She added milk and sugar for those who took it and then bent down to open the cupboard. She found the whisky easily enough. 'This one, mummy?'

'That's the one, dear,' Marion confirmed. 'Your father was

saving it for tomorrow. But I don't think he'd object.' There was unlikely to be much in the way of celebrations the following day. 'We could all do with something warm inside us.'

'As the actress said to the bishop!' Betsy threw in, with a chuckle. Nobody laughed, but Emma looked up from her phone and managed a slight smile.

'Do you want it separate, Aunty?' Vicki asked, lifting the bottle, 'or with the coffee?'

Betsy waved a hand expansively. 'All in, if you don't mind, lovey. Bit of Irish coffee. It will do me the world of good.'

'What about you, Emma?' Vicki asked.

'Just coffee for me,' she called back. 'Thank you.'

'Akash?'

Her boyfriend glanced up from his guitar. 'Er...yeah, go on, doll. Just a drop. You having one yourself?'

'No, I'd better not.' It would not be terribly sensible in her condition. Vicki finished pouring out the whisky and quickly strained the tea for Nicholas and Akash. Then she lifted a couple of the mugs and moved across to the dining table to hand them over. 'There you go, Aunty. And tea for you, Nicholas. Did you want a whisky with that?'

Nicholas looked back from the wood burner. 'No, thank you.'

Marion had finished laying the table. She gazed across at the pots on the hob. 'We should really get the dinner on. Would you go and give your father a call?' she asked. 'He's up in the bedroom. You know what he's like. He can be easily distracted. Tell him we're all waiting.'

'All right, mummy.' Vicki finished handing out the hot drinks and then moved through the door into the utility room. There was plenty of light in there just now. Someone had left the bulb on in the bathroom. The plywood door was open too, just a crack. Vicki ignored that and headed for the workshop. She stopped on the step, however, when she heard a slight noise behind her.

Emma had followed her out from the kitchen. 'Oh, looks like somebody's in there already.' She had noticed the light on inside the bathroom.

'I don't think so,' Vicki said, looking back. 'The door's open. I think someone just left it on.'

'Oh, right.'

She left Emma to her ministrations and carried on through into the workshop. There was less light in here and Vicki had to watch her step. She shivered, as the temperature plunged around her. This was one of the coldest places in the house. There was a bit of a breeze too. That was often the case in the workshop, because of the gaps in the roof. The snow didn't seem to make any difference to that.

Vicki made her way carefully across the hangar, manoeuvring around all the junk, but then hesitated as she reached the stairs leading up to her dad's bedroom. The exterior doors at the far end of the workshop were open. She blinked in surprise. A small desk was usually parked in front of them, blocking the way; but the desk had been moved and the glass doors were wide open. Several inches of snow had tumbled forward onto the concrete floor, where the desk had previously stood. But it was not the snow which caught Vicki's attention.

A figure was standing outside, in the cold. Vicki stepped away from the stairwell and peered across at him. 'Robbie?' Even in the dim light, she could not fail to recognise her own brother. What was he doing out there? He seemed to be bending over. She stepped towards him, manoeuvring herself around the singed remains of a sideboard. 'Robbie, what are you...?'

He pulled himself up sharply at the sound of her voice. His clothes were spotted with snow and his eyes flashed with fear as he looked back at her through the double doors.

Vicki caught a glimmer of something, in his right hand. He was holding a knife. A kitchen knife. 'Robbie!' she cried out again, her throat catching in horror. 'What have you done?'

Her brother dropped the blade and backed away from her, his legs dragging awkwardly in the snow. All at once, he turned and scrabbled out of sight around the side of house.

Vicki made no move to follow him. She was staring at the knife he had dropped. A thin film of blood covered the blade.

Emma did not make a sound. She didn't even cry out, when she caught sight of Giles Wilkerson sprawled across the bathroom floor. For the briefest of moments, she thought he must have had a fall. Perhaps he had slipped on the wet tiles. But then she saw the blood and the wound in his back and her mouth dropped open. *Bloody hell.*

She put a hand on the frame of the door to steady herself and gazed down at the body incredulously. Somebody had stabbed him in the back. His jumper was torn in several places, each of the rips circled with blood. Emma gazed at the wounds, dumbfounded. She had seen her fair share of dead bodies over the years. It was unavoidable, when you worked in a veterinary clinic. But that was animals, not people. Giles Wilkerson was curled up awkwardly between the wash basin and the toilet, his arms and legs forced into strange angles in the confined space. There was blood everywhere. With Dave, out in the plunge pool, there had been mercifully little. But here, it was all over the place, some of it congealed across Giles's brightly coloured jumper, a lot more spread out across the floor. The bathroom tiles were angled slightly, to allow the run-off of the water, and the blood had oozed downhill. It was the gash across the neck, though, that really caught Emma's attention. This was no accident, she realised with a shudder. Someone had deliberately slit his throat.

She took a moment to calm herself down. *What am I going to do?* She let go of the bathroom door and forced herself to look closely at the body. He couldn't have been dead long. Perhaps fifteen or twenty minutes. Emma wasn't a nurse, but she had some idea how these things worked. Twenty minutes ago, she had been sitting in the living room, tapping away at her phone, looking through some old texts. Nobody out there had heard a thing. *Bloody hell*, she thought again. Minding our own business while Giles was being hacked to death. Emma's heart pounded as she tried to make sense of it. Who would do something like this? To Giles, of all people? Who on earth would want to kill him, and in such a brutal way?

150

Her thoughts skipped back to the conversation she'd had with Marion Wilkerson. The older woman was convinced there was a stranger in the house. Was that possible? Someone hiding away? Even now, staring down at Giles, Emma didn't believe it. A madman, sure. Whoever did this must be absolutely deranged. But a stranger skulking about unnoticed in the dark? It made no sense. *No, one of us did this.* Emma felt strangely certain of that. *And they must have killed Dave too*, she realised abruptly. Had all this been planned from the start? The break-in, then the fire, and now Giles. Could the same bloke – or woman – be responsible for everything?

A prickle of fear rose up her back and Emma fought back the urge to throw up. Who the hell would do all that? And what was the point? There was no logic behind it that she could see. Someone must have lost the plot. Trying to burn down the house, for God's sake. Were they trying to kill everyone? Emma rose up from the body and stepped backwards, pulling the bathroom door closed behind her. *This is a bloody nightmare.* The enormity of it all was beginning to overwhelm her. And there was no guarantee it was over yet. Emma pressed her back against the door and breathed deeply. *Get a grip*, she told herself. *Just take a moment and breathe.* She closed her eyes and tried to follow her own advice.

There were voices out in the kitchen, the vague mumble of conversation. The stone walls were usually an effective dampener, but a sudden laugh from Betsy cut its way though, her voice always the loudest of the loud.

It must be one of them, she realised, with a grim certainty. But she had no idea who. They were a strange old bunch, but could one of them really be a murderer?

She steeled herself, moving back towards the living room door. She would have to break the news, tell them what had happened; and then all hell would break loose. They would know it was one of them who had killed him. Emma could already picture the horror and the panic; the accusations, the suspicion. Nobody would believe Giles's death was the work of vagrants. And there was no-one in authority to take charge of the situation.

151

She yanked open the door and moved into the living room.

The scene was unchanged. That was the really bizarre thing. Emma had only been gone a couple of minutes, though it felt like a lot longer. Nicholas was standing in front of the wood burner, as he had been before, warming his hands. Betsy was chuckling away at the dinner table, knocking back her Irish coffee. Akash was over on the sofa, strumming his guitar. The coffee Vicki had made Emma was steaming on a small table by the sofa. The whole tableau appeared so utterly normal, it was almost absurd. Emma hesitated at the door, her eyes flicking from person to person, trying to recall if any of them had left the living room in the past half an hour. Had anyone popped out to the loo? In all honesty, she couldn't remember. But one of them must have done. Marion, perhaps? Or Betsy? Or maybe Nicholas?

There were two notable absentees. Vicki had left the room just ahead of her; and Robbie, the brother, she hadn't seen for some time. *Did he do it?* Emma wondered, with a start. Could he have killed his own dad?

'Are you all right, dear?' Marion asked, gazing across at her in concern. 'You look as if you've seen a ghost.'

'No, I...' Emma hesitated. Maybe it wasn't such a good idea, blurting it all out in front of everyone. She managed to keep her voice level as she said, 'Marion, can I have a word, in private?'

'Yes, of course, dear.' The woman stepped away from the stove and moved across to her. Betsy observed them with interest as Emma wheeled back and Marion followed her into the utility room.

'What is it, dear?' she asked, as the door swung shut behind them. 'What have you found?'

Emma swallowed. 'Marion, I'm so sorry. I don't really know how to tell you this. It's Giles.'

'What about him?'

'I...found him.' She indicated the bathroom door. 'He's...'

Marion moved automatically in that direction but Emma lifted a hand. 'I wouldn't. I found him in there. I'm so sorry. He's dead.'

152

'Dead?' The other woman stopped, not quite understanding. 'He's been murdered, stabbed.'

'No, that's not...it can't...' Marion shook her head and resumed her path towards the open door.

'Marion, I really wouldn't. You don't want to...'

But it was too late. She had already pushed back the door. She let out a low moan as she caught sight of the body on the floor.

'I'm so sorry. I just...I found him in there. I was going to the loo. The door was open.'

Marion stepped forward and crouched down next to the body. She stared in horror at the vivid gash across her husband's neck, but then reached out and took his hand in hers.

Emma hesitated. 'You shouldn't...' It wasn't a great idea, touching the body; but she could hardly blame the woman for doing it.

Marion was silent for some time. There were no tears, no sobs of despair, just dumb incomprehension. 'Oh, you silly man,' she breathed at last. 'What have you done?'

Vicki knew something was seriously wrong, the moment she stumbled back into the utility room and caught sight of her mum standing next to Emma. Her head, at that point, was full of her brother; the image of him out in the snow, holding the bloody knife. 'I've just seen Robbie, outside,' she blurted, her mind still locked on the extraordinary sight. 'He's run away.' It was only when she saw the expression on her mum's face that she began to grasp the significance of that; the reality of what must have happened. 'Mum, what is it? What's going on?' But in her heart, she already knew the answer.

Marion closed the bathroom door, her maternal instincts taking over, a natural desire to protect her daughter from such a horrible sight. 'Vicki, I'm so sorry.' There was no way to sugar coat the news. 'It's your father...' She did not need to finish the sentence.

Vicki let out a silent cry and Marion stepped forward automatically to embrace her. 'Not daddy. No, please. It can't be.'

'I'm so sorry, dear.' Her mum clutched her tightly. 'I'm so sorry.'

'But Robbie. I saw...'

'You saw him?' It was Emma's voice that cut through the fog. 'You saw Robbie, outside?'

Vicki nodded, her face pressed hard against her mother's breast. She pulled back momentarily, her face pale and uneven. 'Where is he? Daddy? What...what happened to him?'

'He's been stabbed,' Emma informed her grimly. It was what Vicki had expected to hear, but still the words cut through her. 'I'm sorry, Vicki. He's in the bathroom.'

Vicki gazed numbly at the plywood door. 'In there?'

Emma nodded. 'It's not a pretty sight.'

'What's this about Robbie?' Marion regarded her daughter seriously. She seemed to be holding herself together, for now. Vicki did not know how. 'You saw him?'

Vicki managed a half-hearted nod.

'Where did you see him?'

'Out...out there...' She gestured vaguely in the direction of the workshop.

'Show me,' her mum said.

Vicki led them through into the workroom. The women threaded their way across and Vicki pointed numbly at the open doors on the far side. Marion put an arm around her daughter's shoulder.

Emma moved in to take a closer look. 'There are footprints!' she observed, peering out into the semi darkness.

'That's Robbie,' Vicki said. 'I...I saw him run away.'

'Hang on. What's that, in the snow? It looks like...Christ, it's a knife.' The steel blade had been partially covered over, but a few spots of blood were still in evidence.

Vicki looked away. The enormity of what her brother had done was only just beginning to sink in.

Her mum let go of her shoulder and stepped forward, scrabbling up onto the ice. She was not dressed for the outside – no gloves or proper boots – but that did not stop her as she crunched forward to recover the blade. Her legs sank a few

154

inches into the snow, but Marion did not even blink as she reached out and grabbed the knife.

Emma squeezed Vicki gently on the shoulder. 'You saw your brother? Out there?'

'Yes.' It was a struggle for Vicki to keep her voice level. 'He…he was holding that knife. He must…he must have…' The very thought of what her brother had done overwhelmed her now and she let out another sob. Emma drew her in and allowed Vicki to bury her head in her chest. Despair racked through her. This was a nightmare. *Surely he didn't do it? How could he?* It had to be some sort of mistake. *How could Robbie…?*

'There are footprints leading around to the front,' Marion observed, sliding back into the workshop. 'He must be making for the main road. We'll have to go after him.'

Vicki pulled back. 'Mummy, no!'

'We can't leave him out there. He'll freeze to death.'

Emma was not convinced that was a good idea. 'It's getting dark outside, Marion. We can't just head blindly into the snow.'

'Be that as it may. I'm not going to let my son freeze to death, no matter what he may have done. We have to bring him back.'

'All right, look,' Emma agreed. 'I'll come with you. But we need to get properly kitted up. Get some boots on, grab some torches. And we'll need to tell the others what's going on.'

'There isn't time, dear.'

'He's not going to get far in this, is he?' Emma gestured to the mountain of snow outside. 'We'll be able to follow his trail for a while yet. But we've got to tell the others what we're doing. Safety in numbers.'

For a moment, it looked as if Marion was going to dismiss the idea, but at the last moment she relented. 'Very well, but quickly, dear.' As always, she was putting any difficulties out of her mind and focusing on the practicalities. That was her mum all over, Vicki thought. And it was the only thing to do, when her dad…when daddy… Vicki buried her head once again in Emma's breast. She couldn't believe it. Her daddy, dead. It was impossible.

'Let's get you back to the others,' Emma said, quietly.

They moved as one towards the utility room and then on to the living room.

Akash was standing in the doorway, waiting for them. 'We thought we heard voices,' he said. 'What's going on?' He took in their grim expressions. 'Vicki, what is it?'

'She's had a shock,' Emma replied, her arm still around the younger woman. 'Get her in front of the fire. Give her some tea.'

Akash embraced his fiancée and led her gently into the living room, across to the wood burner. He pulled up an armchair in front of it so that she could sit down, but Vicki clung onto him tightly. 'It was Robbie,' she mumbled, staring blindly at the flames through the open metal door. She didn't want to believe it, but it was true. 'Oh, God, it was Robbie. He's killed him, Akash. He's killed my dad.'

Emma hefted her left foot onto the dining chair and started lacing up the boot. Nicholas Samoday, who was now sitting on the opposite side of the table, regarded her in alarm. 'Giles is dead? He's really dead?' The young man exchanged a horrified look with Betsy Klineman. 'Was it an accident?'

'No. Somebody killed him,' Emma replied bluntly. 'A knife to the back. The workshop doors were wide open.'

Betsy was gobsmacked. 'You don't mean them vagrants, from last night? They broke in? Again?'

Marion cut across her before Emma had the chance to reply. 'It wasn't the vagrants, Betsy,' she said, looking back grimly from the kitchen cupboard. 'It was Robbie. It was my little boy.'

Betsy snorted in disbelief. 'Don't be daft, Marion. Your Robbie wouldn't kill anyone. Least of all his own dad. He's all mouth and no trousers. I've always said it. He wouldn't hurt a fly.'

'Someone just killed him,' Emma pointed out.

Betsy shook her head. 'I can't believe he's dead. I mean,

Giles, of all people.'

'You can look if you want,' Emma shot back, too tired to be polite.

'But little Robbie wouldn't... I mean, look, I know he's had his problems. I was telling Nicholas, wasn't I? He's had a few problems, I said, these last few years. But he's a good lad at heart. He would never hurt anyone. He was the sweetest child. I used to bounce him on my knee.'

Not so sweet now, Emma thought. 'Vicki saw him, with the knife in his hand. He ran away. Why would he do that, if he hadn't done anything wrong?'

'He's run away?' Nicholas looked across at the window. 'Out there?'

'He ran like the clappers,' Emma confirmed, placing her boot back on the floor and sliding her other foot into the second one. 'Four feet of snow. He's not going to get far. We're going after him.'

Akash was perched in front of the wood burner, next to Vicki. 'I should come with you,' he suggested. Vicki looked up in alarm. 'He might be dangerous, doll. You don't want your mum going out there on her own, do you?'

'Robbie won't hurt me,' Marion said firmly. She had grabbed a couple of torches from the kitchen cabinet and placed them down on the table. They were small but probably more effective than a phone torch.

'Still, safety in numbers, eh? Better if there are three of us.' Akash put his hand on Vicki's shoulder. 'You don't mind, doll? We've got to find him. Your Aunt Betsy will look after you. You'll be safe as houses in here.'

'Course you will,' Betsy agreed, pulling herself up. 'And you could use a bit of muscle, Marion, in this weather. It's bitter out there and Robbie might not come back willingly.'

Marion was not in the mood to argue. 'Very well. Thank you, Akash. But be quick. There are some boots over there in the corner. You've got your gloves?'

Akash nodded, rising up from the armchair. He leaned over and gave Vicki a quick kiss, then straightened himself up and moved across to the boot rack.

Emma laced up her second shoe and gazed across at him, as he grabbed a spare pair and shifted around the sofa to put them on. Akash wasn't exactly muscular but an extra pair of hands couldn't hurt. It would probably be better, when the time came, for her and Akash to approach Robbie, rather than his mother. Sure, Marion seemed calm enough at the moment – focused on the task at hand – but there was no telling what she might do when she found her son. He had just killed her husband, for Christ's sake. God, what must she be thinking right now? How long had they been married? Twenty-five years. Over half her life. And her own son holding the blade. Why did he do it? Emma wondered, still not quite believing it. Why kill his own father? And why now? The evidence was pretty damning, but Emma didn't want to jump to conclusions. Was it at all possible that he hadn't done it? So many other things had happened, these past few hours. Could he really be behind it all? Killing his father was one thing – she could just about understand that – but his uncle too? And starting the fire? *None of it makes any sense.*

Her thoughts returned reluctantly to her own boyfriend and the peculiar circumstances of his death. Surely Robbie didn't kill him too? What possible beef could he have had with Dave Flint? It was his dad he despised. And even if he had a motive, from a practical point of view, how had he managed to shift the body, if he had clobbered him in the house? Surely it would have taken at least two people, to drag him all the way next door? And why bother to move him at all? Maybe Marion was right and there was somebody else here. Nobody had broken in through the workshop doors, though. Emma had taken a good look and they had definitely been opened from the inside. The knife had come from the kitchen too, so it was obviously an inside job. Whatever the truth, it seemed increasingly obvious that the whole thing had been planned. It wasn't just a random act of violence. Somebody was working to a plan, trying to cause as much mayhem as possible. And working to a plan did not sound like Robbie at all.

Betsy had no great love for Dave, Emma recalled, as the older woman moved across to the fire. There had been a bit of sparring between them over dinner last night. And, by all accounts, she and Giles had something of a chequered history too. Betsy had shagged him behind Marion's back, before they were married. In fact, hadn't Giles left Marion for a time to hook up with her, before changing his mind? But that was all decades ago. Surely it was water under the bridge?

What about Nicholas, the current boyfriend? He was staring quietly at Akash, as the other bloke laced up his boots. What did they really know about him? His mum had been at the Wilkersons' wedding, all those years ago, according to Betsy. She was a schoolfriend of Marion's, who had died young. That fact snagged on Emma's mind. Could somebody here have been responsible for her death? Perhaps Nicholas knew about it and was looking for revenge? No, that was straining credibility too much; but Emma could not rule out the idea entirely.

Then there was Akash, the laid-back boyfriend. Giles had never said as much, but Emma had the distinct impression that he rather disliked his daughter's fiancé. He probably thought him a bit of a wastrel, or even a gold-digger, considering how much money Giles had stashed away. Akash had proved himself to be a useful bloke in a crisis, but could there be something nasty lurking behind that amiable facade?

And what about Vicki? Her distress seemed genuine enough, but Emma didn't know her well enough to rule out a bit of play acting. She would probably get a fair whack of money, with her dad six feet under. Then there was the wife, Marion, always so calm and practical in a crisis. She wasn't exactly the lovey-dovey type. Had she loved her husband or did she just tolerate him? By the sound of things, she had been a reluctant emigrant. Starved of company out here, so far from home. Probably a little too enamoured of her French teacher. Perhaps she had confessed as much to Dave, or he had overheard something. Maybe he'd reacted badly to the idea of her cheating on Giles and had threatened to expose her. No, that was too thin, too nebulous. In all probability, Robbie had killed his dad. Vicki had seen him with the knife. He had argued with Giles and it had then spilt over into violence. That was the simplest explanation.

Akash had returned to the rack by the window to grab a coat. 'Hey, I can see some lights out there,' he said, peering out through the snow-clogged glass.

Marion looked up sharply. 'Is it Robbie?'

'No, no. Up on the road. On the hill there.' He stuck his head close to the window. 'It must be a gritting truck or something.'

Emma dropped her foot and dusted herself down. 'Civilisation,' she whispered, half in jest.

Marion handed her a walking stick. 'We should get going, dear,' she said, moving towards the utility room door. 'We'll follow his footsteps from out of the workshop. Akash, are you coming?'

The bloke nodded. He stopped at the fireplace and bent down to give Vicki a kiss. 'Be careful,' she told him. 'Do be careful.'

'Don't you worry, doll. We'll be back in no time.' He kissed her again and then moved off after Emma and Marion.

Chapter Ten

The last time Emma had gone outside, it had been a cool, crisp morning with barely a breeze. Now, the wind was a steady howl, the air alive with snowflakes and the sky getting darker every minute. Emma pulled up the hood of her coat and stabbed the end of her walking stick into the ice, hauling herself up onto the semi-permeable snow, which was stacked as far as the eye could see beyond the workshop doors.

Marion was already outside, surveying the trail. She was wearing a thick windcheater and some hefty boots. Robbie's footprints were easy enough to make out: a small trench led along the side of the house and around to the front. Even in the time it had taken them to throw on some clothes, however, the trail had become fuzzy and misshapen.

Akash scrambled up onto the snow next to Emma. He wobbled slightly, dropping his torch and almost losing his balance. Emma had to shoot out an arm to stop him from falling on his arse. He flashed her a grin as he found his feet. He did not have a walking stick. He crouched down to recover the torch, which he stashed in his coat pocket. For now, there was enough light for them to see by.

Marion regarded the pair of them impatiently. 'We should get along,' she said. Emma indicated for her to lead the way, and Marion moved off at a quick pace. The snow had compacted a bit over the course of the afternoon. The woman's feet sank a little but plopped out again quickly as, without looking back, she hurried around the side of the house. Emma and Akash followed on as best they could. *Good thing I had a bit of practice this morning*, Emma thought.

At the corner of the house, Marion stopped and gazed out across the expanse of white. She had a scarf pulled up across her mouth. The wind was making it difficult to stand upright, let alone move forward, though the house was providing a little cover. Marion grasped the wall with a gloved hand and peered forward into the gloom.

'Looks like he's heading for the main road,' Emma said,

coming to a halt beside her. The trail led across the field diagonally, towards a lane – invisible now – some seventy or eighty metres distant.

Marion lifted a hand to protect her face. The snowfall, though less severe than earlier in the day, still stung a little. 'Can you see him anywhere? My eyesight isn't what it was.'

Emma screwed up her eyes. The footprints were overwhelmed, in the distance, by the glare of white.

Akash slipped into position beside them. 'Hang on a mo,' he said, gazing across the bitter landscape. A thick line of fir trees on the far side of the lane gave some indication of distance. The trees were swaying viciously in the wind, their looming presence serving to darken the picture considerably. On the near side of the lane there was a sprinkling of bushes and here at least there was some sign of life. 'There!' Akash exclaimed, pointing a gloved finger. 'He's over there!'

Emma followed his direction but, try as she might, she couldn't see anything. She wiped the frost from her face and then saw a blur of movement, this side of one of the bushes. Between it and a small outhouse; some kind of shed, belonging to the farm next door. The outline of that helped to give a little context to the darkness and finally Emma saw him. There was Robbie, scrabbling forward inch by inch. He looked to be on his hands and knees.

'He's not having much luck,' Akash observed. 'He'll never get to the main road at that rate.' By the looks of it, he had barely covered a third of the distance.

Marion was breathing deeply, concerned for her son.

'We'll catch him,' Emma said, placing a hand on her shoulder. 'We'll bring him back.'

Marion pulled herself together and nodded. 'Of course we will, dear.' She took a firm grasp of her walking stick and, once again, set off across the field.

He's not moving much, Emma thought, as she made to follow. Was he in trouble? Robbie had pelted out into the snow without any preparation. Did he even have a coat on? Emma couldn't see for sure.

Her foot sank into the ice and she stumbled, swearing, as her boot stuck fast and refused to budge.

Akash slid to a halt beside her. 'What's up?'

'I can't get my foot out,' she said, leaning over and trying to pull at her leg.

'Here, give us your hand.'

Emma extended an arm and Akash grabbed it, returning the favour from earlier on. He yanked hard, pulling her towards him and, with an inelegant plop, her foot came clear of the hole; but only her foot. She clutched onto Akash to steady herself and glanced back. Her sock had half come out of the boot with her foot, but the boot was stuck fast behind her. Emma laughed, the absurdity of the situation momentarily overwhelming her.

Akash was grinning too. 'Hey, Marion, hang on a mo! Emma's lost her boot.'

Up ahead, the older woman came to a halt.

Emma plonked herself down on her knees and, with Akash's help, quickly managed to dig out the boot. That done, she sat down, pulled up her now wet sock and, unlacing the boot, slid her foot back inside. 'Oh, yuck!' she exclaimed. The inside was filled with ice. She laced it up all the same, as best she could with her gloved hand, aware of Marion's impatient gaze. Then she grabbed her walking stick and pulled herself up.

'All right, dear?' Marion called back.

'Yes, fine.' She stifled another laugh. 'Although to be honest, I'd be quite happy never to see another drop of snow so long as I live.'

Akash was in agreement with that. 'You and me both.'

'Let's get on then.' Marion moved off without another word. Akash and Emma exchanged a glance and then followed.

Robbie had not yet realised he was being followed. The howl of the wind had cut off the sound of their voices and he was probably too caught up in his own problems to bother looking back. The only lights to be seen – apart from the farmhouse windows behind them – were some kind of heavy vehicle moving slowly along the main road.

'What did I say?' Akash grinned, gesturing to the lights on top of the hill. 'A gritting lorry. If we could get up there and have a word…'

Emma rolled her eyes. 'What, in this weather? It'd take us hours.'

Even with the odd stumble, however, they were making better progress than Robbie Wilkerson. They would soon be within shouting distance. He didn't seem to be moving at all. *He must be well and truly stuck.*

'Robbie!' his mum called to him, now that they were drawing near. 'Just stay put! We're coming for you!' Her voice cut across the wind, loud but concerned.

The air was not quite as thick with snow now and Emma caught a sudden surge of movement up ahead. Robbie had seen them at last. He freed himself from whatever obstacle he was caught up in, and scrambled once again across the ice, deaf to their entreaties.

'Don't be an idiot!' Emma shouted after him. 'We're not going to hurt you! Come back to the house. We can talk about this!'

Robbie showed no signs of listening. In fact, he was picking up the pace. Marion called out again, but the trio had hit a difficult patch of snow.

Emma growled. If he had a mind to, Robbie could drag this out for hours. A new approach was probably in order.

Akash had the same idea. 'What do you reckon?' His eyes were gleaming. 'Speed things up a bit?'

'All or nothing?' She nodded. Skim the top of the snow, run like the wind and use their momentum to carry them forward. It was worth a try. They would probably fall arse over tit, but what the hell. In the absence of a decent plan it was their best bet. 'Let's do it!' Emma said, launching herself forward, kamikaze style.

Marion dug a pole into the ground and stared after them in surprise, as Akash quickly followed suit.

Robbie could see them coming now. They were close enough, even in the semi-darkness, to make out his weary, despairing face, his hair and eyebrows covered in snow. He wasn't wearing a hood or even a coat, the poor sod, just the same blue sweatshirt he had been sporting back at the farm. He must have left the house in one hell of a hurry. His hands were trembling as the cold cut through him.

'Leave me alone!' he bellowed. 'Keep away from me!' He grabbed the edge of a snow-covered bush and tried to stabilize himself, as he manoeuvred around the obstacle. Emma was within kicking distance now, but she had no way of stopping herself. The only way to break the momentum was to fall over or collide with something; and the bush was directly in front of her. She slammed into it and Akash followed her a second later. The two of them bounced off and fell backwards, collapsing in an awkward heap on the ground. A pile of snow dislodged from the bush and showered down on top of them, half burying the duo.

The impact had rippled through the branch Robbie was holding, causing him to lose his balance too. He fell forwards, on the other side of the bush, but he was quicker to regain his feet. He had no socks or shoes on.

Emma disentangled herself from Akash. *Christ,* she thought, catching sight of the naked feet. *No wonder he was having trouble.* His shoes must have got stuck in the snow, just like her boot.

Robbie lost his footing a second time and collided with another bush. 'You keep away from me!' he snarled, as Emma moved towards him.

'Calm down!' she said, abandoning her walking stick where it had fallen. She raised her hands and tromped slowly forward. 'We're not going to hurt you.'

Robbie was now sprawled out across the snow. He was breathing heavily, like a wild animal, cornered and desperate.

Akash dusted himself down and moved in cautiously. 'Look, mate,' he said, 'we just want to get you back into the warm. Your mum's here, she's worried about you.' Marion was trudging up behind them now, moving with greater care than either of the youngsters. She at least had managed to retain a modicum of dignity.

The sight of his mum provoked a strong reaction. Robbie scrabbled to his feet again. 'Keep her away from me!' he bawled. 'All of you, keep away.' He tried to run, but Akash had

165

been slowly circling left and, as soon as Robbie picked a direction, the other bloke launched himself forward, thudding into his waist, bringing him crashing down onto the icy ground. Robbie kicked back, screaming and spitting, but Akash had the measure of him. He yanked an arm firmly behind his back and then pressed a knee into him, keeping him face down in the snow.

'Here, give us a hand,' Akash called, as Robbie continued to struggle.

Emma came forward and grabbed his other arm. 'Robbie, stop! This is ridiculous.' she said.

Marion came to a halt in front of him. 'Robbie, that's enough!' she snapped.

At the sound of her voice, all life seemed to go out of him. He let out one last strangled sob and then gave up the fight.

Marion glanced at Akash. 'That's all right, dear. You can let him go.'

Akash removed his knee from Robbie's back. Emma stepped backwards too, then crouched down and offered a hand, to help Robbie sit up. He looked dreadful, his hands raw and shaking in the extreme cold, his hair covered in snow and ice, his face a white sheet, a cheek bleeding slightly where it had brushed against the prickly bush. 'I didn't do it,' he muttered, his eyes dashing from person to person. 'I didn't lay a finger on him. I just found him there, in the bathroom.'

Emma grimaced. She wasn't sure if she believed that. 'Vicki saw you with the knife. She saw you run away.'

'Of course I bloody did.' Despite his wretched state, there was a flash of anger in Robbie's eyes. 'You don't think I was going to hang around, do you?'

'You thought we'd blame you? When we found your dad?'

'I didn't care what you thought,' he snapped. 'I just wanted to get the hell out of there. I wasn't going to be next in line.'

'What do you mean?' Emma frowned, not quite following.

'The knife in the back. It was going to be me next, wasn't it? They tried once already.'

'They?'

'Him. Her. You. I don't know. Someone in that house. It

166

could have been you.' He shrank back from Emma and Akash. 'It could have been either one of you.' His whole body was shuddering, and not just from the cold. 'I don't know you from Adam, either of you. You could have started that fire. Murdered my dad. Tried to kill me.'

'Robbie, that's ridiculous,' Emma said.

'And now you're going to frame me for his death.'

Marion raised a hand. 'Robbie, that's enough. I'm having no more of this nonsense. Dear, you're freezing half to death. We can't talk out here. You're coming back with us to the house and we're going to discuss this like adults.'

Robbie shrank back once again. 'Mum, no, I can't...'

'You'll do as you're told, dear. And when we get back you are going to tell us exactly what is going on. And no fairy stories, Robbie. I want the truth. It's high time you took some responsibility for your actions.'

Robbie was having none of it. 'I'm not going back there. Not to that house. No chance. I'm not going to let you stab me in the back.'

'For heaven's sake,' Emma said. 'No-one's going to hurt you. But we can't leave you out here. You'll die of exposure.'

'I don't care. I'd rather freeze out here than go back there.'

'That's enough, Robbie!' Marion snapped again. It was the first time Emma had seen the woman come close to losing her temper. 'Your father has just died. Have some consideration for me at least.'

'What do you care?' Robbie snapped back. 'You never loved him.'

'Of course I did. How dare you say that!' Marion's patience was finally beginning to run out.

'Shagging your French teacher, behind his back. For all I know, it might have been you who stabbed him.'

'That's enough!' Marion stepped forward and raised a hand, as if to strike him, but then pulled back at the last minute.

'It's true, though, isn't it? You never loved him.'

Marion bit her lip, struggling to bring herself under control. 'Robbie, this isn't the time...'

'It's true!'

Emma glanced from one to the other, curious to see how Marion responded. The woman closed her eyes. 'Robbie, I loved your father very much. We had our difficulties. He could be a stubborn man, on occasion. But I would never betray his trust. Giles never had any reason to be jealous of me.'

'So you say.'

Marion let out a low sigh and gazed across at Akash. 'We need to get him out of the cold. Akash, dear, would you help him onto his feet?'

'Sure.' Akash reached forward to help, but Robbie brushed him off.

'I'm not going back to that house.'

Emma rolled her eyes again. The bloke was half dead already but he was as stubborn as a mule and there was no reasoning with him. It looked like they would have to drag him all the way back to the farmhouse. She gazed across the field. Actually, they were closer to the neighbours' house than they were to the Wilkerson farm. The lane Robbie had been making for curved in a bit on its way up the hill. 'We could take him there,' she suggested, indicating the house belonging to the French couple. 'You've got a key, haven't you, Marion?'

'I have,' the older woman confirmed. Marion had let herself into the building that morning, to check the phone, when they had gone to retrieve Dave's body. She still had it with her.

Akash seized on the idea. 'At least it will be warm in there,' he suggested. 'Out of the wind.'

Robbie had his eyes closed now, but his teeth were chattering. 'All right,' he stuttered. 'Next door.' He opened his eyes and looked up, trying to gather a bit of energy. 'You might need to give us a hand.'

Emma moved in to help. Between her and Akash, they managed to lift the poor sod, trembling, back onto his feet.

Marion observed them closely. 'Very well,' she said, gazing down in concern at her son's exposed feet, which were now little more than two lumps of ice. 'And when we get there, Robbie, and you've warmed up, you are going to tell us everything. Do you understand? You are going to tell us everything that you know.'

168

Betsy Klineman carried the loaf to the dining table and began to cut it up. Vicki was staring vacantly at the table in front of her. The soup was bubbling away in a pan on the stove and Aunt Betsy was chattering away, trying to normalise the situation; but all Vicki could think about was Akash and her mum out in the snow, and her brother too. She gripped her hands together tightly. Better to focus on that, she thought, rather than her dad. She hadn't really wanted Akash to go outside. After everything that had happened, she needed him to be here. More than that, she needed him to be *safe*. The thought of any harm coming to him – after what had happened to her father and Uncle Dave – was beyond endurance.

'Get some warm food into you, that's the thing,' Betsy babbled as she sliced the bread. 'It's a shame to waste it.' She buttered a small slice and shoved a plate onto the mat in front of Vicki. 'It'll do you good.'

'I'm not really hungry,' Vicki murmured, without looking up. How could she eat anything, at a time like this? She doubted she would even have the strength to chew the bread. One thing did catch her attention, though: the flash of the bread knife as her aunt resumed cutting the loaf. It was just like the one she had seen in Robbie's hand. The knife covered in blood. Her father's blood. Vicki closed her eyes and struggled to banish the image from her mind.

Nicholas was tending to the soup. 'Careful, lovey,' Betsy admonished, looking across at him, standing in front of the stove. The broth had risen up in the pan and was about to spill over. At Betsy's suggestion, Nicholas lifted it from the hob and moved it to one side. 'In a world of his own, that one,' Betsy chuckled. 'I was telling your mum last night, we're a right old pair, Nicholas and me. Neither of us can cook. But you can't go wrong with a tin of soup, can you?' It was Betsy who had volunteered Nicholas to prepare it. The young man was looking a little pale and needed something to occupy himself with. Not that there was much for him to do. There wasn't even a tin to open. All the vegetables had been chopped up and put into the pot beforehand. Vicki watched as he turned the heat down on the hob and then returned the pan to the ring. Her dad had prepared that soup. It was one of the last things he had done.

'I can't believe he's dead,' she whispered, abruptly. 'I can't believe Robbie would…'

Betsy put down the bread knife. 'Try not to think about it, petal. We don't really *know* that he did it, do we? Like I was saying to your mum, those doors in the workshop, they were wide open. Anyone might have come in and caught him by surprise.'

Vicki frowned, trying to clear the fog from her mind. 'But you should have seen the look on his face. Why would he run like that, if…?'

Betsy returned to her seat. 'I don't know,' she admitted.

Nicholas lifted the saucepan away from the heat a second time. 'I think it's just about ready,' he called. His hands gripped the handle tightly, as if afraid he might drop it. 'Are there some bowls somewhere?'

'Not bowls. Let's have mugs, shall we?' Betsy suggested. 'There's nothing like a nice warm mug to get your hands around.'

'Where are they?'

Vicki gestured vaguely. 'In the bottom cupboard, just at the end.'

Nicholas abandoned the saucepan and reached for the cupboard. His movements were stiff and mechanical. What must he be thinking? Vicki wondered. He had come here for a quiet weekend – the only person he knew was Aunt Betsy – and then all this had happened. She watched as he pulled out a couple of mugs and placed them on the work surface to the left of the cooker. His hands were shaking. *He must be scared too,* she thought. These last few hours would be enough to put the wind up anyone. He grabbed a third mug and placed it next to the others, then stopped abruptly.

Betsy pushed back her chair and walked over to him. 'It's all right, lovey,' she said, squeezing him gently. 'I'll do it.' She moved him out of the way and picked up the pan. 'Don't want you spilling it all over the place, do we? It was like I was saying,' she called back to the table, 'neither of us can cook. We need all the help we can get.' Betsy began to pour out the soup, one mug at a time, while Nicholas hovered awkwardly to her right. 'You sit down, lovey. I'll bring it over to you.' By now, even Betsy was beginning to look a little strained.

A minute later, they were seated around the table and Betsy had handed out the steaming hot mugs. 'Mind you don't burn yourself!' she warned.

'I don't think I can...' Vicki felt her stomach heave at the prospect.

'Have a nibble at least. Try some of the bread. You need to keep your strength up. I was saying to your mum, in your condition, you need all the food you can get. You're eating for two now, aren't you?' She indicated the buttered slice on Vicki's plate. 'Come on, it'll do you good.'

Vicki let out a sigh. 'All right.' It was clear her aunty wasn't going to let her say no. She took the bread and dipped it tentatively into the mug, then forced herself to take a bite. It took some effort to swallow it. She lifted the mug and took a sip of soup as well. The broth was hot and spicy.

'There you go!' Betsy exclaimed, lifting her own mug. Nicholas, who was sitting next to her, at the head of the table, was not eating either. 'Help yourself to some of this,' she suggested, pushing the breadboard in his direction. She grabbed a chunk for herself and dunked it in the soup. Her face lit up as she swallowed a mouthful. 'That's better! I'll say this for your dad, he certainly knew how to cook, didn't he?'

Vicki choked back a sob and pushed the mug away. Her eyes flicked across to the clock on the wall, forcing her thoughts back to Akash and her brother. 'What's taking them so long?' They had been gone for over forty minutes.

'They'll be fine, petal. Don't you worry. They'll be back in no time.'

Nicholas was staring at his mug. He had a piece of bread in his hand but he hadn't touched it yet. 'Do you think they'll find him?' he asked quietly.

'Oh, I'm sure they will,' Betsy said, determined to look on the bright side. 'In no time. I told you, that Marion is a force of nature. I was saying to her this morning, if anyone can find out what's going on, it's you.'

Vicki put down her soup. 'I can't bear to think of them getting lost in the snow. And Robbie's all on his own out there. What if they don't find him?' Whatever he had done, he was still her brother. 'He might freeze to death.' The image of Uncle Dave swam back into her mind, the eyes under the water. 'Do you think...do you think he might have...I mean, Uncle Dave?'

For once, it was Aunt Betsy who let out a sigh. 'I don't know, lovey. We shouldn't jump to conclusions.' She grabbed another piece of bread, but stopped herself before dipping it in her soup. 'There was a break-in last night, wasn't there, people ransacking the place. There's no reason to think young Robbie had anything to do with that. You saw the damage they did this morning. Some hooligans. I said to your mother, some people can be so vindictive, slashing everything like that.'

'But all that's happened since then,' Vicki insisted. 'The fire. And now daddy. It can't all be down to vagrants. That doesn't make sense.' She looked up and was surprised to find Nicholas nodding in agreement.

'It doesn't,' he said, his voice quiet but unequivocal. 'I don't think there ever was a break-in. Or any vagrants. It was all a lie.'

'You can't be sure of that,' Betsy said. 'None of us were in here this morning to see it, were we? None of us could have...'

'I was here,' Nicholas said. He put down the bread and placed his hands around the steaming mug in front of him. 'I saw it.'

Vicki stared at him in surprise. 'Nicholas, what do you mean?'

'I...I saw what happened, last night. I saw your brother. It must have been three or four o'clock in the morning.' He swallowed hard. 'I...I know exactly what he did.'

Chapter Eleven

Robbie sat with his knees held against his chest. Perhaps it wasn't such a good idea coming here, Emma thought. Robbie looked awful, shivering uncontrollably on a blanket, his back pressed up against the washing machine. The farmhouse had been empty for some time. The French couple who owned it were away in Bordeaux. Marion had let them all in with the spare key. The place was bloody cold, though it was a relief to be out of the wind. Emma had found a thermostat and flicked it on, but it would take a while for the heat to kick in and warm the place up. Luckily, Akash had had a brainwave. He had turned on the oven in the kitchen, left the door open and sat Robbie next to it. With that and a few blankets Emma had found in a cupboard upstairs, they would soon have the poor sod warmed up. In fact, there were enough blankets for the four of them. Emma wasn't exactly feeling toasty herself.

It felt a bit odd, clomping round a stranger's house like this, rifling through their linen drawers. But the owners had given Marion a key in case of emergency, and if this wasn't an emergency, Emma didn't know what was. She gazed around the room. It was a modern building, fully renovated, with polished floors and wide floor-to-ceiling windows. Emma was sitting cross-legged, opposite the oven. Marion was seated to her left, directly in front of her son.

The older woman seemed to be coping well in the circumstances, the lines of her face accentuated by a set of overly bright kitchen lights. Betsy had said Marion was a force of nature and she wasn't wrong. Somehow, after all she had been through today, the woman was still managing to keep her head together. Emma marvelled at that. It was not an easy thing to do. Emma was only just managing to hold herself together, trying hard not to think about Dave, ignoring the hole in the window which they had passed on their way back to the farm. Just concentrate on the now, she thought; on the shivering figure in front of her.

Robbie was denying everything, despite the persistent

questioning from his mother. 'It's the truth, I swear it,' he said, pulling the blanket tighter around his body. Marion had given him such a look when he'd said he wasn't responsible for his dad's death. 'I didn't lay a finger on him. Why would I?' The heat from the oven was having some effect. The ice in Robbie's hair had melted and was dripping down onto the blanket. 'Oh, I hated him for a time. God, did I hate him. He was so bloody minded. He would never listen. He wouldn't believe a word I said about anything. Even when I was telling the truth. I was angry, I admit that. But I wouldn't *kill* him. We…we were getting somewhere, this weekend. He was starting to accept things, starting to believe me. We talked, really talked. He said he was going to sort things out. Make things right. Like a proper dad. He was going to look after me, he said, he was going to protect me. I had no reason to want to hurt him. Why would I want to do him in?'

Akash had pulled up a chair and was looming over the group. He pulled off his woollen bobble hat and scratched his curly dark-brown hair. 'What do you mean, protect you?'

'Protect you from what, dear?' Marion asked.

Robbie hesitated, closing his eyes. 'It's my fault,' he breathed. 'It's all my fault.'

Emma had a horrible feeling she knew where this was heading. 'This has something to do with Dave,' she guessed unhappily, her skin beginning to prickle. 'You had something to do with *his* death, didn't you?' Her stomach lurched as Robbie let out a sob, confirming her fears.

'I didn't mean to kill him,' he declared, mournfully. 'I really didn't. I just…I got so angry.'

Emma regarded him in horror. 'You mean, you were the one who…?'

'I'm sorry. I'm so sorry. I never intended to hurt him. Not like that. But if you knew what he…if you knew what that bastard did to me.'

Emma pressed her fingers into the palms of her hands. It was true, then. Robbie had killed him. Bloody hell. He had killed Dave. 'What do you mean, *did* to you?' she asked, unable to mask the anger in her voice.

'You think you know someone,' Robbie said, his head drooping now, his eyes unfocused. 'You trust them. But you don't really know them at all.'

Akash leaned forward in his chair. 'You're talking about Mr Flint? About Dave?' Robbie nodded. 'What did he do? Mate, what did he do to you?'

Robbie looked up then. His eyes were raw, his expression one of utter dejection. 'You wouldn't believe me.'

'I'll believe anything just now,' Akash said.

'It was when I dropped out of uni. You remember?' He looked to his mum and she nodded briefly. 'I was fed up. It wasn't going anywhere. It was a waste of time. I knew dad would hit the roof, but I didn't care. I wanted to go off travelling, see a bit of the world, not sit in some lecture hall. Dad flipped when I told him. We had a monumental row. He didn't care what I thought. Didn't care what I wanted.'

'He only ever wanted what was best for you,' Marion said. 'He had such high hopes for you. We both did.'

'It was what *he* wanted, though. University. A career in the City. It was never what I wanted. But he didn't care about that.'

'What has this got to do with Dave?' Emma cut in. How did a row between Robbie and his dad lead to a death out here?

'I'd left my digs. Cleared out all my stuff and come home. But I wasn't going to stay there, not after dad started having a go at me. The atmosphere in that house. I just wanted to get as far away as possible. But I didn't have anywhere to go. I didn't have any money. So I gave Uncle Dave a ring.' He laughed bitterly. 'I asked him if I could doss down with him for a couple of nights, while I sorted things out. He said sure, come on over.' Robbie's eyes hardened at the memory. 'I dumped my stuff. I was in such a foul mood. I just wanted to get pissed, forget all about it. So that's what we did, the pair of us. Got absolutely hammered. It was the first time I'd seen him drunk, Uncle Dave. Properly drunk. He wasn't supposed to be drinking then. He was still having treatment, for the cancer. Dosed up to the neck on all sorts of drugs. But you know Dave. Anything for a good time.' He caught Emma's eye. 'And he was sympathetic. I was moaning about dad, and he was

175

listening and agreeing with me.'

'So what happened?' Emma asked cautiously. Now that it came to it, she was not sure she wanted to hear the answer.

'One minute, we're having this heart to heart. You know, guy talk. He was all sympathetic, like. Said how dad had shafted him too, all those years ago, when they were in business together. Left him without a penny. And then, the next thing I know, he's making a pass at me.'

Akash rocked back in his chair. 'No way! Mr Flint?'

'Yeah, Mr Flint.' Robbie did not disguise the contempt in his voice. 'I tried to push him off. I thought he was having a laugh at first, but he wouldn't stop. He pushed himself onto me, forced me down.'

Emma shook her head, not wanting to believe it.

'I tried to stop him, I yelled at him to get off of me, I tried to push him away, but he was so bloody strong. He pinned me down on the sofa and pulled my trousers down. And then he… then he…' Robbie's voice faded away as the memory of what had happened overcame him.

For a time, nobody spoke. Emma felt her throat constricting. This was her Dave he was talking about. The gentle giant. The guy she had dated for more than two years. It couldn't be true, could it? Dave had never been violent with her, never shown much of a temper, even when he was pissed. Oh, sure, he was a bit of an animal in the sack; and adventurous too. She could hardly forget that time they had had a threesome with some random bloke. But there was never the slightest hint of coercion. Nobody had ever been forced to do anything. And yet…and yet, looking at Robbie now, his eyes cast downwards, his voice cracked, the wretched expression on his face, she could not doubt that he was telling the truth.

'Afterwards,' Robbie continued, his voice a blank monotone, 'I think I must have blacked out. I was still there on the sofa in the morning. Dave came in to see me. "Uncle Dave". He apologised. He said he didn't know what had come over him. He'd never done anything like that before. He said it must have been the medication he was on. For the cancer. He was on some sort of new drug, he said. It was screwing him up,

176

playing with his head. But that was bull, total bull. I told him so. And I got the hell out of there as quick as I could. Phoned up a mate, dossed down on his sofa for a couple of days.' He lifted a hand and wiped his nose. He looked across at his mum then, shamefaced. 'That's it,' he said.

Marion regarded her son calmly. 'I'm sorry,' she said. 'I had no idea. I would never have believed Dave capable of anything like that. Why didn't you tell anyone about this at the time?'

More to the point: 'Why didn't you go to the police?' Emma asked.

At that, Robbie snorted loudly, a little colour returning to his cheeks. 'You must be joking. How could I go to them? They wouldn't believe me. I had a record. Shop lifting. Drunk and disorderly. You don't honestly think they'd listen to a word I said, do you?'

Probably not, Emma agreed. But even so. 'So what did you do?'

'I went to see dad. What else *could* I do? I went back to the house, to tell him exactly what his best mate had just done to me. I was so angry, so ashamed.'

'That was the Friday,' Marion recalled. 'We had a few people over that weekend. Friends and family, to celebrate Vicki's eighteenth.'

'It couldn't have been worse timing.' Robbie pressed his lips together bitterly. 'All the old friends. Apart from Dave. He was coming on the Saturday. I was so upset. I thought dad would listen to me, this time. But he didn't want to know.'

'You told him what had happened?' Emma asked.

'I told him everything. What Dave had done. But he didn't believe me. He said I was making it up. Trying to get back at him. I'd told him so much rubbish over the years – so many lies – he thought it was just more of the same. Crying wolf, just to hurt him. As if I would make up a story like that. But he wouldn't listen. I got so angry, that he wouldn't believe me, that he wouldn't take my word on anything. It made me sick. He was my old man and he couldn't even stick up for me, after what I'd been through. I wanted to deck him. I just…I hated him then, more than ever. As much as I hated Dave. I had to get away. I had to get as far away from all of you as I could.' His mother included, it seemed.

'He didn't speak to you about any of this?' Emma asked Marion.

'I had no idea. I knew they had rowed. I assumed it was about university. That was what Giles told me. I had no idea that it had been about anything like this. If I'd known…'

'I couldn't talk to you,' Robbie said. 'How could I? I couldn't tell you about that. Not ever. I had to get away. Get away from everything.'

'And that was when you stole the credit cards?' Emma suggested, recalling what she had heard about that particular weekend.

'Yeah. I didn't care what I did then. But I needed some cash. So I stole the cards. Any ones I could find. Then I booked a flight. Got on a plane. Got as far as Madrid, before anyone caught up with me. And I ended up in prison. Dad never came to see me. He didn't care at all.'

'Of course he cared, Robbie,' Marion insisted. 'But he was a proud man. And then he had his accident.'

'Yeah, I heard about that from Vicki. Jumping out of a plane. Tosser. It was his own bloody fault. I didn't care. He broke his leg. So what? I didn't want anything more to do with him.'

'You were out of prison by then?' Emma asked.

'Yes, a few days out. I went back to the house. I knew there would be no-one there. They were all down at the hospital. I'd made up my mind. I was going to go away for good. I was going to see the world, like I'd always intended. Find a place I liked and maybe settle down there. Anywhere but England. But I still had the money problem. I needed cash. So I hacked into dad's account, on his computer. It wasn't difficult. He kept all his passwords on a sticky by the desk. I transferred a few grand to my account and that got me started.' His mum pursed her lips in disapproval, but Robbie ignored her. 'I knew he wouldn't call the police. He didn't have a choice, the first time. It wasn't just his card I'd nicked. He had to phone the police. But now it was just him and I knew he wouldn't do anything.

178

He was probably glad to see the back of me. So I took the money and off I went, travelling across Africa. I don't regret it. Had the time of my life.' Robbie managed a half-hearted smile. 'But in the end, I had to come home, didn't I? It was fun while it lasted, but I didn't find anywhere I wanted to settle down. So I came home, found myself a place to live down in Cornwall. Did a few odd jobs to cover the rent. Vicki kept in touch, told me what you and the old grouch were up to.'

'She's a good girl,' Marion said. 'I worried about you. Every day, I worried.'

'I know. I'm sorry, mum. Vicki told me what you were up to. Said you'd come out here to France, the two of you. Didn't see that coming, but what the hell. Good luck to you, I thought. She texted me, when she heard about the anniversary, telling me everyone was coming out here to celebrate. Aunt Betsy and Uncle Dave. That really pissed me off. I was trying to put it all out of my head, but the thought of dad and Uncle Dave palling up together again, it made me so mad. How could dad do that? How could he even talk to that bastard?'

'I was the one who suggested inviting him,' Marion said.

'He could have said no, couldn't he? But he didn't believe me. He automatically took Dave's side. Didn't question him for a minute. Didn't even think for a second that I might have been telling the truth. And I thought, sod that. I'm going to make him listen. I'm going to bring it all out into the open. I'm going to confront the bastard. Dave, I mean. In front of dad. I'm going to prove to him that I was telling the truth. Make Uncle Dave deny it to my face.'

Emma's eyes widened. 'And that's why you came out here?'

'Yeah.' He nodded grimly. 'Hopped on a ferry. Stole a moped. Had to be done. I thought, if he did it to me, your Dave, he must have done it to other people. It's never just a one off, is it, that sort of thing?'

That was not a happy thought. 'I've been going out with him for two years,' Emma said. 'I never saw any indication...' How could she not have seen it?

'People like that, they know how to cover their tracks. Probably even kid themselves they aren't doing anything

179

wrong. And you weren't exactly living in each other's pockets, were you? You never actually lived together.'

'No. No, we didn't,' Emma admitted.

'I do remember one incident,' Marion recalled. 'Shortly before Giles and I were married.'

'Oh?'

'I wasn't there myself. But there was some sort of misunderstanding over the entertainment at Giles's bachelor party. Vicki was asking me about it earlier today. At the time, I thought it was blown out of all proportion.'

'What happened?' Emma asked.

'As I understand it, Dave took a few liberties with an exotic dancer.'

'A stripper?'

'Yes. At the party. She reported him to the police. But nothing was ever proved.'

Robbie at least was not surprised. 'There you go. It was there from the start.'

Emma was keen to bring things back to the present. They still hadn't got to last night. What had Robbie done then, that was what she really wanted to know. She kept her voice calm as she said, 'So you came out here, and confronted your dad? Before Dave and I got here?'

'Yeah, just before. He was mad, I tell you. Went ballistic. Didn't want me to be here. Didn't shout or nothing, that was never his way. But God, was he angry. He didn't want to be embarrassed in front of all his guests. Not again, not on your anniversary. He wanted you to have a good time, he said. He wanted everything to run smoothly. When I told him why I was here, that knocked the wind right out of him. I was going to confront Dave and I was going to shame him in public. He didn't know what to say to that. He didn't want the fuss. But it shook him. The fact that I had come all this way, just for that. That I was still going on about it, after three years.'

'You think he started to believe you?' Emma asked.

Robbie shrugged. 'I don't know. I expected him to send me packing. But he couldn't turf me out into the snow. Especially not when I'd just been knocked off my bike. Perhaps he did

180

believe me, or at least thought there might be something in it. He didn't want any kind of scene, that was obvious. You know dad. Hates to be embarrassed in public. So he said, look, if you promise not to upset anyone this evening – if you behave yourself – then when everyone has gone to bed, I'll speak to Dave. I'll tell him what you said and I'll get the truth out of him.'

'He was going to confront him?'

'So he said. He looked as if he meant it. And I thought, what the hell. I've come all this way. Why not give the old sod one last chance to make things right? It didn't stop me having a go in the morning, if he bottled it. So I said fine, you talk to him tonight, get him to admit it. Then tomorrow, it'll be my turn.' Robbie shook his head. 'It wasn't going to be easy, though. Holding my temper with that bugger in the house. I just wanted to punch someone.'

That was certainly the impression Emma had got when she had first met him. 'Is that why you smashed the bathroom mirror?'

Robbie laughed abruptly. 'That had nothing to do with me.'

'That was Giles, I'm afraid,' his mother put in.

Emma's jaw dropped. '*Giles* smashed the bathroom mirror?'

'It was an accident, he said. I presumed he had lost his temper. He never shows…he would never show his anger in public. But sometimes he would take out his frustration on an inanimate object.' Marion gave a half smile. 'He probably threw something at it.'

'He was angry 'cos I had put a spanner in the works,' Robbie said.

'No, dear.' Marion grimaced. 'If what you say is true, then he must have been angry with himself. Angry that he hadn't believed you before. Angry that he had blamed you when he should have been blaming your Uncle Dave.'

'Maybe,' Robbie conceded. 'When Dave got here, yesterday afternoon. When I saw him at the dinner table. God, I just wanted to ring his bloody neck. He was all smiles, all jokes, as if nothing had ever happened. Hardest thing I've ever done, keeping my temper that evening. And he was making jokes

181

about me, taking the piss. I couldn't stand it.'

'That's why you left dinner early?' Emma suggested.

'I had to get away. I'd give dad one last chance. Let him sort it out. And then, come morning, it would be my turn.' Robbie pulled up his blanket a little further. 'So I left them to it. They stayed up late, by all accounts. Had a few drinks. I couldn't sleep. I was listening out, but I couldn't hear nothing. The whole thing was going through my head. I still wasn't sure if dad really believed me. I thought he must be going through the motions, being the dutiful father. Better late than never I supposed. But whether he really believed me...'

'I'm sure he did,' Marion said.

'He accepted something had happened, but he probably thought I was exaggerating. He thought it must be a misunderstanding. Like at the stag do. That was dad all over. Always putting his mates before his family.'

'That's not true,' Marion insisted.

'Isn't it? I don't know. Well, anyway, when everyone was fast asleep, dad made some excuse to get Dave out away from the living room and down into the barn. Didn't want to have that conversation in the kitchen, where they could be overheard. Not that dad ever raised his voice.' Robbie scoffed. 'You wouldn't believe anyone could get so angry without ever raising his voice, but that was my dad. It really used to piss me off.'

Emma leaned forward. Her hands were shaking now, as they moved towards the climax of the story. 'So the two of them went down into the barn together?'

'Yeah. Dad's got a wine rack buried away down there somewhere. He said he was going to show Dave a really rare vintage. Switched on the light, closed the door. Bolted it, probably. And then, over the wine rack, they talked.'

'You didn't hear the conversation, though?'

'No. Like I say, I was upstairs in my room. Knowing dad, he'd have taken his time, worked his way around the subject, not just blurted it all out. I did think about sneaking down and having a listen, but I had no idea what time it was going to be. It was only later dad told me what had happened, and by then it was too late.'

Marion grimaced, staring at her son. 'What do you mean, dear?'

Robbie's face blackened. 'He didn't deny it, Dave, when dad asked him. He admitted it. That I'd stayed over with him, that we'd both got drunk. But of course he made out it was all a misunderstanding. He thought I was coming on to him, he said. The medication he was on, it confused him. In any other circumstances...' Robbie growled contemptuously. 'All that bull. He said he was so upset about it afterwards, so angry with himself. Tried to apologise to me, but I scarpered before he got the chance.'

Emma scratched her nose unhappily. 'What did your dad make of that?'

'He wasn't happy. All this time, he'd thought it was a fairy story, that I was just making it all up. Like I say, he was probably just going through the motions, to get it out the way. And now it turned out, I wasn't lying at all. Dave had admitted doing it, just like I said he had. Oh, it was all a "misunderstanding", but that didn't change the facts. His best mate had shagged his own son. Forced himself onto him. Dad just couldn't get a handle on that.'

You can hardly blame him, Emma thought. 'So what happened next?'

'Dave tried to laugh it off, said it was all in the past, no harm done. But dad was having none of it. He was furious. Dave tried to leave. He said it was getting late and they could talk about it another time. But dad wasn't having that. Dave was halfway up the stairs at this point, but dad wasn't going to let him walk away. He wanted to have it all out, there and then. He'd never been so angry, he said. He grabbed Dave's jumper and tried to pull him back. Dave must have lost his footing on the steps. He came crashing down and smacked his head on the concrete.' Robbie shuddered, picturing the scene in his mind's eye. 'He just lay there on the ground. Not moving. There was no blood or nothing. But there was a loud crack, dad said, when he hit the floor. We think he must have fractured his skull.'

Emma shivered. 'Oh, Jesus.' So it had been an accident,

after all. It hadn't been deliberate. But then why…?

'I don't know how long it was before he came to get me. Dad, I mean. I heard him on the steps, the A frame out in the workshop. His head popped up. He didn't say anything. He looked dreadful. I could just about make him out, on the top of the ladder. He put a finger to his lips and gestured for me to come down. I grabbed my shoes and followed him. Didn't need to get dressed. I hadn't bothered to take anything off, it was so bloody cold up there. We got to the living room and I asked him what was up, but he shushed me until we got into the barn. Then I saw the body.' Robbie drew in a heavy breath before continuing. 'There he was, lying at the bottom of the stairs, all sprawled out. I couldn't believe it. I'd wanted to expose the bastard. I hadn't wanted to kill him. I came down the steps and dad closed up the door behind me. The metal door. Then he told me what happened. And you know what?' His eyes lit up. 'I was glad. I never loved my dad more than at that moment. And I was glad Uncle Dave was dead. I'm sorry Emma, but that's the truth. I couldn't help it.'

Emma dipped her head. 'I…I understand.'

'It felt like, I don't know, a liberation. To be rid of him at last. To be rid of the taint of it all.'

'So it was all an accident,' Marion said, with some relief. 'It was all…'

'No.' Robbie cut across her grimly, his eyes hardening once again. 'That was just the start of it. Dad was in a right old panic. You couldn't blame him. It was his fault, even if it was an accident. He didn't know what to do. He didn't think anyone would believe him. Anyone could see there had been a struggle. He'd ripped his jumper, pulling him back. The police would come, and we'd have to tell them everything. What Dave had done to me. What I had done, coming out here. What dad had done. And there I was, listening to it all, thinking, you know what? I don't care. The bastard's dead. That's all that matters. And then…' Robbie closed his eyes and took a slow breath. 'And then he moved.'

'Moved?' Emma's eyes widened.

'Dave. He started to move. Started to groan. He wasn't dead

184

at all. Probably had a fractured skull, but he wasn't dead. He'd just been out cold.' Robbie started to tremble, as he remembered. 'And that was when I flipped. I'd felt so relieved, thinking it was all over, that we could just start again. And then to see him there, his hands groping about, struggling to pull himself up. I couldn't stop myself. The anger just boiled up inside me.'

A chilly silence descended. No-one wanted to interrupt, but Robbie had ground to a halt, caught up in himself. It was Marion who eventually broke the silence. 'Oh, Robbie. What did you do?'

He swallowed hard. 'All that sporting gear, up against the wall, at the bottom of the stairs. I didn't even think about it. I just grabbed the baseball bat and I…I went at him. I hit him and hit him. He didn't even cry out, lying there on the floor. He didn't struggle at all, but I kept on hitting him, and hitting him. Even after…even after he was dead, I just carried on. I couldn't stop, until dad grabbed my arm and pulled me away.' Robbie lifted a trembling hand to his face and wiped his eyes. 'And then we just stood there, me and him, for an age, staring down at the body. The life drained out of me. I couldn't help myself. I felt so bloody cold. I was…I was in tears.' There were tears now as he remembered. 'Dad took me in his arms. He told me it wasn't my fault. He even stroked my hair, the silly sod. He said we'd get it sorted. It would be okay. He'd protect me. But he wasn't fooling anyone. Not even himself. I'd screwed it up for both of us. Just like before.'

'Oh, Robbie,' Marion said.

'The thing is, mum.' He wiped his eyes again. 'I don't regret it, even now. I just can't. That bastard. He had it coming.'

Emma looked away. She was struggling with her own emotions, torn between sympathy and horror. 'And so you decided to cover it all up?'

Robbie nodded. 'What choice did we have? We didn't want to end up in prison. We talked it over. It was my idea to drag him outside. I thought, let someone else take the blame. Those vagrants the gendarmes had told you about. Why not blame it on them? It was a crazy idea. We didn't really think it would work. But we didn't have anything to lose.'

'I can't believe Giles would go along with that,' Marion said.

'You didn't see him, that night. He was falling to pieces. He'd been wrong about Dave, right from the off. He said he felt so guilty. Not about him dying, although that too, but how he hadn't believed me in the first place. Helping me to cover it all up, he wasn't doing it to protect himself. He didn't care about that. He was doing it for me, mum. And for you. You'd made a life for yourself out here. He didn't want everything to come crashing down. We grabbed some boots and a jacket from the rack and headed out into the snow. It was a long shot but it was worth a try. We lucked out on the weather. There was a bit of a lull just then. I took the baseball bat and hurled it off into the distance. It would get covered over pretty quickly. By the time the police found it, there'd be no fingerprints on it. Nothing to tie it to us.'

'But why did you drag him all the way over here?' Emma asked. 'Why dump him in the plunge pool?' That was the part that had really shocked her, the calculation of it.

'It wasn't the original plan,' Robbie admitted. 'We were going to just leave him out in the snow, as far away from the house as we could get. It wasn't as deep then as it is now, but it was easier to move across country rather than downhill. We half dragged him, half carried him. Dad managed all right, even with his dodgy leg, but I did most of the heavy lifting. The plunge pool was his idea. He'd been next door a few times and knew the layout. If we dumped him in there, under the cover, it would be ages before anyone found him, even when the snow thawed. And the longer he was out there, the less evidence there would be, the less connection to us.'

'You broke the window, too?' Emma asked, out of curiosity.

'Yeah. Not my brightest idea. I had a stone caught up in my boot. I thought that would add to the illusion. The vagrants, smashing the place up. That was on the way back, though. First, we had to drag the body up the steps and into the pool. It was a hell of a job. In the dark too. Although dad did have a torch with him.'

186

That must have been the light Mrs Pavan saw, Emma realised.

'Afterwards, we headed back to the house. Got out of our wet clothes. We came back into the living room, as quietly as we could. Kept the lights off, tried to dry ourselves off. We didn't want anyone to know we'd been up and about. I've no idea what time it was.'

'It must have been about four in the morning,' Nicholas said, his eyes fixed on the dining table in front of him. His blonde hair hung down in a sideways fringe, partially covering the top of his face. 'I didn't really want to get up,' he said. 'I don't like creeping about in the middle of the night. But I had to.'

Betsy smiled. 'If you've got to go, you've got to go.'

Vicki was sitting opposite the older woman. She did not smile. Her eyes were fixed on Nicholas. The accusation was hanging in the air. Not only had her brother killed her dad, but according to Nicholas he had something to do with Uncle Dave's death as well. Even now, with all the evidence before her, Vicki did not want to believe it; but she had seen the knife in Robbie's hand, and the blood spattered across the snow. *He killed daddy. He really did.* The two of them had often argued, but never in her worst nightmares had she imagined Robbie would do something like that. Part of her wanted to run and hide – she didn't really want to hear any more – but Vicki could not tear her eyes away from Nicholas's nervous, pale face. Deep in her heart, she knew he was speaking the truth.

His eyes flicked from left to right as he recalled the dreadful events of the previous night. 'There was no light on in the living room,' he said, glancing across at the door leading through into the master bedroom. 'It was pitch black. I opened it up just a crack.' He looked across at Betsy. 'I didn't want to wake you up.'

'Not much chance of that!' she cackled. 'A herd of elephants wouldn't wake me up. I was dead to the world.' With her earplugs in as usual. 'I was saying to your mum, Vicki, that mattress is to die for. I slept like a log last night. Didn't hear a thing.'

Nicholas took a slow breath and then continued. 'I saw a shadow moving about. I...I didn't know who it was. I hadn't opened the door very wide. I thought, it must be someone up and about, like me. Getting a glass of water or something. It...it sounds silly, but I didn't want to bump into them, whoever it was.'

Vicki could understand that. It was always embarrassing, stumbling across someone in the dark in the middle of the night. 'Was it Robbie?' she asked.

'Yes. He was here. But not just him.'

'Robbie and...Uncle Dave?'

Nicholas shook his head. 'No. Robbie and your dad.'

'My dad?' Vicki blinked in surprise.

'They were together, in here. I...I couldn't see all that much. There was a bit of a glow from the wood burner but that was it. They couldn't see me, through the crack in the door, but I could see them.'

'What were they doing?' Vicki asked.

Nicholas hesitated. 'It was strange. They...they were moving the sofa.' He raised a finger and gestured vaguely in the direction of the couch. 'I thought they were trying to shift it for some reason, but they just turned it on its side.'

Vicki nodded vaguely, remembering how she had found it that morning.

'I couldn't make any sense of it,' Nicholas said. 'But they grabbed the armchair too and upended that. Gently. They didn't throw it or anything. Then your brother took the bin from over there.' He nodded towards the kitchen area. 'And started scattering the contents across the floor.'

Vicki was struggling to understand any of this. 'You mean daddy and...and Robbie, they... the break-in. The vagrants. That was all staged?'

'I saw them do it,' Nicholas confirmed, his eyes fixed once again on the table in front of him. He had barely touched his soup and it would soon be getting cold. 'I...I didn't know what was going on. They seemed to have gone mad.'

'It does sound pretty barmy,' Betsy agreed. She was still

chewing on some bread. 'They must have done the same thing in the barn. Marion was saying, wasn't she, they turned everything over in there.'

'I didn't see that,' Nicholas confessed. 'I...I couldn't see into the barn, although the door was open. One thing I did see, though. I didn't really think anything of it at the time. But there were some clothes, lined up in front of the wood burner. Coats hanging up there and some boots on the floor in front of them. It was only later that...that I realised what that must mean.'

Betsy understood what he was getting at. 'It was them who went outside. That's what you're saying, isn't it? It wasn't vagrants who killed Dave. It was...' Her voice trailed away. For a brief moment, even she was speechless.

Vicki shook her head. In one horrible moment, she saw it all. Her dad and Robbie, working together. They had killed Uncle Dave. They had put on their coats and dragged him outside together and then hung them up to dry afterwards. No, it was too horrible. Too dreadful to even consider.

'Why would they do it, though?' Betsy was struggling to understand. 'Why on earth would they kill Dave?'

'I don't know,' Nicholas admitted, his hands trembling. 'But they did. They must have done.' His voice was wavering, trying to keep an even tone. 'They killed him and...and then dragged his body through the snow. I only saw the aftermath, when they came back here and tried to cover it up.' Tears were beginning to flow down his cheeks. 'They murdered him, in cold blood. And I don't know why!'

Vicki regarded him incredulously. 'Why didn't you tell us? Why didn't you tell us that you had seen them do it?'

'I...I didn't know,' he protested. 'I didn't know what they were doing. Last night, I mean. I had no idea what any of it was about. I...I didn't know anyone had died. All I'd seen them doing was moving the furniture around. Emptying their own bins. What could I say about that? It was their house. I didn't want to embarrass anyone. And it upset me, seeing it all like that. I don't know why. I...I think I knew something was wrong.' Nicholas frowned. 'Your dad, he came over to the wall. There, by the front door.' He indicated the empty space between the door and the window. 'He grabbed hold of the painting on the wall, one of his landscapes. I closed the door pretty quickly, so he didn't see me there; but in the morning, when I looked again, I saw it had been torn to pieces. He must have slashed it. His own painting. That was when I really started...when I really started to worry.'

Vicki was perplexed. 'Daddy would never destroy one of his own paintings.'

Aunt Betsy was not so sure. 'He might do, lovey. Think about it. If he did...if the pair of them really did kill your uncle, for whatever reason...well, they'd have to make a good job of covering it up, wouldn't they? Make the place look like a bomb had hit it. And it worked, didn't it? None of us doubted it for a second. I remember saying to your mum: those vandals, it's not right them coming in here. I didn't doubt it for a minute.'

'But why would they do it?' That was the question that Vicki could not even begin to understand. 'Why would they kill Uncle Dave?'

'I don't know,' Nicholas said again, raising a hand to his eyes. 'I only wish I did.'

'But surely when you saw the painting this morning; and when you heard Uncle Dave had gone missing, why didn't you say something then?'

'I...I didn't know what to think. I was lying in bed, all last night, trying to make sense of what I'd seen. And then, by the time we did get up, everything was in a whirl. Dave had disappeared and everyone was heading off to look for him. I knew then that something bad must have happened, but I didn't imagine...I didn't want to think...' Nicholas let out a strangled sob. 'I didn't want to believe anything might have happened to him. Not now. Not when...' He broke off, tears flowing once again. Betsy reached across and gave his arm a gentle squeeze. He swallowed and tried to recover himself. The whole thing had hit him hard; and he wasn't even a member of the family. 'I hoped that I was wrong and that...that everything would be fine. But when you and Akash came back and you told us what you'd found, I...I didn't know what to do. It was as if the whole world had fallen apart. Would anyone believe me, if I accused your dad and your brother? The phone wasn't working, so we couldn't call the police. For all I knew, your father might have cut that off himself. We were on our own, with no help coming. And your dad and your brother...the pair of them, they seemed to have everything planned out. They had their story prepared, they had the people ready to blame. And I...I just sat there, listening to it all. And I thought, they're going to get away with it. They'd killed someone and they were going to get away with murder.'

'The truth would have come out,' Aunt Betsy insisted, 'It always does in the end, doesn't it?'

'Not this time,' Nicholas said, his whole body trembling. 'When they brought the...the body back here. When I saw him lying there. Oh, God, I felt sick. It just...I wanted to throw up.'

'You *were* sick,' Betsy pointed out. 'All over the floor.'

'I almost fainted.'

'I couldn't even look,' Vicki said. She had run off to the bedroom before they arrived. 'I didn't want to see him like that.'

'It wasn't pleasant,' Betsy agreed. 'But still.' She gave Nicholas a look. 'You hardly even knew him. Dave. I mean, it was shocking and all that, but...'

'That's the worst thing,' Nicholas admitted quietly. 'I didn't know him at all. We sat next to each other on the plane out, but I was...I was too shy to really talk to him then. He went to sleep and I just sat there, watching him. It was only at the dinner table last night that I really...' His face lit up. 'Seeing him laughing and joking. He was so alive. And then...then they took all that away from me. I was so happy, at dinner, for those two hours. I never thought I'd get to meet him like that.'

Vicki frowned, struggling to understand.

'And then they killed him,' Nicholas said. 'They took his life and now I'll never...I'll never be able to...' He stopped. 'I was so angry. I've never been so angry. I...I didn't know what to do. No-one was going to believe me. Your brother, and Giles, they were going to get away with it. I...I had to do something. I couldn't just let...' His lips pressed together. 'I wanted to hurt them, don't you see? I couldn't stop myself. I wanted to lash out. I saw all those paintings, stacked up, out in the workshop. All your dad's watercolours. And I just...I lost it.'

Vicki let out a gasp. 'You mean it was you who started the fire?'

'I wanted to burn the whole place down. You must believe me, it was just...I was lashing out. I was so upset. But...but it wasn't enough. I couldn't bear it. What they had done. I couldn't let them get away with it.' Nicholas's hand slid across the table and grabbed the bread knife in front of him. 'I didn't have a choice. You must understand that.' He looked up then and finally met Vicki's eyes. 'It was my dad, you see. They killed him. They killed my father.'

'Uncle Dave?' Vicki's eyes widened in disbelief. 'He was your dad?'

Nicholas nodded grimly. 'And they had to pay the price.'

Chapter Twelve

'I found him lying there, in the bathroom,' Robbie Wilkerson continued. 'I'd just come for a slash. The door was closed, the light was on. I knocked, but there was no reply. Then I opened the door and saw him lying there.'

Emma was watching him intently. They had been talking for some time now and her legs were beginning to go to sleep, but her attention was still keenly focused. Robbie was adamant that he had not laid a finger on his dad. Apparently, he had not started the fire either.

'That had nothing to do with me. I stubbed out that bloody cigarette. You know I did. You were there when I did it.'

'You think someone else started the fire?' Emma asked. 'Deliberately?'

'Of course they did. Burning dad's stuff like that. It had to be deliberate. Someone must have seen us last night. It's the only explanation. They must have seen what we did. The fire was their way of getting back at us.'

'Your dad seemed pretty sure it was an accident.'

'So he claimed. I suppose it was easier just to blame me, say it was all my fault. Perhaps he thought I'd done it on purpose. I don't know. Either way, it scared the hell out of me. All his paintings, all his magazines, destroyed. It was obvious someone was trying to get at us. They had to be. Dad reckoned I was imagining it. How could anyone know, he said? And if they did, why didn't they just tell everyone? But I was spooked, I can tell you. I didn't want to go back to my room. I could have choked to death up there.' Robbie had gone out to the barn instead; and some time after that, he had found his dad's body.

Emma looked up, as Akash returned to the kitchen. The curly haired bloke had disappeared off upstairs to the bathroom. She gave him a half smile as he sat down next to Marion. Robbie's mum was gazing impassively at her son. Emma could not begin to imagine what she was feeling right now.

'I panicked,' Robbie continued, reliving the moment. 'When I saw him there. All that blood. I didn't think about dad at all. I just thought, I'm next. It's going to happen to me too. They'd already set light to the place, nearly choked me to death. Now someone had killed my dad. Stabbed him in the back. Jesus.' Robbie shuddered. 'I loved him, the old sod. I really did. He was stubborn as a mule. Never gave an inch. But I loved him.'

'You were more alike than either of you would admit,' Marion said.

'I hated him too, sometimes. He wouldn't ever listen to me. But then, this last day or so, we found something. It sounds stupid. What we did to Uncle Dave, I never meant it to happen. But he stood up for me, my dad. He was looking out for me, at the end, trying to help me. And then someone...'

'That was why you ran away,' Emma guessed. 'You were frightened.'

He nodded bitterly. 'I wasn't going to hang around, was I, to get my throat slit? I had to get away, before...' He shrank back, pressing up awkwardly against the door of the washing machine. 'I didn't know who it was, that was the worst thing. It could have been any one of you. I had to get away. I ran out into the workshop. I was going to grab my stuff from upstairs and then head off. Out into the snow. I'd take my chances out there rather than risk staying home. Then I saw the doors open. The workroom doors. And I thought, hang on, maybe it wasn't one of us after all. Maybe all that bull we fed you about the vagrants, it had come true. Somebody really had broken in. But then I took a closer look. The doors hadn't been forced. Someone had shoved that old desk out of the way. It looked like they'd been going outside, not coming in. That was when I saw the knife. It was lying out there on the snow. Someone must have thrown it out there. It can't have been there for more than a few minutes. I went out and grabbed it. I could see the blood on it. From dad. And that was when Vick saw me. Caught me red-handed.' He laughed bitterly. 'I knew straight away what she was going to think. So I dropped the knife and I just ran. I ran as fast as I could.

Not very fast, Emma thought, *in this weather*. But had Robbie run because he was afraid or because he thought he was going to be blamed? It didn't matter. It was clear that Robbie had not killed his dad. Which begged the question, who did?

Marion took Robbie's hand in hers and clutched it tightly.

'I'm sorry, mum. It's all my fault.'

'It's not your fault,' she told him firmly. 'We should have been there for you. We should have listened to you.' The air was warm now, the open oven door having done its job, and some colour had returned to Robbie's cheek. His expression, though, was more that of a lost child.

'Dad really never told you anything. About...?'

'Dave? No. I had no idea. I would never have allowed him to come here, if I had.' She looked down at his hand in hers. 'What you did, dear, what you and your father did, it was in the heat of the moment. It was an accident. You lost your temper, Robbie. That's all. If you'd been thinking straight...'

'I'd still have done it. I didn't mean it to happen, but he deserved it. What he did to me.'

Emma didn't want to dwell on that. 'What about Giles? If you didn't kill him, then who did?' That was the most important question now.

Robbie didn't have an answer. 'I thought it might be you,' he admitted, bluntly, looking at Emma. 'You or Akash. Or Nicholas. I don't know any of you. Anything about you.'

Akash grinned. 'It wasn't me, mate,' he declared. He almost seemed to be enjoying this. But that was probably just his manner. People had different ways of coping in situations like this.

'But if the vagrant thing was all rubbish,' Emma said, thinking it through, 'and if Robbie didn't kill his dad either, then you're right, it must have been one of us. One of us here or somebody back at the house.' That was not a happy thought.

'We ought to get back there,' Marion suggested, a note of urgency creeping into her voice.

'I'm not going back to the house.' Robbie pulled his hand away from her.

'We don't have a choice, dear,' she said. 'Your sister could be in danger.'

She might even be *the danger*, Emma thought darkly. So much had happened, these last few hours. There was no way of knowing who might be behind it all.

Akash pushed back his chair and stretched his arms above his head. 'Better if we're all together. Don't worry, Rob. I'll keep an eye on you.'

Marion untangled her legs and rose wearily to her feet. 'We'll need to find you a pair of shoes. But we must hurry.' She stepped around her son and switched off the oven. Then she gazed across the kitchen floor. A pool of water had formed all around them. 'I shall have a lot of explaining to do when the neighbours get back,' she reflected, absently. But the owners of this house were the least of their problems.

They needed to get back to the farm, before it was too late.

Nicholas's hands were trembling as he grasped the bread knife. For a moment, there was silence. Vicki's heart was in her mouth, watching him holding the blade; but he gave no indication that he intended to use it. She could not even begin to make sense of what he had just said. It made her dizzy, the implications of it. 'Uncle Dave?' she stuttered, unable to stop herself. 'He was your father?' The young man nodded, his eyes fixed on the knife in his hand, his whole body shaking.

Aunt Betsy was keeping her cool. She caught Vicki's eye, imploring her to keep calm as well. Any sudden moves might lead to disaster. 'He must have met her at the wedding,' she guessed, keeping her voice level. 'Is that it?' She looked to Nicholas for confirmation.

'I...I don't know,' he said.

'Did *he* know?' Betsy asked. 'That you were his son?'

'I...I don't think so.' Nicholas hesitated. 'I don't think she ever told him about me. It was only a...a brief affair, I think.'

'That sounds like Dave,' Betsy said, forcing a smile.

'I never knew who my father was. Not until...not until a few weeks ago. When I found out, I so wanted to meet him. That's why I came here this weekend, with you. I wanted to see him, to find out what kind of man he was. If we got on, I was going to tell him who I really was. That...that was the plan.' His voice broke apart as he added, 'And now I'll never get the chance.'

Vicki was struggling to maintain her composure, as the reality of the situation began to hit home; the truth of what Nicholas must have done. 'You...you killed my dad,' she breathed, barely daring to articulate the words. Part of her just wanted to run away; to push back her chair and bolt from the room. But she knew she could not; that she had to stay calm, for her own sake and for the sake of her aunt.

'I didn't want to do it,' Nicholas declared unhappily. 'I didn't want to kill anyone. But I was so angry. I didn't know what to do. When you came back here this morning and told us Dave was dead, that he was lying at the bottom of the pool, I just...I couldn't believe it. I didn't want to believe it was possible.'

Vicki remembered how pale he had looked, how shocked he had been when he'd heard the news, even before Akash and the others had gone out to recover the body.

'It was like someone had put a noose around my neck,' Nicholas said. 'I went to my room. I sat on the bed. I...I tried to make sense of it all. And then I remembered what I had seen them doing, last night, and it all began to make sense. I knew what they had done, your dad and Robbie. They killed him. They really did. And I was sitting there in my bedroom, looking through the door into the far room. Dave's room. I was so upset. I was trying to figure out why they would do it. And then I saw that painting on the wall, a landscape your father had painted. Just like the one he'd slashed in the living room. I couldn't stop myself. I was so angry. I stormed into the room and ripped it off the wall; and I smashed it. Tore the canvas, threw it on the floor.'

Vicki shuddered, picturing the scene.

'It didn't help at all,' Nicholas admitted. 'I tried to calm myself down. He was out there, your dad, in the kitchen, pretending to be shocked. I...I didn't know what to do. I couldn't confront him. I didn't know what he might be capable of. I didn't understand...I still don't understand why he would ever do something like that. I...I tried to pull myself together. I thought, I have to wait until someone in authority gets here.

197

Then I could tell them. But I'd already destroyed the painting. It was lying there on the floor, all ripped up. I couldn't just leave it there. So I gathered it up. I was going to put it in the drawer, hide it away with the linen in there. Then I found that old key in the bottom and I guessed it must be for the workshop door. So I put the painting out there, piled up with all the others. After that, I came back to the living room. You were both here, you remember? You and your dad.'

Vicki nodded. She had been too caught up in her own grief to pay Nicholas any attention. As far as she could recall, he had just sat quietly on the sofa, looking at his phone, while Aunt Betsy had chatted away, trying to keep their spirits up.

'I couldn't bear it, sitting there. Seeing Giles, your dad, fussing about. I wanted to throttle him. I wanted to scream and shout. But I just froze. I couldn't do anything. And then…and then they brought the body back and that was the end of me. Seeing him lying there and…and knowing what they had done. I couldn't bear it. I wanted to kick and scream. I wanted to lash out. I could barely stop myself from retching. But I decided then and there, I had to do something. I…I couldn't wait for the police. Even when they did come, they might not believe me.'

'So you decided to take the law into your own hands,' Betsy said.

'I didn't have a plan. If you'd asked me then, I…I couldn't have told you what I was going to do.'

'But you went back to the workshop and lit that fire?'

'Later on, yes,' he admitted, 'when there was no-one around. I…I didn't really know what I was doing. I just wanted to burn the place down. Burn all Giles's books, all his paintings. Make your dad feel some of the pain that I was feeling. I wasn't trying to hurt anyone. At least, not then. I…I came in through the bedroom. Got the matches from the drawer. There was a cannister of petrol out in the workshop, next to the mower. I'd seen it there earlier on. I poured a bit of that onto the books, to help get it going.'

'What about Robbie?' Vicki asked quietly. 'Did…did you know he was upstairs, at the time?'

'I knew. I'd heard the floorboards creaking. But I didn't

care. Maybe the fumes would overwhelm him. That would serve him right.'

Vicki shuddered again. 'It was you who knocked over the ladder.'

'It wasn't...yes, I did. I put it on its side. Although I didn't really think the smoke would kill him. He must have been lying down, listening to music. He didn't hear me do it. Then I set the fire going and...and went back to my room. Akash came by, a minute or two later, looking for some candles, and I made myself scarce. I wasn't sure how long it would take to go up. I'd only used a little bit of petrol. But Emma and Akash discovered it almost at once, much quicker than I'd hoped.'

'We could all have been killed!' Vicki exclaimed. Betsy shot her a warning look, her eyes flicking down to the knife, but for a moment Vicki did not care. 'Why would you do that?'

'I didn't want to hurt anyone,' Nicholas protested again. 'But I...I was getting more and more angry. Even after the fire. Giles blamed that on your brother. And he was so calm about it. And I just...something inside me snapped. I couldn't bear to look at either of them, but your father...his horrible, smug face. I had taken a knife from the kitchen, while everyone was fussing about over the fire. I was worried that your dad would realise what I had done, that he'd guess that I knew about last night. I needed something to protect myself with.'

Vicki frowned. 'But you were in the bathroom with me during the fire. Helping me put the hose on the tap.'

'After that. I went out to get a second bucket of water, but it wasn't needed. I grabbed a knife from the kitchen drawer. And then, things calmed down a little. Everyone seemed to think the fire was an accident. But your dad knew better, and so did Robbie. I...I just sat and bided my time. I'd made up my mind then. I knew what I was going to do.' Nicholas's voice was now a grim monotone. His hands had stopped trembling. 'I...I waited until your dad went upstairs to his bedroom. Then I nipped back into the master bedroom.' Vicki had a vague recollection that he had gone off to fetch an extra sweater. 'I went through into Emma's room, and waited. I...I heard him come down the stairs, your dad. Then I...then I followed him and…and…' He gazed at the blade, almost without comprehension. 'I was in a rage. I didn't know what I was doing.'

'You're a monster,' Vicki cried, jerking back from the table. 'How could you do that?'

New tears were beginning to stream down Nicholas's face. 'I…I didn't want to hurt anyone,' he cried again. 'I just got so caught up in…' His voice trailed away. For a moment, there was silence.

Betsy left it a couple of seconds, gazing at him sadly, and then said, 'Why don't you put the knife down, lovey? It's over now, isn't it? We're not exactly any threat to you. A couple of girls. And we've done nothing to hurt you, have we?'

'No. No, you haven't,' Nicholas agreed. He lifted his head and shot Betsy a sad smile. 'I'm so sorry you got caught up in all this. I thought you'd laugh, when you found out the truth, that Dave was my father. I…I never expected anything like this.'

'I know, lovey. I know.' She reached a hand forward across the table. 'Put the knife down, eh?' She made to cover his hand in hers. At the last second, Nicholas snatched it away. He jerked backwards so hard, the chair fell away from under him. Betsy rose up, coming round the side of the table. 'Here, let me…'

The knife had fallen from Nicholas's hand. He scrabbled for it, just as Vicki was pushing back her own chair. Aunt Betsy stretched out a hand, offering to help him up, but he shrank away from her, mistaking her intent. He rose up quickly, then swerved left and shot a hand out, grabbing Vicki by the arm.

She let out a scream as he pulled her in towards him. All at once, Vicki felt a knife – the hard, serrated bread knife – pressed against her throat.

It was pitch black outside as Emma and the others made their way back towards the farmhouse. Akash had a torch in his hand and was leading the way, setting a brisk pace. The wind had died down now and the snow seemed to have hardened a little, making their progress easier. Emma dreaded to think what they would find when they got back to the house. Probably, everything was fine. But if somebody there had been handy with a knife once before, then there was no telling what they might do next. Always assuming the person who had killed Giles was one of the three they had left behind. *Robbie was right*, Emma thought, *it could just as easily be one of us.*

A scream rang out from the building up ahead and Emma almost lost her footing. The group were now about thirty metres from the house. Robbie and Marion were a little in front of her, with Akash ahead of them.

Marion froze at the sound of her daughter's voice. 'That's Vicki!' she exclaimed. Emma was already pushing past her. Akash caught Emma's eye and the two of them broke into a run, slipping and sliding towards the house as quickly as they could. Marion followed behind, abandoning her walking stick and grabbing Robbie's hand, propelling her son forward.

Emma reached the corner of the house first. Her heart was hammering. *Please God, let them be all right.* The barn doors, a few feet in front of her, were closed up and snow was piled high in front of them. Akash was already moving past them towards the front door. He stumbled up a set of unseen steps and by a frosted window, then skidded to a halt, half colliding with the doorstep.

'Vicki! It's me!' he called urgently, banging on the locked door. There was no response from within.

Emma stopped at the window and peered inside, but she couldn't make anything out. Akash continued banging on the door.

Marion had reached the corner of the house, having abandoned Robbie momentarily. He had slipped over and was struggling back onto his feet. Marion slid a hand into her coat pocket. 'Here!' she called, producing a set of keys and tossing them forward.

Emma caught them easily. She spun around and tossed them to Akash, but he fumbled the catch and had to dip down in the snow to recover them. Then he searched for the right one and inserted it in the lock. Emma slid over to him as he pushed open the door.

Together, they tumbled into the living room, a small avalanche of snow accompanying them inside. Emma lost her balance and crashed heavily onto her backside while Akash fell forward, his legs propelling him further into the room. He collided with the sofa and came to an abrupt halt.

Emma groaned, pulling herself up. She had landed badly, but she didn't have time to worry about that. Where was Vicki? She glanced around. Betsy Klineman was standing to her left, in front of the door leading down to the barn. The door itself was closed. Betsy was bending over a second figure.

'Vicki!' Akash had rebounded from the sofa and caught sight of his fiancée, who was lying spread-eagled across the floor, just beneath the window. He let out a cry of horror. 'She's not...?'

Betsy looked up and shook her head. 'She's all right, lovey. She's just had a fright.'

The figure on the floor let out a groan. Emma moved across and almost collided with Akash as the two of them sought to help the young woman.

'Doll, what happened?' Akash breathed, crouching down in concern. Vicki rolled onto her side and clutched the back of her head. Emma leaned forward and helped the girl to sit up.

By now, the other family members had appeared at the front door. 'Vicki, are you all right?' Marion called. She stepped down into the room, her hand to her mouth, staring at her daughter.

Emma had her arm around the young woman. Vicki was trembling, not meeting anyone's eye. 'What happened?' Emma asked her. She looked up at Betsy, who was looming over them. 'Where's Nicholas?'

'It was him,' Vicki declared. The sound of his name had brought her suddenly to life. 'He killed daddy.'

Emma boggled. 'Nicholas did?'

Akash was holding Vicki's hand, trying to reassure her.

'It was him all along,' she breathed. 'I thought he was going to kill me.'

'Here, let's get you up,' Akash suggested. Emma gave him a

hand and, between the two of them, they helped Vicki to her feet. They were going to move her across to the sofa, but Vicki had other ideas. She broke away and ran straight into the arms of her mother.

'I thought he was going to kill me,' she mumbled again. 'I was so scared. I was so frightened.'

Marion held her daughter tightly. 'It's all right now, dear,' She stroked her hair. 'It's all over.' Her voice was the soothing balm that Vicki needed. Marion's eyes, however, were focused on Betsy, who was standing over by the barn door.

The older woman shrugged her shoulders, for once finding it difficult to speak. 'He went mad,' she managed eventually. 'Nicholas did. He grabbed the bread knife from the table. Confessed to everything. Killing Giles. Then he grabbed hold of Vicki. You should have seen him. He was like a wild animal.'

'I thought he was going to kill me,' Vicki whispered again. 'He dragged me over to the door.'

'He didn't want us following him,' Betsy explained. Vicki had been a hostage, nothing more. 'He got to the door, told me to keep well back, then pushed her over and disappeared.'

'How long ago was this?' Emma asked.

Betsy shrugged. 'Just now. A couple of minutes. We were sitting at the table there, weren't we? He told us everything. Admitted it all. He set fire to the workshop, he said, and stabbed Giles. He seemed to think Giles had killed our Dave.' Her eyes flicked uncertainly to the front door, where Robbie was now standing. 'Him and Robbie. He said he saw them. That was why he did it, he said. Just admitted it all, straight out. I was saying to Vicki, I couldn't believe it. But then he just went mad.'

'Where is he now?' Robbie asked. His hands were gripping the frame of the door. 'Where's Nicholas?'

'I don't know.' Betsy shrugged. 'He ran out, through the barn.' She jerked a thumb to the metal door behind her. 'He locked up behind him. I heard the bolts go. He must have headed out from there off into the snow. Like you did.'

Robbie stepped forward into the living room. 'There's no-one outside.'

'We just came past the barn doors,' Emma explained. 'They were all locked up.' She moved over to the window to peer outside. 'No one could have come out that way. Which means…'

A loud crash from behind the metal door confirmed her fears. Nicholas was still in the barn. It sounded like he had knocked something over.

Akash was on the case already. He pushed hard against the door but – as Betsy had said – it was bolted on the far side. He pressed his shoulder to it, but it would not budge. 'Can we get in from the outside?'

Marion shook her head. 'Not any more, dear. We made sure of that, after last night.'

'Right. Brute force it is, then.' Akash took a step back and rammed his shoulder against the door. 'Ouch!'

'Here, let me try.' Emma moved forward and bashed her own shoulder against it, but with no more luck.

Akash threw in a couple of kicks, then tried again with his shoulder. 'I can feel it shifting,' he said, after the third attempt. 'I'll take a run up.'

'Be careful!' Vicki called to him, looking up. 'Don't forget the stairs on the other side!'

Akash shot her a wink. 'Don't worry about me, doll!' Emma stepped aside as he hurled himself at the door at full speed. This time, it did the trick. The bolts flew apart. Akash pulled himself up just in time, rebounding unceremoniously onto his backside as the door flew open. Better that, though, than crashing down the stairs.

Emma gave him a hand up. Then she stepped through the door. A light was on inside the barn. The others hung back but Emma and Akash moved straight in, down the steps, past the moped and the shroud covering Dave Flint. All the while, her eyes were scanning the enormous space, peering into the gloom for any signs of movement. It did not take long to see him.

Nicholas Samoday was suspended in mid air, his body hanging from a piece of rope tied to a beam beneath the hayloft at the far end of the barn. The tennis table had been dragged over and parked in front of the bench. Nicholas had launched himself off it. Emma let out a gasp as she saw the legs kicking. He was still alive. His mouth was foaming, his body jerking left and right. There was blood everywhere. The table hadn't been high enough to break his neck.

'We've got to get him down,' Emma breathed, shuddering at the awful sight.

There was an iron saw on top of a nearby sideboard. Akash grabbed it and rushed forward, clambering up onto the ping pong table, just behind Nicholas's still twitching body. Emma meantime grabbed hold of his waist, which was writhing in front of her at head height. As Akash set to work, attempting to cut the rope, Emma did her best to try and carry his weight.

A scream from behind signalled the arrival of the others. Vicki again. Emma did not look back, but she could hear someone rushing across the barn. That was Marion, coming to help. But it was too late. Before Akash could finish sawing the rope, Emma felt Nicholas's body go limp in her arms. She held on regardless, with a little help from Marion, while Akash completed the grim task; and then they lowered the body gently to the ground.

Chapter Thirteen

Robbie had only given them half the story. Now Betsy provided the other half. 'You've got to be joking,' Emma breathed, as the woman repeated the tale she had been told. 'Dave was Nicholas's dad?' Emma's mouth fell open. 'Bloody hell.'

Vicki was staring across the barn as her mum helped out with the body. She looked a little shell-shocked, which was hardly surprising. Betsy had her arm around her, while Marion and Akash drew down Nicholas's body and laid him out. Robbie was standing nearby, watching closely, his face unreadable, his back to the stone wall.

Emma had already stepped away. She was shivering too, delayed shock kicking in. She had felt Nicholas die in her arms; felt the life go out of him. The death throes of an animal, just like at the clinic. She had witnessed it a thousand times. But this was something different and, like the image of Dave in the plunge pool, she knew she was never going to be able to expunge it from her memory.

She gathered herself together and walked calmly across the barn, to where Betsy and Vicki stood waiting. Emma opened her mouth to say something, but no words came out. *It's over*, she thought, throwing a half-hearted smile at Vicki. That was some comfort at least. But there were so many questions. Dave was Nicholas's father? Emma couldn't even begin to get her head around the idea.

Betsy was babbling away, trying to explain it all, in her usual extravagant fashion. 'I couldn't believe it either. I was just saying to Vicki, I've been going out with him for – what? – three months. Nicholas, I mean. He was so shy. Wouldn't say boo to a goose.'

'He never told you, about Dave?' Emma glanced down at the concrete floor, aware of the older man's body lying nearby. Two bodies now, to lay out. Three, actually. Giles out in the bathroom as well. What the hell were they going to do with them all?

'He never said a word,' Betsy confirmed, still caught up on the matter of Nicholas Samoday. 'It just goes to show, doesn't it? It's always the quiet ones.'

'And Giles, he killed him, because of Dave?' Emma asked. 'He saw them do it? Robbie and Giles?'

Betsy nodded. 'Some of it, anyway. That's what he told us, isn't it, lovey?' She looked down at Vicki, who was still clutching her tightly. 'He said he lost his temper. He wanted to burn the house down and kill the pair of them.'

Vicki confirmed that with a nod. 'That was why he killed daddy,' she breathed. 'He would have killed Robbie too, if he'd been able to. I was so worried about him.'

'He's safe now,' Emma reassured her, as Betsy stroked the girl's hair.

Robbie was leaning against the wall, watching as Akash and his mother pulled the tennis table out of the way. He wasn't offering to help. All the life seemed to have gone out of him.

'Is it true then?' Betsy asked, meeting Emma's eyes. 'Robbie killed Dave, like Nicholas said?'

Emma drew in a breath but confirmed it with a nod. 'Him and Giles, together. It wasn't planned. But they did kill him. With a baseball bat.'

That provoked a reaction from Vicki. 'Daddy would never...'

'That wasn't your dad,' Emma assured her quickly. 'But he was involved. And Dave wasn't exactly guiltless either.' She looked away for a moment. There was no point sugar coating the truth. It would all come out eventually, what Dave had done to Robbie. It was better to deal with it now. She kept it as brief as she could, aware of Vicki's eyes on her as she spelt out the horrible details.

'Uncle Dave?' Vicki whispered, incredulously.

Emma shrugged. 'I can't explain it. He wasn't the man I thought he was. Who any of us thought he was. But it's true. Ask your brother. That was what started it all.' She filled in the rest of the details as quickly as she could. 'Robbie lost his temper, when Dave came round. And that was the end of it.'

Vicki gazed across the barn at her brother. 'Oh, Robbie...'

Betsy pulled her head close once again. 'It's all over now, lovey. It's all done with. We're safe.'

'But daddy…'

Emma scratched her head. She crouched down and gazed for a moment at Dave Flint's body, lying under the sheet. The great lump. It was all his fault. Better for everyone if he had never come here. 'Did he know, do you think? Did he know that Nicholas was his son?'

'He had no idea,' Betsy said. 'At least not according to Nicholas. He said to us – didn't he? – he was hoping to pluck up the courage to tell him this weekend. Once he got him on his own. But he never got the chance, the poor little lamb.' She frowned. 'Well not…' For once, even Betsy was at a loss for words.

Across the room, Akash had found something interesting on the floor. 'Hey look at this. It must have fallen out of his pocket.' Akash picked up the bit of paper and handed it to Marion. She unfolded it and scanned it briefly.

Emma lifted herself up. 'What is it?' she asked.

For a moment, Marion did not reply. Then she came over and handed it to Emma. 'It's a photocopy of Nicholas's birth certificate,' she said. 'Look at the father's name.'

Emma did not need to look. 'David Flint. Betsy was just telling me.' She glanced down at the document. Nicholas's mother was listed as Mary Samantha Samoday. Marion's old friend, the one who had been at her wedding. The father, of course, was Dave.

'Betsy, you knew about this?' Marion was perplexed.

'Not until twenty minutes ago!' Betsy exclaimed. 'I had no idea. I only knew his mum to talk to, not much more. She was your friend, really. Dave must have hooked up with her at the wedding. You remember, I said to you, she was there?'

'Yes, I remember,' Marion said. 'We lost touch soon after that. But I don't recall Dave talking to her at the wedding. Not that I was paying close attention.'

'He probably got her number then and met up with her later,' Emma suggested.

'It's possible, dear. He always was a bit of a ladies man.'

'I'll say,' Betsy threw in, with a chuckle. 'A real skirt chaser. I used to say to him, leave some of them for the others.'

Marion looked down at the certificate sadly. 'I was sorry to hear when she died. That was a few years later, of course.'

Emma nodded. 'After Nicholas came along.'

Vicki had been paying close attention to their words. 'It's true then, what he said?' She looked up. 'Dave really was his father?'

'It looks like it,' Emma confirmed, showing her the document.

Marion's face softened at the sight of her daughter. 'How are you doing, dear? Perhaps we should get you back into the kitchen, away from all this?'

Vicki nodded and disentangled herself from her aunt.

'I'll put the kettle on,' Marion said. She gave a nod to the others and the two of them moved away.

Emma stayed put. There was a second piece of paper, alongside the birth certificate. It was a printout of a web page, a social media profile belonging to Dave Flint. She showed it to Betsy. 'It looks like Nicholas must have been looking him up online,' she said. 'It can't have been easy. Dave or David Flint.' There were probably hundreds of them. 'Nicholas must have found a copy of the birth certificate and looked him up; but he wouldn't have known which Dave Flint was his.'

Betsy had gone very pale. 'Until I told him,' she admitted, shaking her head. She stared down at the page. 'I recognised his mum's name. It's not exactly common, is it? I said, I used to know a girl called Mary Samoday. And it turned out that was his mum. Marion's old friend. So, of course, I started to tell him about the wedding, didn't I? Showed him a couple of old photos. Pointed out a few faces.'

'And Dave would have been right there,' Emma guessed. 'The best man at the wedding. That was why he wanted to come with you this weekend. He'd finally found the Dave Flint he was looking for.'

'He never said a word,' Betsy asserted, incredulously. 'You'd have thought he'd have said something, wouldn't you. As soon as he realised?'

'Was it all a coincidence, do you think? I mean, him meeting you like that, at work?'

'It must have been. He was just a temp. Came from an agency. I don't think he could have known who I was.'

Emma was not so sure. It was amazing what you could dig up on the internet. But it might equally well just have been a matter of chance.

'He was keen on coming out here, though,' Betsy recalled. 'When I said to him about the reunion. He said, "I'd like to meet some of your friends." Of course, I was going to invite him anyway – show him off and all that – but he did say he wanted to come.'

'I'll bet he did,' Emma said, gazing thoughtfully across the barn.

'Not a nice way to go,' Akash thought, holding Vicki tightly to him. He had cut his finger, sawing at the rope – just a tiny nick – and Marion had provided a plaster. It wasn't that which had taken the wind from his sails, though. A man hanging himself. 'What a day, eh?'

Vicki was in a daze too. The couple were nestled up together on the sofa in the living room. Mum had handed her a mug of coffee, once she'd seen to Akash, but Vicki had barely touched it. 'I couldn't look,' she said, remembering the scene which had greeted her when she stepped into the barn. No matter what Nicholas had done, it was a horrible way to die. Vicki was still finding it hard to believe that that quiet, lonely young man had killed her father. It was true, though. She had heard it from his own lips; and she had felt his desperation too, in those awful seconds when he'd dragged her over to the door. By rights, she should hate him for what he had done, for what he had put them all through. But somehow, Vicki could not help feeling a little sorry for him. Nicholas had never had a real home. He had never had a father, until this weekend, and then it had all been snatched away from him.

'He lost it in the end,' Akash concluded. 'Man, did he lose it. After what he did to your dad, well, there was no coming back. Probably for the best, he topped himself. Not the way I'd have chosen to do it, though.' He pulled Vicki closer to him, his eyes fixed on her. 'Are you all right, doll? When I heard that scream...'

'I thought he was going to kill me. But he wasn't. He just wanted to get away; to buy a bit of time to...to do what he was going to do. I don't think he really meant to hurt me.' She could not forgive Nicholas for what he had done to her dad, but she was at least beginning to understand it. Maybe Akash was right. Perhaps it was better that it had ended this way. 'It's all such a mess,' she sighed, burying her head in his shoulder.

'We'll get it sorted, doll. You and me.'

Vicki nodded, shifting her head sideways.

Marion was at the kitchen sink, on the other side of the living room, doing some washing up. She had switched the radio on and a voice from the BBC was burbling away quietly. That was mum all over. Keeping busy, whatever happened. It was her way of coping.

'What will mum do now?' Vicki whispered to Akash. No amount of activity could hide the enormity of what she had just lost. 'Without daddy?'

'She'll be all right. She's a trouper. Just give her time, doll. You've got to grieve, haven't you? And we'll be there for her.'

Vicki reached for her coffee and took a sip, as she listened to the radio. The weather in England had taken a turn for the better, according to the forecast.

Akash glanced at the clock on the wall. 'It's not even seven thirty. Is it just me? I'm famished.'

'You're always hungry,' Vicki said.

'Too right. Got to build my strength up. If the phone doesn't come back on by the morning, someone's going to have to trudge up that hill, see if we can't flag somebody down.'

'I'll come with you,' Vicki said. She did not want to be separated from Akash again, even in daylight. Every time someone went outside, something horrible seemed to happen. 'The police. They'll want to interview Robbie, when they get here.' She shuddered at the prospect.

'It's not going to look good, is it?' Akash agreed.

Robbie had admitted to killing Uncle Dave; a moment of madness, he had said, rather than premeditated murder; but he would still be held to account. Vicki was struggling to come to terms not just with all the deaths, but what Uncle Dave had done to her brother, to set it all off. Part of her did not want to believe him capable of that – forcing himself on Robbie – but she knew her brother would not lie about it. And at least it was a mitigation, of sorts. The jury would take that into account, when Robbie came to trial.

'Aye, aye. Talk of the devil,' Akash said.

Vicki's brother had moved quietly into the living room. Without a word, he came and sat down on the armchair, adjacent to the two of them.

Akash regarded him quietly. 'Not the best of days, eh?'

'No,' Robbie agreed darkly. 'At least it's over with now. That bastard got his comeuppance.'

Vicki frowned, not quite sure if he was referring to Dave or Nicholas.

'Are *you* all right, Vick?' Robbie leaned forward, concerned.

She nodded. 'I think so.' There was barely any emotion left in her now.

'I should never have come here,' he grumbled.

'What's done is done, Robbie.'

'Yeah. You said it.'

Akash tried to break the mood. 'So, you staying the night?'

It was a facetious question, but Robbie answered it anyway. 'I don't know.' His eyes flicked across to the front door. 'I don't think it'll make much difference either way.' The police would catch him, if he tried to run.

Vicki put down her mug and regarded her brother seriously. 'Robbie, I didn't know. About Uncle Dave. You should have told me.'

'How could I? Even my own dad wouldn't believe me.'

'I would have believed you, Robbie.'

'Yeah, perhaps. God, what a mess.' He slumped back into his chair. 'Are you going to visit me? When they lock me up?'

'Of course I will. We both will,' Vicki said.

'When the little one's born, we'll bring him along to see

you,' Akash added. 'You can change his nappy.'

'Or hers,' Vicki added.

'I can't wait.' Robbie gazed down at his feet, his face dark. 'I'm sorry, Vick,' he said quietly. 'I'm sorry all this happened. It's all my bloody fault.'

Marion had been listening in to their conversation. 'What's done is done, dear.' She gazed across at him from the kitchen. 'But we will always be here for you. The kettle's just boiled. Do you want a cup of tea?'

Robbie rolled his eyes. That was the cure for everything in the Wilkerson household. 'Yeah, go on.' He looked across at her for the briefest of moments. 'I'm not going anywhere,' he added.

The departure hall at Bergerac airport was not as jam-packed as Emma expected. When the airport had reopened, a few days ago, there had been a mad flurry of activity, but things had calmed down a bit now. Emma and Betsy had arrived early in any case, just to be on the safe side. Emma was seated on the usual plastic chair, one of a long row of identical seats. She was tapping away at her phone as Betsy bustled across the hall towards her. The older woman had a broad grin on her face. She was carrying two plastic cups from the coffee machine. 'I kept putting the coin in and it kept coming back,' she said. 'I had to swap it with a nice man, over there. I was saying to him, I can't do without a decent cup of coffee, can I?'

Emma raised an eyebrow ironically. 'Decent?'

'Well, something like that, anyway. Here you go, lovey.' She handed the plastic cup across.

Emma took a quick sip. It felt a bit strange, being back here at the airport, after all that had happened. She had organised the bookings, making sure she and Betsy were seated together, as they had been on the way out. Looking around the departure lounge, barely half full but busy enough, it seemed almost as if the last ten days had never happened. Almost.

The French police had questioned them at some length. The inspector at the station spoke perfect English. He was quite a good looking bloke. The farmhouse had been roped off for the duration. They were forced to stay in a cheap hotel for two or three nights. Then the farm had flooded, when the snow thawed. But that was the least of their worries. The press had got hold of the story and they had had a field day. None of them had been able to leave the hotel without people taking photographs and following them around. Thankfully, the authorities back in England had contacted Dave's family beforehand and told them what was going on. Emma had phoned his brother and passed on the bare facts of the case. He didn't seem all that surprised, which really bothered Emma. *How could I have missed it*? She kept asking herself that over and over again. She had been going out with Dave for two years. *How could I not have realised what he was really like?*

Betsy slurped her coffee. 'It'll be good to get home,' she said. Emma gazed at the woman thoughtfully. From her manner, you wouldn't have guessed she had just lost a lover, let alone two very old friends. Betsy could talk the hind legs off a donkey, but Emma was coming to admire her; the way she brushed it all off and carried on as if nothing had happened. It was probably the best way to deal with it. Betsy was one of those people who bustled through life, without anything ever sticking to her. 'I've got so much to do,' she continued, without pausing for breath. 'I feel awful, leaving Marion out here. I said to her this morning, if there's anything you need, anything at all, I'm on the end of the phone. I can always pop back anytime you like. The people at work have been so understanding. I said to my boss, you won't believe what's happened, but they'd heard all about it.' She chuckled. '"Take all the time you need," they said.'

They could probably use the peace and quiet, Emma thought, with a smile. Her lot had been understanding too, back at the clinic, even though a friend of hers had had to work double shifts. 'Poor Marion,' she said. 'At least she's got Vicki to keep her company.' Vicki had decided to stay out in France for the time being. The death of her dad had hit the girl hard and it would take a while for her to get back on her feet. The baby would help, when it came along. 'At least she's got

Akash, to look out for her.' Akash didn't have a job, so he could stay here for as long as he was needed.

'He's going to make such a good dad,' Betsy gushed. 'I was saying to Vicki last night, he's a keeper, that Akash. Never mind what anyone else says. Giles didn't like him. He thought he was such a layabout, a dreamer. But I said to him, no, I said, when push comes to shove, I reckon that's someone you can rely on.'

Emma nodded. Akash had proved surprisingly capable. 'It's a good match,' she agreed, taking another sip of coffee. 'Do you reckon Marion will stay out here, in France, now that Giles is gone?'

Betsy shook her head. 'I can't see it. I was saying to that guy in the hotel. You know, the one with the teeth. He was asking me about it. I was saying to him, if Robbie is transferred to an English prison, she'll want to be near him. She won't want to be in another country, will she?'

'No. I don't suppose she will.'

Robbie had been arrested shortly after the police had arrived at the farm. The trial was some way off but there seemed little doubt he would be convicted. In all likelihood, he would be allowed to serve his time in a British jail.

'He was wrong, you know,' Emma said. 'Robbie. He said to me he thought there was something bad at the heart of his family. Something malignant. But there really wasn't.'

'No, just the one bad apple.' Betsy agreed. 'We're a pair, aren't we? Your David and my Nicholas.' She sighed theatrically. 'They weren't wholly bad, you know. Either one of them. Things just got a little out of control, that's all.'

Emma laughed. That had to be the understatement of the century. 'Even so, when I get back, I'm going to try to put all this behind me as quickly as I can.'

'Quite right, lovey. Find yourself some nice young man and have a bit of fun. Take your mind off it. That's what I'm going to do.' Betsy took a final slurp of coffee. 'You're right about the family, though. Robbie and the others. I've always said, they're good people at heart.'

'His dad loved him,' Emma said. 'Even if he could never

really show it. I think Giles would have gone to jail to protect him, if it had come to it. And Vicki and Marion will always look out for him. Robbie doesn't realise how lucky he is to have them.'

'He knows it, lovey. He'll breeze through prison. He's done it before. He's as tough as an old boot, that one. They all are. Even Vicki, when it comes to it.'

A roar of an engine interrupted them; a plane coming into land, not a hundred and fifty metres away. 'That's us!' Betsy said, beaming.

Emma nodded and put down her coffee. It would be good to get home.

Also Available On This Imprint

Murder At Flaxton Isle
by
Greg Wilson

A remote Scottish island plays host to a deadly reunion...

It should be a lot of fun, meeting up for a long weekend in a rented lighthouse on a chunk of rock miles from anywhere. There will be drinks and games and all sorts of other amusements. It is ten years since the last get-together and twenty years since Nadia and her friends graduated from university. But not everything goes according to plan. One of the group has a more sinister agenda and, as events begin to spiral out of control, it becomes clear that not everyone will get off the island alive...

Available Now On This Imprint

The Scandal At Bletchley
by
Jack Treby

"I've been a scoundrel, a thief, a blackmailer and a whore, but never a murderer. Until now..."

The year is 1929. As the world teeters on the brink of a global recession, Bletchley Park plays host to a rather special event. MI5 is celebrating its twentieth anniversary and a select band of former and current employees are gathering at the private estate for a weekend of music, dance and heavy drinking. Among them is Sir Hilary Manningham-Butler, a middle aged woman whose entire adult life has been spent masquerading as a man. She doesn't know why she has been invited – it is many years since she left the secret service – but it is clear she is not the only one with things to hide. And when one of the other guests threatens to expose her secret, the consequences could prove disastrous for everyone.

Also Available On This Imprint

The Gunpowder Treason
by
Michael Dax

"If I had thought there was the least sin in the plot, I would not have been in it for all the world..."

Robert Catesby is a man in despair. His wife is dead and his country is under siege. A new king presents a new hope but the persecution of Catholics in England continues unabated and Catesby can tolerate it no longer. King James bears responsibility but the whole government must be eradicated if anything is to really change. And Catesby has a plan...

The Gunpowder Treason is a fast-paced historical thriller. Every character is based on a real person and almost every scene is derived from eye-witness accounts. This is the story of the Gunpowder Plot, as told by the people who were there...

Available Now On This Imprint

The Pineapple Republic
by
Jack Treby

Democracy is coming to the Central American Republic of San Doloroso. But it won't be staying long...

The year is 1990. Ace reporter Daniel Parr has been injured in a freak surfing accident, just as the provisional government of San Doloroso has announced the country's first democratic elections.

The Daily Herald needs a man on the spot and in desperation they turn to Patrick Malone, a feckless junior reporter who just happens to speak a few words of Spanish.

Despatched to Central America to get the inside story, our Man in Toronja finds himself at the mercy of a corrupt and brutal administration that is determined to win the election at any cost...

Printed in Great Britain
by Amazon

70715339R00132